NEKOMONOGATARI

CAT TALE

(WHITE)

NISIOISIN

VERTICAL.

NEKOMONOGATARI
Cat Tale

(WHITE)

Translated by Ko Ransom

NEKOMONOGATARI (SHIRO)

First published in Japan in 2010 by Kodansha Ltd., Tokyo.
Publication rights for this English edition arranged
through Kodansha Ltd., Tokyo.

Published by Vertical, Inc., New York, 2018

ISBN 978-1-945054-49-5

Manufactured in the United States of America

First Edition

Vertical, Inc.
451 Park Avenue South, 7th Floor
New York, NY 10016

www.vertical-inc.com

CHAPTER SNUG

TSUBASA TIGER

CHAPTER SNUG
TSUBASA TIGER

TSUBASA HANEKAWA

001

Though the tale of Tsubasa Hanekawa is my tale, it is not one that I can tell. That's because I can't even define the extent to which I am me. I believe there was once a great author who said he found it hard to believe that he was himself down to the tips of his outstretched toes, but I don't even need to extend my legs. It's uncertain whether my very heart is my own.

Am I me?

What am I?

Who am I?

Who—is me.

What—is me.

For example, could we really say that I am these thoughts that so closely consider this pointlessness? Maybe we could say that, if we're only going to say it. These are only feelings, thoughts, and maybe even memories, but we might say that they're nothing more than accumulated knowledge. If we're saying that I am my experiences, does that mean we can also say a human with the exact same experiences as me would actually be me?

That there could be a me other than me that was still me?

In that case, if I were being unlike myself, would I no longer be me? What to think about that, how to feel?

To begin with, the name Tsubasa Hanekawa is already unstable.

My family name has changed a number of times.

So I can't look for my identity in my name, not even a bit. I understand on quite a deep-rooted level the idea that names are nothing more than signifiers. We could even say I understand it on a bodily level.

In facing an aberration, nothing is more important than knowing its name—or at least, that's supposed to be the first step in the process. So maybe the fact that I never recognized my name as my own was a major reason I haven't been facing myself.

In that case, I need to begin by knowing my name.

I need to know Tsubasa Hanekawa as myself.

Then maybe I can define myself for the first time.

Of course, when I think about how Araragi most likely doesn't worry himself into a standstill with these kinds of ideas, my self-imposed stalemate seems silly and absurd. He can become a vampire, lose his humanity, and be dragged into the other world by a host of different aberrations, but he always continues to be Koyomi Araragi, with his unshakable self, his unshakable ego, and I feel embarrassed when I think about that.

Maybe he doesn't realize it.

It's clear to anyone around him, as clear as day that he always continues to be himself no matter the place or time, but just maybe he doesn't realize it.

He doesn't have to realize it.

Koyomi Araragi can be Koyomi Araragi in confidence.

That's probably why he can always tell his own tale.

That's why I love him.

Tsubasa Hanekawa loves Koyomi Araragi.

In the end, any me I can speak about would have to begin there. Amusingly enough, that is the only certain thing in me. Like when I'm studying alone at a library desk and suddenly decide to write the name "Koyomi Araragi" in the corner of my notes and can't help but smile.

That is all my tale needs to be.

Of all sixty stories about the adventures of Sherlock Holmes, the famed detective created by Sir Arthur Conan Doyle, only two shorts exist that are narrated not by his assistant, Dr. Watson, but by Sherlock Holmes himself. These are controversial works among Sherlockians, even treated as apocryphal at times, but in one of them, "The Adventure of the Blanched Soldier," Mr. Holmes begins with these words:

"The ideas of my friend Watson, though limited, are exceedingly pertinacious. For a long time he has worried me to write an experience of my own. Perhaps I have rather invited this persecution, since I have often had occasion to point out to him how superficial are his own accounts and to accuse him of pandering to popular taste instead of confining himself rigidly to fact and figures. 'Try it yourself, Holmes!' he has retorted, and I am compelled to admit that, having taken my pen in my hand, I do begin to realize that the matter must be presented in such a way as may interest the reader."

Like most, I was fascinated by Sherlock Holmes's near-superhuman abilities as I read about his exploits, which is why I was taken aback when he abruptly gave voice to these "true feelings."

To be frank, I was disappointed.

Why would this man who had made one extraordinary display after another now choose to say such a human thing? I felt betrayed.

But now I understand. I understand his humanity, which could no longer bear the gap between him as the "superman" spoken of by Dr. Watson, and him as himself.

His feelings of wanting to make an excuse for himself.

Ultimately, those two stories are positioned as the outcome of a renowned detective's assistant talking back to him: "Then why don't you write it yourself!" Let me say here from the start that this tale is the same for me.

A tale to let you know that contrary to Araragi's portrayals of me as some kind of historical saint or holy mother, I am but a human being.

To let you know that I am a cat, and that I am a tiger.

And that I am a person. A tale of betrayal made to let everyone down.

I don't think I'll be able to tell it well, the way Araragi can, but I'd like to play it by ear and try my best. I imagine that's the way anyone would talk about his or her own life.

Now.

The time has come to wake from this nightmare.

002

Rumor has it that Araragi dutifully gets woken up every morning by his little sisters Karen and Tsukihi. That their efforts are tireless, regardless of whether it's a weekday, weekend, or holiday. He seems quite bothered by it, but from where I stand, they just sound like close siblings to me.

Actually, I'm just plain jealous.

Honestly, truly.

How many older brothers exist in this world so loved they're woken up each and every morning? But more than anything—it may not be Araragi himself I'm jealous of here, but Karen and Tsukihi, who get to see his sleeping face every day.

Really, jealous as can be.

Honestly, truly.

So, how do I, Tsubasa Hanekawa, get up each morning? Just as Araragi has his sisters, Roomba wakes me up every morning. Of course, Roomba isn't the Hanekawa family cat, nor the eccentric name of little sister Roomba Hanekawa. It is indeed, simply, the automatic vacuum made by iRobot, the Roomba 577 if you were to call it by its model number.

This high-performance vacuum cleaner, timer set to go into action automatically at six each morning, *klonks* into my head and wakes me up.

A refreshing start.

Still, Roomba generates a good bit of noise while it cleans, as all vacuums do, so really I'm awake by the time it creeps down the hallway toward me—and yet I keep my eyes closed, waiting for that *klonk* to come, not getting up until my head is bumped, perhaps because I yearn for that feeling of someone waking me up, that feeling of being woken up.

Like I'm Sleeping Beauty, to put it poetically.

Well, no—nothing about the situation could be poetic when it's a vacuum cleaner waking me up.

Sleeping Beauty. Did I really just say that about myself?

I must be nothing more than a nuisance from Roomba's perspective, some sleeping person blocking the hallway it's cleaning.

That's right, I sleep in the hallway.

I sleep on a futon in the second-floor hallway of a house.

I used to think it's normal and utterly natural, but apparently it isn't. Ever since I unwittingly talked about this and lost a friend, I've made it a point not to discuss the matter too openly.

Even then, I don't particularly desire my own bed, not after all this time.

It's become natural.

I don't want to change what's natural.

I never had the childish thought of wanting my own room, and you know, I did talk about this with my classmate Miss Senjogahara after we became friends, because it felt like it would be okay to tell her.

"Hey, that's nothing," she replied. "My place doesn't even have a hallway."

Maybe it seemed like a first-world problem to Miss Senjogahara, who lives with her father in a one-room apartment, and I didn't see it as a problem in the first place.

No.

Maybe I'm wrong.

To take a guess, perhaps I don't want this house to become "my place." Like the opposite of how an animal marks its territory—maybe

I want to distance myself from this house.

Not even a trace.

Not leaving any whatsoever at this house.

Maybe that's what it is.

…Let's put aside why I'm having to take guesses about my own heart and mind, or why I can only say "perhaps" and "maybe."

"Well, however I feel about it, it's not going to matter a few months from now, so I should try not to think too much," I say to myself as I fold my futon.

I don't have much trouble getting up in the morning.

In fact, I don't really understand what it feels like to be "still asleep" after waking up.

My consciousness being on or off is, in my case, probably more clear-cut than it needs to be.

If you feel sleepy, then just sleep.

That's what I end up thinking.

"That must be where I don't match up with other people. Araragi tells me things like, 'What you find only natural to be able to do is nothing less than a miracle for me' all the time—but 'miracle' is going too far, isn't it," I continue to talk to myself.

I don't do it when I'm outside, but I can't keep from talking to myself when I'm in the house. Because if I don't, I feel like I'd forget how to speak.

I do think that's an issue.

I also think it's an issue that I naturally begin to smile when I think of Araragi as I speak to myself.

I place my futon in the closet and go to the bathroom to wash my face.

Then, I put in my contact lenses.

Back when I wore glasses, I was so terrified of sticking lenses directly onto my eyeballs that I didn't even want to consider the idea, and when I first started using them, I was indeed so terrified that I practically kept my eyes closed throughout the whole ordeal (that's a figure of speech), but now that I'm used to it, it's no problem at all.

We can get accustomed to anything.

In fact, with a burden lifted off of my nose and ears, it's more comfortable.

When I think of my future starting next year, though, whether it's contact lenses or glasses, I'll be hindered in a way. I've been wondering lately if I should just be brave and go through with LASIK surgery while I'm still a student.

After making myself look presentable, I head to the dining room.

There, someone who should be called my father and someone who should be called my mother are, as always, eating breakfast separately at the same table.

They don't even look at me as I enter.

I don't even look at them, either.

Something entering your field of vision doesn't mean you've looked. The heart's eyes can always be averted. It may be hard to see with the heart, but it is easy not to.

The only sound to echo through the dining room is the voice of the TV anchor reporting the day's top stories.

Why?

The news anchor, surely at a distant television station, feels closer to me than these two persons in the same room.

Why indeed.

To the point that I want to greet her with a "good morning."

Speaking of which, how many years was it since I last uttered the words "good morning" in this house? I tried searching through my memories only to come up with nothing. I did remember saying good morning to Roomba five times (as mentioned earlier, not just mumbling in my sleep but plainly. There's something oddly alive about the way that automatic cleaner moves), but I seriously couldn't recall a single time I said it to the persons who should be called my father and my mother.

Not even once.

Huh.

That is surprising.

I once said to Araragi something like, "I think, for my part, I've tried to meet my parents halfway," but it seems those words weren't truthful. Then again, it's not like everything that comes out of my mouth being a lie is anything new.

I am made of lies.

An existence far from the truth—that is who I, Tsubasa Hanekawa, am.

Even my family name is a sham.

I close the door without a sound and head to the kitchen, not the table. To make breakfast, yes, but that isn't to say I don't feel like delaying, for as long as possible, the moment when I have to approach the table where those two sat.

I know resistance is futile, or rather, empty.

Allow me that degree of resistance, even so.

It's not exactly a coup d'état.

The Hanekawas' kitchen, which I would personally prefer not to call my home's, has a lot of cookware. It has three cutting boards and three kitchen knives. It also has three each of milk pans and frying pans. That is to say, there is three of everything. If you want to know what this means, then yes, the three of us living in the house each use our own separate sets of cookware.

This is another anecdote whose telling lost me a friend.

I have too many of these kinds of anecdotes to count, like how we each prepare our own bath and then drain the tub for it to be refilled, or how we do our laundry separately, but it's strange.

I don't find any of this odd, and no matter how many friends I lose, I don't feel like the Hanekawa household ought to adopt the ways of other homes.

Since we leave the house at about the same hour, our breakfast times "happen" to coincide, but it's like finding seats at the same table in a cafeteria, there is no conversation, and none of us ever makes breakfast for the other two while we are at it preparing our own.

I select my personal cookware and commence my domestic chore.

But I don't make an elaborate breakfast like that wording might suggest.

I dish out the single serving of rice I cooked, prepare my miso soup, rolled omelet, grilled fish, and salad (I'm told that's too much,

17

but I'm the type to go for hearty breakfasts), and ferry it to the table over three trips. I then take one last round trip to pour myself some tea. There'd be no need for four-and-a-half round trips if someone helped me, but of course, no one in this house does. Even Roomba doesn't help out to that extent.

I sit down thinking how nice it'd be if Araragi were around to help me.

"Thank you for this meal," I say putting my hands together and pick up my chopsticks.

I've never heard the other two mouth those words; nonetheless, while I don't say "good morning" or "good night," I seldom fail to show my thanks before and after a meal.

Especially after spring break. Not even once since then.

After all, the words are for the plants and animals that will become my flesh and blood, once alive before they were made into food.

Lives killed for my sake, of all creatures.

Thank you. I humbly accept you.

003

I finished eating breakfast, changed from my pajamas into my school uniform, and immediately left the house. I understand it takes Araragi about eighty pages to leave his home, but that's all I need. It seems clear this is the difference between having a family that won't let you leave your room and not having one.

Anyway, today was the start of a new term at school.

It was a relief to know that.

It felt, from the bottom of my heart, like I'd been saved.

I felt like I owed my life to each new trimester that came along.

Days off are days for walking—but even then, there's only so much wandering one can do. I could even put a delinquent to shame. While acting as Araragi's private college-exam tutor was, in some sense, something I did to improve his grades, it must have also been a handy excuse for not returning to my house.

Which is why having school—was a relief.

I let out a sigh of relief.

Then again, it didn't matter. Walking around, being a home tutor. Going to school.

In any case, I would always have to return to that house in the end, and nothing could depress me more—and yes.

The act I'm describing is strictly "returning" to that house and not "going home."

Tytyl and Mytyl realize in the end that the bluebird of happiness was at home all along, but where should someone with no home go to seek it out?

Perhaps she's seeking the wrong thing?

Should she be seeking not a bluebird but—say, a white cat?

Anyway, if you'll allow me to say something a little negative—even if the bluebird of happiness is at your own home, that doesn't mean a beast of unhappiness isn't lurking there, too.

As I walked pondering such thoughts—why, if it wasn't a little girl with pigtails appearing in my way.

"My goodness. If it isn't Miss Hanekawa."

The little girl—Mayoi Hachikuji—turned around and approached me with a charming trot. Every move she made was just too adorable. I wondered how aware she was that her cuteness drove Araragi mad.

"It seems that classes are resuming today, Miss Hanekawa."

"Yup. That's right."

"Applying yourself to your studies really is extraordinarily taxing. I may only be an elementary schooler, but I, too, spend my days overcoming one trial after tribulation. You could even call the crushing amount of coursework I faced during summer break its own kind of military history."

"Huh…" Noting that the girl's tongue never seemed to suffer any slips except when she was speaking to Araragi, I engaged her. "So what are you doing now, Mayoi?"

"Searching for Mister Araragi," she said.

My goodness.

Now it was my turn to use the line.

I could understand Araragi wandering around in search of Mayoi, but the opposite was truly rare.

No, had something similar happened before? I wanted to say that Shinobu had gone missing then—could something like it have happened again?

"Oh, no," Mayoi denied, picking up on my groundless concern from my expression. "It isn't as if anything serious has happened. It's only that I forgot a little something at Mister Araragi's home, and I was hoping to have him return it to me."

"You forgot something?"

"Just look."

Mayoi presented me with her back.

I couldn't find anything to look at there other than a cute little back, but when I gave it some more thought, the fact that there was nothing there was the strange part. What was charming about Mayoi was the big backpack she wore no matter where or when.

That backpack was absent.

What was up?

"Um, hold on. Mayoi, did you just say that you forgot something at Araragi's house?"

"That's right. He hauled me there yesterday," Mayoi complained, her back still facing me. "And I carelessly forgot my backpack then."

"Hauled?"

"Forcibly hauled."

"You're making it sound even more criminal…"

I decided not to pursue the matter any further. If I asked again, she might say she was assaulted. Whatever the case, Mayoi seemed to have forgotten her backpack at Araragi's home.

What a bold thing to forget.

"In that case, why don't you just go to Araragi's?"

Her coordinates were all wrong.

Why was she here?

"I of course began by visiting the gentleman's home. But he seemed to have already left, and his bike was nowhere to be found."

"Hm? Does Araragi leave for school this early, though?" While *I* do, wanting to get out of the house as soon as possible, even if Araragi wanted to, his sisters wouldn't let him go so easily. You could say he's in a constant mild state of house arrest, so if he left home early, he must have had something very important to do before heading to school…

"Or he *must have finished having* something very important to do and hasn't come home since last night."

It wasn't that he left early.

21

Maybe he hadn't come home yet.

"Ah, the thought never occurred to me. I should have known I could count on you for an impressive feat of inference. Yes, that is a possibility. Perhaps an intractable case came up after I somehow managed to flee from Mister Araragi's home."

"Yeah." I decided to ignore the fraught, already plenty intractable *somehow managed to flee*. Pursuing it any further felt like it might shine a light on a lot of regrettable facts.

"But whatever the case, it seems unlikely that Mister Araragi would have gone straight to school at this hour, which is why I'm here, bravely searching for him at random."

"Looking for people isn't your strong suit, Mayoi, is it?" What sort of haphazard approach was she taking? Did she really expect to find him that way? It wasn't just a shot in the dark, she didn't know which way she was aiming.

"Well, well, but it's exactly what led me to you, Miss Hanekawa. My tracking abilities are nothing to sneeze at."

"How forward-looking..."

"Be that as it may, I don't know whether or not you could count yourself fortunate for having met me today."

"Hm? Why? People in my circle say that anyone who meets you is guaranteed to have something good happen that day. You're spoken of as a lucky item."

"Please stop making up strange legends about me..."

My source, of course, was Araragi.

No one can outdo him when it comes to spreading false rumors.

He has what it takes to be a pretty good teller of ghost stories.

"Okay, if I see Araragi at school, I'll tell him you were looking for him."

"Thank you very much," Mayoi said, politely bowing down her little head, before going back the way she came in her still-charming trot.

Obviously, Mayoi doesn't have long conversations with me the way she does with Araragi. I envy him for being able to talk on the same eye level with cute little girls like Mayoi, and yes, I suppose I envy Mayoi for being able to chat on and on with Araragi.

Araragi seems to find it completely natural.

To me, it's far more of a miracle than anything I do.

I'm jealous.

"Well, then! Let us meet again soon, Miss Hanekawa!"

Mayoi was kind enough to turn around once more and wave her hand from a distance.

I waved back.

"Yep! See you later!"

"What's about to happen with me and Mister Araragi is an episode for the next volume!"

"Don't be so crass with your foreshadowing."

That wasn't even foreshadowing, it was just an ad for a program.

Following in Araragi's footsteps, I at least managed to get one quip in at the end.

004

Meet an aberration and you'll be drawn by aberrations—they say.

Apparently.

Whether they mean drawn in, drawn together, drawn out, or even drawn and quartered, the possibilities seem closely related if you really think about it, making it all a chaotic mess—but according to Mister Oshino, people who have "encountered" an aberration, even once, are more likely to meet one again for the rest of their lives.

He said there was no rhyme or reason to it, but I think you can assign one. A realistic reason, nothing mysterious or inexplicable.

It could of course just be my tricky, bad habit of ascribing a reason to everything.

Basically, though, it's a matter of memory and cognition.

Everyone has experienced learning a new word or phrase and suddenly running into it everywhere.

For example, when I learned about "jellied meats," I was inundated with them whether I was reading a newspaper or novel or watching television or a film.

It's not just words. The same phenomenon occurs with music and names, too.

If you know it, you know it.

You know it more the more you know it.

Knowledge equals cognition, memory.

It's just what you know.

In other words, a circuit for recognizing "it" has formed in your head, and from out of the torrent of information flowing into you each day, you're able to scoop up what you used to ignore.

Aberrations are everywhere.

Aberrations are only there.

It's merely a question of whether or not you notice them.

That's why *the first time* is so important.

Your very first is your most important one.

For Araragi, it was a demon.

For Miss Senjogahara, it was a crab.

For Mayoi, it was a snail.

For Sengoku, it was a snake.

For Miss Kanbaru, it was a monkey.

For Karen, it was a bee.

And for me—it was a cat.

Now, if you're wondering why I've started to talk about this all of a sudden, it's because there was one in front of me at that moment.

One what?

An—aberration.

"Ack…"

Normally, in encountering an aberration, people must think: Ghosts aren't supposed to exist in this world, *yokai* aren't supposed to exist in this world, what I'm looking at can't be an aberration.

They must.

But at that moment, I was thinking nothing but the absolute opposite.

I was wishing with all my heart that "it" was an aberration in front of me.

After all—a tiger?

It was a tiger.

A tiger, prowling right in front of me.

Yellow and black stripes.

The very picture of a tiger.

It happened soon after I saw Mayoi off—I turned the corner and there was the tiger. No, even phrasing it that way imparts no sense of reality, no taste of an actual occurrence.

Since it doesn't, it had to be unreal.

It had to be an aberration.

Actually, it was going to be an issue if it wasn't an aberration, whatever the facts of the matter—I stood less than fifteen feet from it. I could almost reach out and touch its stripes. If the tiger were real and not an aberration, say one that had escaped from a zoo, my life was surely over.

I was so close that I couldn't even run.

I'd be eaten.

Humbly accepted into its stomach.

I'd be passing the baton along in the race of life.

By the way, they say that any sufficiently advanced technology is indistinguishable from magic, but any excessive aberration is indistinguishable from reality, too.

Its uniquely feral scent, its even majestic presence, it was all so intense that lacking in reality, it yet seemed like realness itself; but I was okay, the dearly beloved television anchor hadn't said a word about a tiger escaping from its zoo.

<...nn>

The tiger—growled.

It didn't care to let loose an affected <Roar!> the way predators do in manga.

Then, coming to a halt, the tiger glared at me.

Oh no.

Our eyes had met.

Whether the tiger was real or an aberration—meeting eyes was a bad idea.

With a real tiger, of course, that was reason enough to get attacked—and if it was an aberration, it recognizing me was bad news, almost as bad, no, even worse than me recognizing it.

I instantly averted my gaze.

I put the tiger outside of my visual field.

Though this didn't provoke the tiger into moving, again, at the same time, I couldn't move from my spot, either—whether it was animal or aberration, my reaction to it ended up being lukewarm.

If I wanted to run, I should have run—why wasn't I running away? I'd be safe if I just ran.

Why not do it?

I.

"......"

How long did I stand there like that?

People often describe these situations as seeming to take hours, or the opposite, as happening in a flash, but to be honest with you, I didn't have the space to think about it at all.

I have a surprisingly narrow mind.

Able neither to be here nor not here, which makes me sound like an aberration myself—and then, at last.

<Hm. White.>

Thus—spoke the tiger.

Aberration confirmed.

<White—and how transparently so,> it said (not appending a <Groar!> or anything, of course)—before starting to swing its four stopped legs forward without further ado and loping, lumbering past me.

As someone who'd never seen the creature we call a tiger up close before, I had no sense of perspective for this subject that had been fifteen feet ahead, but as soon as it passed by my side, it was impressed upon me that the position its torso occupied was higher than my head, that it was too huge, once again, to be real.

I probably shouldn't have turned around.

If it was passing by me, I ought to have let it pass—it had decided to take its eyes off of me, so why follow it with my own?

But I.

White.

White—and how transparently so.

Ensnared by the words the tiger had spoken to me, I thoughtlessly, carelessly—

Turned around.

How completely foolish.

I'd hardly learned my lessons from first term, including Golden Week. How was I going to take Araragi to task about anything now?

No, when it comes to me.

I'm far worse than Araragi.

"...Oh."

But, fortunately.

Or maybe not? It's difficult to say.

Well, of course, it clearly wasn't. But.

There was nothing there when I turned around—forget tigers, there wasn't even a cat.

Just a plain street.

The same path to school as always.

"Oh, jeez."

I said that not because the tiger had disappeared but having glanced at the watch on my left wrist.

Eight thirty.

It seemed like I was going to be tardy for the first time in my life.

005

"You have to hear this, Miss Senjogahara. I met a tiger on my way to school today."

"Did you, now. So, Miss Hanekawa, am I obligated to listen to the details of this story? When you say 'You have to hear this,' is that not just a lead-in but an earnest request?"

As we'd walked in little groups back to our classrooms after the beginning-of-term ceremony, I'd run up to Miss Senjogahara, who was in my class.

Then I'd told her about my morning.

With a slightly bothered expression, however, she'd treated me to an openly bothered reaction.

Yet instead of pushing me away altogether, she urged, "What?"

She'd chopped off her hip-length hair at some point during summer break before going straight to her grandparents' home on her dad's side, so I wasn't sure about Araragi, but a short-haired Miss Senjogahara was a new sight for me.

She always had very neat features, and any hairstyle, short or long, would look like a perfect fit on her, but the trim wiped out any trace of the air of a "cloistered princess" that surrounded her during our first term. It stirred quiet controversy among the rest of our classmates (possibly more than when I cut my hair), but in my opinion, "cloistered princess" is almost an insult for a high school girl, so this was good.

"Did you just say a tiger, Miss Hanekawa? Not a cat?"

"Yup. Not a cat, but a tiger."

"Not a tiger-striped cat?"

"Nope. A tiger-striped tiger."

"Not a tiger-striped striped hyena?"

"I think that would be a regular striped hyena, but nope, it wasn't."

"Don't you think more people would be happy to earn stripes if we called them hyenas?"

"I don't."

Hmm, she nodded.

"This way," she took my hand.

She took me aside.

It seemed like she wanted to break away from the group, as there was a bit of time before homeroom began—and indeed, this was something I hesitated to talk about in front of others in our classroom.

We went behind the gymnasium.

Those words have a somewhat frightening feel to them, but the gym's environs have been under some of the most scrupulous management possible ever since the girls' basketball team's run the previous year; the area in fact feels wholesome and open.

The weather being nice too, this was an optimal situation for girls talking romance, but we were going to make a ghost story bloom.

Maybe I should say "withering" story.

"You saw a tiger... Miss Hanekawa, isn't that something to be very worried about?"

"I think so. Oh, but no, it wasn't a real-life tiger. It was probably an aberration. It talked."

"What's the difference? That doesn't change anything. Even a flesh-and-blood tiger is practically an aberration to a Japanese person."

"Ah."

She was right.

Her way of seeing the world was as bold as ever.

A realistic audacity.

"If someone told me that pandas are monsters, I'd believe it," she said.

"Hmm, I'm not sure about that one."

"What about giraffes? Those are *rokurokubi* right there."

"Zoos must seem like haunted houses to you, Miss Senjogahara."

That might be true, she nodded.

How candid.

"Even so, Miss Hanekawa, what an unexpected thing to encounter—or maybe I should say you're as amazing as ever. A tiger? A tiger? A tiger! It's just, how could you be any more stylish than that? A crab. A snail. A monkey. What was it for Karen? A bee, I want to say? Take that lineup, and then what do you add to it but a tiger. It's like we've all been in a foot race, each one of us careful not to stick out so that we can all cross the finish line together, a friendly, flat competition, and then you go and do this? How can anyone be so insensitive? That might even be cooler than Araragi's demon."

"You always have such a unique way of looking at things…"

"Did it do anything to you?"

"No, it didn't do anything—or at least, I don't think it did. It's hard to know about these kinds of things for yourself, which is why I wanted to ask you. Is there anything strange about me right now?"

"Hmm. Well, you being absent from school is one thing, but it isn't like you to be tardy. That isn't what you mean, though, is it?"

"No."

"Excuse me."

Bringing her face closer, she pored over my skin. Like she was going to lick it. Like she was inspecting my skin, my eyeballs, my nose, my brows, my lips, each individual part. After she was done with my face, she took my hand and examined my nails and the vessels on the back of my hand.

"What are you doing, Miss Senjogahara?"

"Checking to see if there's anything unusual."

"Really?"

"At least, that's what I was doing at first."

"Then what is it you're doing now?"

"Indulging my eyes."

I shook her off.

As hard as I could.

"Ah!" she exclaimed, looking at me with a very disappointed expression—but, well, I'm sure she meant it as a joke.

You might be surprised to hear this, but Miss Senjogahara loves to joke around.

...I hope it was a joke.

Especially because Araragi recently told me about Miss Kanbaru's preferences.

"So," I asked, "what do you think?"

"You're fine. You'll be able to reel them in for another decade with that skin."

"That's not what I meant."

"There's nothing that I can see—it's not as if you've sprouted tiger ears or anything."

"Tiger ears..."

It wasn't a remark I could take in jest as someone who'd sprouted cat ears in the past, and precisely because the analogy was realistic, I let out an exaggerated laugh while giving my head a sly check.

I was fine.

I hadn't sprouted anything.

"But," reminded Miss Senjogahara, "it's not as if something unusual is bound to happen as soon as you encounter an aberration—considering the time lag, we can't relax yet."

"Right."

"We can't rule out the possibility that you'll wake up as a bug tomorrow."

"I do think that's too much of a leap."

She needed to link it to tigers in some way.

Even if she loved Kafka.

"For this stuff," she advised, "I think you ought to be talking to Araragi instead of me. True, I did meet a crab aberration—and it caused me a whole lot of suffering, but that doesn't mean I'm equipped with the methods or the know-how for dealing with it any more than other people."

"Mm. Mmm. Yes, but…"

She was right.

Meeting an aberration doesn't mean you're experienced.

In fact, the more seasoned you become, the further you skid off the career track.

Discussing this with Miss Senjogahara only served to trouble her. It could even end up reopening old wounds.

"But it does seem like Araragi's taking the day off," I said.

"What?" Miss Senjogahara tilted her neck in puzzlement. "Wasn't he lined up there at the beginning-of-term ceremony? His absence going unnoticed says even more about how ignorable he is than his presence going unnoticed."

Heheheh, she laughed.

A shudder ran through me.

The dregs of what Araragi calls her "acid-tongued era" seep out at times.

Then again, the venom had been removed over summer break, and now too, she'd spoken in a way that made it clear she was just kidding.

Humans are able to change.

You could call her living proof of that.

"Well, he says he doesn't need to worry about his attendance record too much anymore, but I do wonder what happened to my beloved darling."

"Don't call him that," I chastised her. That was too much of a change. How were we supposed to accept her as the same character? "Speaking of, actually, I also ran into Mayoi this morning before meeting the tiger. Judging by what she said, he does seem to be—*up to something.*"

"Something, you say." Miss Senjogahara shook her head with what seemed like resignation. Though a bit exaggerated, the reaction accurately expressed how appalled she was. "Same thing as always, I guess?"

"It could be. He can only focus on what's right in front of him."

"Did you try calling him? Or sending him an email or something?"

"Ummm, something stopped me."

I really didn't want to bother him when he was obviously *at work*. I'd have brought it straight to him if he were at school, of course, but I wasn't sure about going so far as to call or text him.

It was less discretion than out of concern for his safety.

"Right," Miss Senjogahara nodded. "I think it'd be fine for you to be a little more shameless."

"Shameless?"

"Or maybe I should say unashamed? He'll never be annoyed by a request from you, no matter what kind of situation he's in. You know that, don't you?"

"Hmm. I'm not sure." I found Miss Senjogahara's remark confusing. "Maybe I don't."

"Or is it out of consideration for me?"

"Oh, no. Of course not."

"Just as long as it isn't."

This time, she let out a sigh.

A deep sigh.

"Well," she said, "it's not like something is bound to happen, so we shouldn't get too nervous—being worried sick would defeat the whole purpose. That'd just make us a pathological *yandere*. Still, since this tiger might attack someone other than you, don't you think we need to talk to Araragi? Whether it's a tiger or a lion, it's not like either of us is capable of fighting an aberration. Aren't you just like me, knowledgeable but inexperienced and only equipped with secondhand wisdom?"

"Sure, but..."

Her phrasing was taking on a certain innuendo.

It was hard to tell if she was doing it on purpose.

I'm sure Araragi would have figured it out and replied with the perfect zinger.

I lack that skill.

"You'd have to be like Araragi and have a pet vampire in your shadow to fight an aberration—well, Kanbaru seems like she might be able to if she felt like it, but we shouldn't ask that girl to do anything unreasonable."

"Yeah," I agreed.

I'd heard about it, vaguely.

The bandage on her left arm, I assumed.

That wasn't an issue of discretion, it was dangerous—as a practical matter. While Miss Kanbaru's aberration trouble had been solved, it was as though she were living with a bomb strapped to her.

Or maybe you could say she was the bomb herself.

But if we did, wasn't the same true for Araragi? Could that be why I wasn't able to call him?

It seemed to be.

But I knew—it wasn't why.

Ultimately, it was exactly as Miss Senjogahara said.

I wasn't able to be shameless with Araragi.

The reason was abundantly clear, no doubt—

"Miss Hanekawa, have you ever asked Araragi to save you?"

"What?"

The sudden question brought me back to my senses.

She'd surprised me.

"Huh? 'Save'? I don't know. It doesn't seem like the kind of word you'd use in a regular conversation... Probably not."

"Okay. Neither have I," Miss Senjogahara said, looking heavenward. "He'd probably save us before we ever said it—and he'd do it reciting some phony quote like 'people just go and get saved on their own.'"

It wasn't a phony quote, it was a real one that I'd heard before. Mister Oshino constantly repeated that line.

"It wasn't just the crab," she continued. "There was the time with Kanbaru, there was Kaiki, there have been a lot of times that he's saved me, both in the open and from the shadows. But I feel like his saving us without us saying anything doesn't mean we don't need to be saying anything."

"Hm? What?"

"Just maybe, well, I think you might be expecting him to save you before you ever say anything."

"...Ah."

Hmm.

Is that how it looks?

But now that she said it, the sad fact of the matter was that I couldn't deny it outright.

I couldn't make my approach—and was just waiting for the other party to approach me?

Was I—well, such a me did exist.

There was a dark me inside me.

And being inside me, it was closer to me than anyone else.

"I think you just ought to rely on him. He's always hoping that you will. If you'd been able to during Golden Week—"

So she said—but stopped mid-sentence.

Maybe she felt she'd gone too far, even though she hadn't said it all.

But rather than apologize, she just acted awkward—nor would I have known how to respond if she'd said sorry.

There was no reason for her to.

"Why don't we go back to class?" I said.

This wasn't particularly an attempt to bail her out. It really was time for us to be heading back, according to my watch. To the point that we needed to run up the stairs.

"Let's," nodded Miss Senjogahara. "I'm not pressuring you or anything, but you shouldn't try to handle your problems all by yourself. You still tend to do that—if you're unwilling to bother Araragi, then get me involved, though I can't do much. Well, I guess I could die with you at least."

Miss Senjogahara casually threw out those outrageous words and began walking toward the school building. Though she may have been rehabilitated, that part of her that you might call her overwhelming strength was still alive and kicking.

Sure.

It wasn't so much getting rehabilitated as getting cuter, to be frank.

Especially in Araragi's presence.

But since Araragi only knows her as she is in his presence, it might take him a little more time to realize that.

Like I was going to tell him.

And so on.

Then, together, we returned to our class—I was afraid we'd missed the start of homeroom, but we hadn't.

Well.

Our teacher, Hoshina-sensei, was already there.

That normally meant that it had already started—but everyone in class, our teacher included, was stuck to the window facing the athletic field. Not a person was seated, so it wasn't anything like homeroom.

What was going on?

What could they be seeing?

"Ah," Miss Senjogahara muttered by my side.

She's a good bit taller than me, so she noticed *it* before I could—to be precise, she took off her shoes and stood on a chair the moment she knew everyone was looking at something. Contrary to appearances, she could be surprisingly proactive.

Lacking her nerve, I simply weaved through my classmates, approached one of the windows, and gazed out of it.

I immediately saw what everyone was looking at.

"...A fire."

My mind was blank, in a haze.

I rarely spoke to myself outside the house—yet there I was, speaking to myself.

Beholding the roaring flames, so powerful it seemed like their sound might reach us despite looking like a speck from where we stood, far away—I ended up speaking to myself.

"My house is on fire."

That house—I'd gone and called it mine.

006

There were two things I didn't know.

First, I didn't know the house I lived in was visible from the window of the classroom where I spent my days studying. I'd had opportunities to stand by the window and gaze outside.

Why hadn't I noticed?

Why wasn't it visible?

I guess it had to be, and I just never consciously recognized it—in other words, according to the reverse of the logic of "Meet an aberration and you'll be drawn by aberrations."

I must have been pushing that house out of my consciousness.

And the other thing I didn't know was how unexpectedly shocked I'd feel if that house burned down—it left me speechless.

It was enough to make my mind go blank.

It was a shock to my system.

Araragi seems to be mistaken about this point, but I'm not all that mature—I harbor the same kind of destructive impulses as everyone else. He placed an excessive level of trust in my character even after the nightmare of Golden Week—or no, maybe he was just pretending to overlook things—but I'd wished time and time again for that lousy house to disappear.

But I never thought it really would.

And I never thought I'd feel such a strong sense of loss.

It wasn't as if I'd been attached to it.

I didn't even feel like I'd thought of it as my house—I let words to that effect slip out of my mouth, but it must have been a momentary failing.

But the unwavering fact was that I felt strongly enough about it to have that moment.

Was that a good thing?

I felt strongly enough.

Yes, that was a fact.

Or was it a bad thing?

You could probably take it either way, but either way, it was too late.

It was gone now.

That home where I'd spent fifteen years of my life.

It was lost forever.

I asked my teacher if I could leave early despite having arrived late, and of course I immediately received permission. I'm not Miss Kanbaru, but I ran back to the house, and while the area was surrounded by fire engines and onlookers, it had already been put out.

Put out.

And nothing was left.

Though the fire hadn't spread to any neighboring homes, the Hanekawa residence was what you'd call razed, without a single column remaining.

Extremely beneficial in making a fire insurance claim, that status was perhaps a saving grace. As vulgar as that sounds, it's of paramount importance.

Oh, wait. No, no.

Of paramount importance, naturally, are human lives—but there was no need to worry about that. I'd been at school, and there was close to no chance that the "other two" who should be called my parents would ever return to the house in the morning.

None of the three inhabitants—considered it a home.

It was a place, not a home.

But Roomba must have gone up in flames, I mourned the passing of the automatic vacuum cleaner that tirelessly woke me up each morning.

Mourned more than the house.

A lot of other things in addition to Roomba, or rather, everything had gone up in flames, but I was a mere high schooler with no remarkable possessions. That wasn't going to be a problem for me.

If you insist, losing all my clothes was a complication.

Actually, it might have been the same for the persons who should be called my father and my mother—neither could have been keeping anything important in the house.

They must have kept anything valuable at work.

That was how I saw it.

That house.

It wasn't a place for keeping anything of value.

They'd get dirty.

In any case, this just meant I was full of things I didn't know—you only ever notice some stuff after a house burns down.

I've never met the man in person, but was this one of those lessons to take home with me that the fraud, Mister Deishu Kaiki, likes to speak of?

I wasn't sure.

I didn't know.

But whether or not I knew—this definitely meant I was being put out on the street.

I had spots to go to for no particular reason on days off because I couldn't stand being at home, but how fortunate I had been to have a place where I could go to bed—either way, the Hanekawas ended up having their first family discussion in a while as a result of this incident.

A discussion?

Well, even I can imagine that normal families wouldn't call that a discussion.

It wasn't anything close to a family meeting.

It was an exchange of opinions.

Not social interaction.

A house burning down naturally necessitated a lot of different complicated procedures—we didn't even know the cause of the fire yet. It was frightening, there were even suspicions of arson—so it was going to be a long-term problem, not something that could be handled by me, who was still a child. What we discussed that day was our most pressing problem. In other words, where we would sleep that night.

With no nearby relatives the Hanekawas could rely on, there wasn't a whole lot of room for debate. We ended up booking the nearest hotel—but even that was a problem for us.

The biggest problem, you could say, or maybe the single issue.

We hadn't slept in the same room in a very long time.

There was me of course, who slept in the hallway, but even the married couple slept in different bedrooms. We couldn't get two or three rooms at a hotel when it would only make this more expensive—

"I'm fine. I'll get a friend to let me stay with them for a while."

Before the discussion could get too deep, I said that.

I proclaimed it.

"Dad, Mom, this is a great chance for you two to spend some time alone together as husband and wife."

I wasn't saying this as an excuse, but as how I truly felt, and I knew that was part of what made me so frightening and inhuman—I'd learned over Golden Week that it was one of my flaws.

I didn't want to go to bed in the same room as those two.

Those personal feelings were no doubt there, but I was putting them far, far aside—and it was very unnatural.

I knew that.

Seeing the fire as a great chance didn't exactly make me human.

Araragi and Mister Oshino had taught me that.

A lesson.

Here I was, not having put it to use—but I just couldn't help thinking those two might go back to being the way they ought to be.

I was able to think it.

Namely, that this could be the last chance for those two, who planned on getting divorced as soon as I ceased to be a minor.

I thought so.

It would take several months to rebuild the house when you factored everything in, and if they spent a few weeks alone together for the first time in fifteen years before we found a place to rent—then just maybe something could happen.

I did think so.

I was able to think so.

I wanted to think so.

The two agreed right away.

They didn't even try to stop me when I conveyed my intention to stay at various friends' houses. In fact, they were visibly happy that I'd suggested it myself.

Well, of course they were.

It was easier for the two of them to be alone than for the three of us to be alone. The fire might have been a reasonably welcome thing for them, too, in that it let them drive off a source of annoyance in their lives.

They were delighted.

And I was happy that they were delighted, so I had to be pretty insane.

007

It put me in a difficult situation, though.

Well, I was from the start, but the greatest difficulty now was the fact that I didn't have any friends who could let me stay with them for a while.

I have friends.

I wouldn't say a lot of them, because my personality is a little problematic, but I feel like I have the kinds of friendly relationships at school that any average student would.

On that note, Araragi likes to talk about how few friends he has, almost boasting rather than roasting himself, but that is the one claim he makes that I will vouch for.

He isn't lying. It's not an exaggeration, he doesn't have friends.

Actually, he was comporting himself so as not to make any friends, for a long time—according to him, it would lower his intensity as a human, or something.

He really believed and really said that.

While he seems to have abandoned that philosophy, he's still in the thick of rehabilitation, and I've never seen him speak to another boy in our class.

In fact, I've never seen him speak to anyone other than me and Miss Senjogahara.

I wonder if he knows that just as Miss Senjogahara used to be the "cloistered princess," he's still being called the "unmovable silence."

So compared to him, I have friends.

People are friends with me.

But when I really think about it, I've never stayed over at a friend's house.

I have zero experience with so-called sleep-overs—hmm.

Now that I'm thinking about it, why is that?

I so loathed spending time at the house, but I never authentically "ran away," either—

Araragi would say it's because I'm a model student, and he probably isn't mistaken, but just maybe Miss Senjogahara's view is the right one.

In other words:

Have you ever asked him to save you?

Not just Araragi.

I bet I can't seek help from anyone other than myself—I don't want to entrust anything decisive to others.

I don't want to let go of the casting board.

I want to define my life on my own.

And so—I became a cat.

An aberration.

I became me.

"Well, it should be fine. I do have a lead, fortunately."

Saying so, not really even speaking to myself but to give myself courage, I began walking, my school bag the only thing I carried. It was the start of a new trimester, our beginning-of-term ceremony, so I had only my pencils and notebooks inside it, nothing much. But it was now my sole possession.

A single bag being the sum total of my belongings made me like Anne Shirley when she first appears—I somewhat enjoyed my predicament, quite inappropriately, so I guess I'm not entirely grave and serious, after all—and as for my lead, it must be obvious.

The ruins of that abandoned cram school.

Apparently it was called Eikow Cram School while it was still in business.

The place where Mister Oshino and Shinobu had lived for about three months—and Araragi lived there too over spring break. So no matter how ruined it looked, it had to feature a bare minimum of facilities a person needed to stay the night.

That was my read on it.

A proper floor and a roof over my head weren't to be taken for granted.

While it was far away on foot, I wanted to save money, considering what I faced, and didn't use the bus.

Mister Oshino used to have a barrier around the place that made it harder to reach than you thought, but it had been removed by now.

You just needed to follow the path.

And you'd get there.

There was obviously no electricity in the building, so I needed to prepare a place to sleep while it was still bright out.

Didn't Mister Oshino and Araragi put desks and chairs together to create beds?

In that case, I'd follow their example.

I passed through the fence, entered the ruins, and began by climbing the stairs to the fourth floor—I chose it because Araragi had told me that Mister Oshino frequently resided there.

In other words, I imagined that the fourth floor was easier to live on than the others, given the living patterns of the previous inhabitant—but this was a swing and a miss.

Or maybe it was closer to striking out.

The first classroom I entered on the fourth floor had a hole in the ceiling.

The next classroom had an opening in its floor.

Not even a proper floor or roof above my head...

As for the remaining classroom, it was so messy it seemed like a wild animal had been set loose inside—almost like Araragi and Mayoi had one of their wild free-for-alls or something.

I felt a tinge of regret. Maybe I'd been too hasty.

I'd been sure the place wasn't this bleak...

Though I already had this location in mind when I declared

my intent to stay at various friends' houses, it was actually a harsher environment than I'd imagined.

Forcing a smile and doing my best to feel excited, I went down to the third floor—where the first classroom I entered had holes in both the ceiling and the floor.

The hole in the ceiling seemed connected to the hole I'd seen in the fourth-floor classroom—wow, really, what happened here? Judging by the edge's color, the damage had to be fairly new… If this was the floor naturally caving in, the building's earthquake-proofing left much to be desired.

My heart was pounding as I ventured onward until at last, I arrived at a classroom whose ceiling, floor, and walls were all in decent shape.

I couldn't let myself feel relieved just yet and went straight to creating a bed. Though it reminded me a bit of a Boy Scout camp, I obviously have never been a Boy Scout.

What I know is only what I know.

It's not experience.

Miss Senjogahara was right about that, too.

It's as if I'm accumulating knowledge, and accumulating senselessness right next to it.

Indeed, improvising a bed by tying together some available desks was nothing more than that, yet not easy. First of all, I didn't have any strings to do the tying. I ended up having to leave the ruins to shop at the closest store.

"Okay, all done. Mister Oshino's bed used one more desk than this, but I'm not as tall as him. This size will do."

Still, making something with your own hands is fun.

The completed bed seemed like a fairly impressive piece of work—unable to hold myself back, I lay down, still in my school uniform.

"Ack."

This was no good.

My high expectations translated into massive psychological damage.

This really was no good.

I felt seriously depressed.

It was the same as sleeping on the floor.

It was rough and bumpy.

Finding it necessary to conduct a control experiment, I tried spreading out on the floor. There didn't seem to be much of a difference after all.

Actually, the connected sections of the desk-bed almost made it the harder of the two to sleep on.

What a terrifying man Mister Oshino was.

He could probably sleep on a bed of nails.

Wondering what Araragi and Shinobu had done, I was reminded that Shinobu was in fact a vampire and that Araragi had been one too during his time here. They weren't going to be useful points of comparison.

Vampires can get a good day's rest inside a cramped little casket, so I didn't have a clue what sleeping entailed for them.

"Bedding. I need bedding..."

Muttering, I left the ruins again.

I had my wallet with me, and it contained my debit card—so it wasn't as if I couldn't go shopping.

It wasn't such a hassle because I needed all sorts of things, and not just plastic strings—but as someone who even had to cut back on bus fares at the moment, I couldn't possibly afford a warm futon. I had to find some kind of substitute.

I remembered reading in some book that newspapers, magazines, and cardboard boxes were very economical ways to stay warm. I would probably be able to get cardboard boxes for free from a department store.

Considering the amount of things I needed to buy, I would have to take the bus back, but I just had to be resigned on that point. One shouldn't skimp on the essentials.

Never let poverty slow the wit.

What a beautiful saying.

For precisely that reason, however, I walked there.

I walked slowly.

One step at a time, like I was packing the earth with my feet.

My absolute essentials were food that would keep and water. I decided to use cardboard boxes as my mattress and newspapers, not magazines, as a blanket. With magazines, I'd have to tear out the pages, something I was afraid I couldn't do. It just felt wrong to destroy reading material, even a magazine. With newspapers, their pages were already separated.

Then came clothes.

I couldn't sleep in my uniform—although Araragi was starting to suspect that I didn't own a single set of casual clothes, of course that wasn't true.

Those two had never behaved like parents for me, but that isn't to say they completely neglected their child.

They did do the bare minimum.

As if they were fulfilling an obligation.

So they did at least buy me clothes—I just didn't want to wear them very much.

And anyway, they all went up in flames.

When they do, it's the end.

It feels like a reset.

Yes—and while it was altogether inappropriate, I couldn't deny a part of me felt refreshed.

Of course, if anything was illusory, it was that freshness.

Reset? No—there had been no reset.

What else was my current situation but an emergency evacuation?

Just because it was gone didn't mean it never happened.

Making my rounds through the department store's general emporium, I saw that clothes were surprisingly expensive. I would have to get on a train, but maybe I needed to go to Uniqlo…or so I was beginning to think when I noticed the hundred-yen shop next door.

That gave me an idea, and when I went over, I found it. They weren't going to be selling pajamas (well, pajama-style sweatshirts and sweatpants) for just a hundred yen, but I was glad to find that they did their underwear. I bought both right away, and I was done shopping.

But I can't show underwear I bought at a hundred-yen shop to

Araragi, the foolish thought ran through my head as I got on the bus as planned and returned to the abandoned cram school.

Mister Oshino never gave off any vibes of everyday life, but he was a human, not a vampire, and when I realized he must have spent three months fighting and struggling like this, an odd wave of admiration washed over me.

Back in the third-floor classroom, I began reinforcing my bed. I used a box cutter to slice up the cardboard, then wrapped two layers around the desk with packing tape. *It's still a cardboard box at the end of the day,* you might think, but this made an overwhelming difference in comfort. I wrapped one more layer of cardboard on top just to be sure, completing my bedding.

All of this had left me quite tired, so I decided to eat.

I had nothing but preserved foods, which meant I didn't need to cook.

Of course, I didn't forget.

"Thank you for the meal," I said.

If you go far enough back, some kind of life had to be sacrificed to create even preserved food. And so, thank you for the meal.

No, even if it didn't contain any morsel of life, the food would become my flesh and blood, so I would gratefully accept it.

Life is precious.

Even if it's not alive.

Still, I was going to tire of such insipid fare eventually, so maybe I needed to buy a gas burner and a pot soon. While my abode was only a temporary one until those two could find a rental, they were busy too, so I could end up living here for quite a while.

"I can just use the toilets and showers at school… And worst case, I can even charge my phone there. I should be able to study in a reading room or the library. What else do I need to worry about…"

I brought up every potential problem and examined it—quickly coming up with a plan to deal with each.

It began to feel less like worrying over the coming days and devising measures and more of a reaffirmation to myself that the darned house burning down didn't affect me at all.

It was like I was making ends meet inside me.

Like I was solving the contradictions.

It was very me.

I gave my thanks again after finishing my meal.

Summer was still going strong so the sun should have been setting late, but it had gotten pitch black out without my noticing. I changed into the pajamas I'd bought at the hundred-yen store, having changed my underwear too, and went to sleep on my brand-new bed.

I wouldn't quite say comfortable.

Strangely, though, I might have slept more soundly than I ever did in the hallway.

0 0 9

Hm?

Didn't we skip over a section number?

Am I just imagining things?

Whatever, it's fine.

The ruins seemed like a place where Roomba could have really shined, but sadly he burned down with the rest of everything in the house, which meant I could no longer rely on him to wake me up in the morning. Even so, I presumed I could wake up at the same time as always.

Humans have something called a circadian rhythm.

This biorhythm is ingrained into our bodies and doesn't falter easily.

Not only that, I was someone who didn't know what it meant to be still asleep—or so I believed until reality intruded.

It wasn't that I overslept.

In fact, I woke up earlier than I'd planned—and I didn't wake up naturally, I was woken up.

But there shouldn't have been anyone who would now that Roomba was gone—

"Miss Hanekawa!"

I was pulled from bed.

Does being still asleep involve incredible images diving into your view? I thought lazily as I waited for my understanding to catch up to my perception—looking at Miss Senjogahara, who was right in front of me with her hands on my collar.

I thought lazily.

She bellowed, "Are you okay?! Are you alive?!"

"H-Huh? Hm? Good morning?"

I gave her a greeting—my first time doing so in a while, actually—still unsure of what was happening.

I was even bewildered.

After all, the normally cool and collected Miss Senjogahara had tears streaming down her reddened face as she stared at me.

"Are you okay?!" she kept asking me.

Still unsure why she was so worried, I nodded, overwhelmed.

"Y-Yeah."

"......nkk." In response, Miss Senjogahara finally let go of my collar, bit down on her lip, seemed to hold back an outburst of tears, and then—"Idiot!" she slapped me across the face.

Roused awake.

And slapped away.

I probably could have dodged them if I'd tried, but she looked so fierce that I just accepted the blows.

No, I probably couldn't dodge them.

Heat pulsed through my cheek.

"Idiot! Idiot! Idiot!"

Not content with hitting me once, Miss Senjogahara did so again and again—her slapping stance deteriorating until she was just popping me in the chest like a child having a tantrum.

It didn't hurt at all.

But it hurt so much.

"Y-You're a girl! By herself! A-And you're staying in a place like this?! What if something happened to you?!"

"...I'm sorry," I apologized.

Well, I should say I was made to—this miniature Boy Scout experience only felt like I was having a bit of fun, and I'd been free of regret or remorse.

Even so.

I was certain I had made Miss Senjogahara, yes, that Miss Senjogahara, terribly worried—

And inappropriately enough, that made me feel a bit glad.

I was happy.

"Uh-uh. I'm not forgiving you. I'll never forgive you," she said, snuggling, clinging, nestling into and hugging me.

She was never going to let me go again.

"I'm not forgiving you. I'll never forgive you, not even if you apologize."

"Okay…understood. I got it. I'm sorry, I'm sorry."

I still reiterated my apology.

I put my arms around Miss Senjogahara and returned her embrace.

And I continued to apologize.

In the end, it took about half an hour for her to stop crying, which brought us to the time that I normally woke up.

010

"I called you constantly since last night, you know," Miss Senjogahara then said, having turned back into her beautiful, nonchalant self. It was incredible how speedily she could switch over. Still, she wasn't quite put together since she couldn't do anything about her red, puffy eyes.

Meanwhile, apparently my bedhead was awful, probably because of my bed (she called me Super Saiyan Hanekawa), so in terms of how put together we looked, the two of us must have been on about the same level.

I couldn't help but be amazed, though, by how normal she was acting, as if all that bawling until a minute ago had just been for show.

I simply found it adorable.

So adorable I almost didn't care about my bedhead.

She told me, "I couldn't even imagine what it'd feel like for your house to be on fire... I thought you might not want to talk to anyone, and I considered not calling you, but I was just too worried. I decided, 'Whatever, just call her!' but you never picked up."

"Oh. Sorry. I had my phone off," I said. "I thought I should try to conserve as much as I can in light of the survivalist lifestyle I'm going to be living."

I hadn't used my cell phone as an alarm clock partly because of my faith in my circadian rhythm, but I also did have another, more pragmatic reason. There was no guarantee that I'd be able to use a power outlet at school (I'm sure my teachers would let me if I explained, but generally, phones are banned at my school).

"God, you're always such a stickler for the rules… Just grab whatever random outlet you find, you don't need to ask," coaxed Miss Senjogahara.

"But that would be stealing electricity."

"I ended up running all around town thanks to that honesty of yours. I talked to various people to come by the intel that you were probably staying over at a friend's house—but no one in class said you were staying with them."

"H-How many people did you talk to?"

"I went through my network."

"……"

Compared to her days of being not just shy but out-and-out paranoid, how she'd grown. But it also meant the whole class now knew I'd gone missing…

My goodness.

"Actually, I should apologize, Miss Hanekawa. I went and met your parents, too."

"What?"

I was surprised.

In other words, had she visited the hotel where those two were staying?

It did seem possible to figure out where they were if you were patient enough… It wasn't as if they were in hiding, and they would have had to inform places like the post office.

Though Miss Senjogahara probably went to the hotel sure that I, too—that I'd be there.

"Oh. You met my dad…and my mom."

"Do you really need to call people like them your 'dad' and 'mom'?" Miss Senjogahara asked bluntly.

Bluntlier.

She seemed disgusted.

Her expression used to tell you nothing about her mindset, but recently her feelings were starting to show.

Whether it was joy or sorrow.

Or anger.

...It seemed like she'd had quite the meeting with those people.

If only they tried a little harder to keep up appearances—they'd been awful towards Mister Oshino over Golden Week, too—but then again, maybe I had no right to think so when I couldn't come up with any appropriate reply.

I wasn't able to paper it over.

"It looks like there's a lot going on. I don't mean to pry, though."

Unlike Araragi, she barely knew a thing about my domestic situation, about the warped and disharmonious Hanekawas, but uninterested in digging any deeper, she put us right back on track.

An impressive feat.

I even felt admiration for her.

"I went around everywhere after that, until this morning, when I finally thought of this place. Well, no, I'd thought of it from the start but didn't want to believe that a young lady would choose to spend the night in these ruins... I thought you would never, that you would never ever, and put if off until last."

"Hm. Hmm? Wait, don't tell me you were up all night, Miss Senjogahara?"

"Even if I didn't tell you, Miss Senjogahara was. Not a wink, it was an all-nighter, in shining armor."

Which is why I cried when I found you—I was so worked up, she explained.

What a cute excuse.

She was playing on "knight," of course.

"It's plenty dangerous for a young lady to be wandering the streets so late, too," I retorted.

"I have nothing to say in my defense."

I'm not the type to ponder the consequences, she added.

Dressed in a very casual outfit, jeans and a T-shirt, she was drenched in sweat. She hadn't been wandering around all this time so much as dashing about as if she were Miss Kanbaru.

"Thanks," I expressed my gratitude as briefly and undramatically as I could before getting off my bed.

My body didn't hurt.

I don't think of myself as particularly talented, even though Araragi insists that I am, but I do seem to have a knack for crafting beds.

Maybe I ought to become an expert craftsman of sleeping beds.

Does that require an apprenticeship in Germany or thereabouts?

"It's fine," Miss Hanekawa said. "It was my own decision—and by the looks of it, I was wasting my time sticking my nose into your business."

"That's not true. I've finally realized how dangerous this was now that you've told me. They say fire drives people mad, and it seems like the house fire got me all weirdly worked up, too."

"You think? I hope that's what it is—but you do terribly dangerous things even when you aren't worked up."

"Do I?"

"Like seduce Araragi."

"Guh."

Guh, indeed.

I didn't know how to rebut that.

I didn't, even though I never seduced him.

The theory that I'd made him the way he was had become surprisingly entrenched out in the world.

"He really was cool...when he first got mixed up with me," Miss Senjogahara mused. "There's barely a trace of that left now, though."

"Is that...my fault?"

"Well, there was also that tiger—I did get excessively worried, true. I'm sorry, it wasn't like me to lose it. Now why don't we get going."

"Get going? To where? School?"

"To my home," she answered as if she were stating the obvious. "And I'm declaring in advance that if you try to resist, I'm going to stick a stapler inside your mouth and whack you on your neck. Is that what it's going to take to bring you with me?"

"……"

When she'd done exactly that to Araragi in the past, there was no way I was going to defy her.

011

Although she'd told me as much, the Tamikura Apartments, where Miss Senjogahara lived, were a terrible sight. Nothing short of decrepit, it was enough to make you think they predated the war.

But while Araragi once made a mean remark about being more worried for its earthquake-proofing than for the abandoned cram school's (his way of showing concern for Miss Senjogahara, in my opinion), the structure felt unexpectedly sturdy as I climbed the stairs.

Maybe old buildings are more reliable that way than the pre-fabs you see these days.

Also, its security features were on another level.

There was even a lock on the apartment door!

Now that I was at a home, I was realizing just how unsafe those ruins were.

"My dad won't be back today because of work. You should stay over tonight."

"What... Really?"

"You see, um...my parents won't be home tonight."

"Why are you rephrasing it like this is a rom-com?"

Miss Senjogahara had a subtle sense of humor both before and after her rehabilitation.

Room 201.

I took off my shoes and entered.

She was telling the truth. There were no hallways.

It was a tidy little, hundred-square-foot room—a bookshelf and a clothes drawer accounted for most of the furniture. She probably made an effort not to own too many things given the place's size, but then Miss Senjogahara never seemed to be someone with many possessions to begin with. Her dad was probably the same way.

"The truth is that I used to live in a mansion—I'd let you have borrowed a whole room back in those days, but alas, my princess, this is all I can do for now."

"Could you not say that like you're Lupin?"

"What would you think if I told you I went to every convenience store I could find and spent a total of ninety thousand yen on a Lupin toy lottery because I had to have a model of his car?"

"I would think you have terrible luck." I sat down and glanced around the room. "You know, it's kind of calming in here."

"Really? Araragi always seems uncomfortable."

"What kind of boy stays calm at a girl's house? But I think I like it here." I was speaking my unfiltered thoughts as they came to me. "It's like my own house."

"Huh."

Miss Senjogahara's expression said that she didn't get it.

She probably didn't.

Of course not. Even I didn't.

I'd blurted out the words.

Like I was speaking to myself.

What was your own house anyway? Yes, the Hanekawa residence that burned down had been a house I'd lived in for fifteen years, making it by definition, or by logical argumentation if we wished, "my own house"; it was "my house" just as I'd uttered as I'd seen it burning to the ground.

But.

Why did this place, Room 201, Tamikura Apartments, make me feel more relaxed than that hallway?

Why did it put my mind at ease?

"It doesn't feel like 'my own house' to me, at least. It hasn't been that long since we moved here," Miss Senjogahara said. "But I guess as far as my last home goes, it's gone."

"……"

That was right.

The house she used to live in, which no one would have objected to calling a mansion, famous in its neighborhood, was now an empty plot of land.

No, it wasn't even a plot.

Was it—a street?

I wasn't sure.

While it had been from a distance, I was able to get a good look for myself at my house burning down—I wondered how it felt not to be informed of your previous home's extinction.

I didn't know.

Another thing I didn't know.

I didn't know—so I stopped thinking about it.

Right.

I wasn't going to mind.

I wasn't going to mind about feeling at ease.

"You should take today off from school," Miss Senjogahara advised, taking off her sweat-drenched T-shirt.

I knew we were both girls, but she was pretty insouciant about stripping. So much so that I admired her.

"I'll take the day off, too," she said.

"What?"

"I'm sleepy. As you might expect." Her eyes were out of focus when I looked more closely. "Right now, I'd sleep with anyone. Even a futon."

"……"

What a way to put it.

"I can barely move my legs. I know I used to be on the track team, but it's been a long time since then. What about you, Miss Hanekawa? It looks like you had a well-made bed, but you couldn't possibly have gotten a good night's sleep in that place."

"Hm? Well, I guess you might be right."

"You have awful bedhead, too."

"Could you not talk about that?" Flustered, I turned in her direction. "It's only the second day of our second term, so we ought to go to—"

"It'd be much stranger for a girl whose house burned down to come to school the next day bright and cheerful like nothing happened. That's where you could be a little less naïve," she told me sternly, having taken off her jeans and turning to me in her underwear.

She looked unwilling to back down.

Despite being in her underwear, she couldn't have looked any braver.

Or less sexual.

"You're not even planning on going to college, right? So you don't need to worry about your attendance record or recommendation letters."

"Well, that's true…"

But the rules.

I wanted to follow the rules.

They were the rules.

"Just take the day off. If you insist on going to school, you're gonna have to defeat me first," she warned, adopting a kung fu pose.

A pointlessly flawless praying mantis stance.

"Sha-shink."

"Could you please not give yourself sound effects? Okay, okay. I'll do as you say for today. And to be honest, it'd be a nice break. I'm glad you're forcing me to do this."

"I hope so. Being a busybody isn't my forte."

She sounded embarrassed, but actually, her way of being a busybody was very much like her.

"Oh, but, but, Miss Senjogahara, what about you? Is it okay for you to take today off too?"

"Me? Well, I'm planning to get into college as a scholarship candidate. Attendance is one thing, but as far as my report card— hmm, right."

Pretending to hesitate for a brief moment, she whipped out her cell phone. As I began to wonder where she was calling, she pinched her nose and started speaking in a hoarse voice.

"Koff, koff, oh, Hoshina-sensei? This is Senjog...koff... Senjogahara. I, I seem to have somehow caught an out-of-season case of the flu... It could be a brand-new strain. Koff, what's that, a fever? Do I have a fever? Yes, it's sitting a little above 107. It broke my air conditioner just now. I'm pretty sure you could pinpoint me as the cause of this year's heat wave. I can swim in my sweat right now. My body hurts so much it feels like it could explode... I know I'll probably give this to the whole class, but I wanted to ask if I could still come to school today. No? Is that so. I understand, that's too bad. I really did want to attend your lesson. Have a nice day."

Ending the call, she wore a guileless look.

"I'm all good now."

Nope, that was hardly all good. "The flu? Why would you go out of your way to tell such a lie? What's wrong with just saying you have a cold?"

"The bigger the lie, the less likely you'll be caught. Don't worry, my primary doctor of long standing can forge a note for me."

"I seriously doubt it."

What sort of doctor jeopardized his or her medical career to help a high school girl play hooky?

For how good of a liar Miss Senjogahara was, she was awful at telling lies.

"And anyway, won't you put on some clothes already?" I requested. "It'd feel awkward if you kept on standing around in your underwear."

"What? But I was planning on taking a shower in a second."

"Ah, got it."

"Will you be taking one too?"

"Ah, yes. If you don't mind."

Now that she mentioned it, my whole body felt like it was covered in dust. I must have sweat a good bit while I was asleep, and the underwear I'd bought at the hundred-yen shop seemed to be in pretty bad shape. The size was a little bit off, to begin with.

"Please go first, though, of course," I said.

"Why are you acting so reserved? Let's get in together."

My prompting was met with a proposition.

With a big smile on her face, too.

A smile as bright as the sun that not even Araragi could have seen before.

"There's nothing to be embarrassed about," she maintained. "We're both girls."

"No, hold on a second. No, no, hold on a lot longer than that. I'm getting a bad feeling about this."

"Oh, you. I'm not planning anything underhanded. Or are you saying you don't trust your friend, Miss Hanekawa?"

"I might not trust a friend who uses that line in this situation…"

"Don't get the wrong idea. I'm not like Kanbaru," she said, her expression turning serious. "I just want to see you in the nude and don't intend to do anything more."

"……"

Miss Senjogahara was starting to take on some new character traits.

While I'd heard about Miss Kanbaru's preferences before, I was beginning to think that their middle-school relationship as the Valhalla Duo may not have been as one-sided as I'd been led to believe.

"Please, Miss Hanekawa. Please take a shower with me!" she entreated, bringing her palms together.

Her new character traits were just so cutting-edge. Was anyone going to be able to keep up?

"I know you and I, as a team, can defeat Sengoku!"

"You're not supposed to know about her yet, in-story…"

There it was. A meta-remark.

We needed to be careful.

About as careful as I was of Miss Senjogahara.

"Well, fine," I relented. "We're both girls, sure, and I'm not particularly opposed to it."

"Oh. I didn't expect you to get on board."

Miss Senjogahara reverted to her usual self.

I really had no idea how serious she was ever being.

It was so ambiguous with her.

"I know I was the one to make the offer, but I always thought of you as someone who'd never cross certain lines, even with a friend."

"Haha, 'certain lines'? Like never letting anyone into your room or never hanging out with anyone outside of school?"

"Yes."

"Well, I don't deny it."

I had that side.

Maybe you could describe it as trampling into someone else's life but hating it when others try to intrude on my own—that seemed to be a perfect description of my relationship with Araragi.

And that's why things turned out the way they did.

"But," I reminded, "how would it make me look if I tried to distance myself from a girl who cried and pummeled me?"

"Guh."

Miss Senjogahara blushed.

She pouted her lips, almost like she was sulking.

She was already wonderful back when she never displayed any emotions, but she was even more wonderful now that she showed a full range of them. It was to the point where I wanted to be the one asking her to take a shower together—or maybe that's going a step too far?

"Oh."

Just then her cell phone, still in her hand, went off. I thought it was our teacher calling back, having realized just how unnatural the excuse had been, but that didn't seem to be the case. To begin with, it was a text.

I asked, "Who's it from?"

"Araragi. Hmm. Judging by what it says, he probably sent it to your phone, too."

"Huh?"

"Why don't you check? Use the outlet over there. Don't worry, I won't bill you for the electricity."

"If you're trying not to sound stingy, that last bit was counterproductive…"

As she suggested, I took my phone from my bag and turned it on. Rather than wait for an incoming message, I manually checked for new ones.

New messages—957.

"Oh," said Miss Senjogahara, "forget all the ones from me. I was so worried."

"Nine-hundred and fifty-six in one night?!"

Nearly all of my inbox's previous messages had been crowded out and was gone from the phone's memory.

Was this my fault?

Shouldn't I actually be demanding an apology?

Thinking so, I rushed to check the newest message—and indeed, the sender was Araragi.

"Not coming back for a while. Dot worry."

No subject, no signature—to be frank, it was utterly bare. Not only that, he seemed to be so pressed for time that he couldn't type out the word "Don't" correctly or fix the spelling. It was a tense message that made you think he mashed it out under pressure.

"While it was expected, he's up to something again—and it looks pretty serious this time," Miss Senjogahara, who seemed to have gotten the exact same message, said with a sigh. She seemed appalled, even. "I don't know the details about spring break, but judging by the text, could this be as bad as then, or worse?"

"You think so too?"

"Yes. But I guess he's grown in that he did send us this message… He used to be really blinkered."

"You're right."

Could it have to do—with Mayoi?

Sure, she was only looking for Araragi to retrieve her forgotten backpack from him, so it might have nothing to do with what he was involved in now, but—

I just had that feeling for some reason.

And I was sure of it.

"No luck. I tried calling him, but I can't get through." Miss Senjogahara, who had started calling him before I noticed (she was way too unhesitant), folded her cell phone shut, not looking particularly let down, and placed it on its charging stand. "He is a boy, after all. I guess I don't have to worry…too much about him. Once he gets back, I'll just force him to hear me brag about how we showered together."

"That doesn't sound like an effective way to harass him."

"I can tell him about how your lines are like *this* and *this*, and *that* is how you are *here*."

"Please stop gesturing."

It was indecent, or rather, erotic.

"In any case," she remarked, "it seems like we're going to have to take care of this tiger ourselves."

"This tiger?"

The tiger—I'd seen on my way to school.

The gigantic tiger.

The speaking tiger.

Now that she mentioned it, she'd said the incident was what had made her excessively worried about me—

"But that tiger—"

"Hm?" interrupted Miss Senjogahara. "My assumption was that the tiger caused the fire, but…did it not? Do you know what caused it?"

"No, they don't know yet—" It might have been arson, a firefighter had told me—the tiger, the tiger as the cause—"so we don't know."

"I see. Then maybe I was jumping to conclusions. Being a former member of the track-and-field team."

"That hardly merited saying it with a dashing look."

"All right, Miss Hanekawa. Why don't we go take that shower. We'll even take Araragi's for him."

"Let's keep Araragi out of it."

"I'll get a good look at your nude body, enough for both me and him."

"Could you just get enough for yourself, at the most?"

"Fine," she agreed readily.

Then again, any resistance would have been troublesome.

"In fact," she conceded, "now that I really think about it, naked girls or their underwear don't excite him anymore."

"Is that true?"

"Yup. He's at a new stage after all of his experiences in the last few months. Now he says just seeing a girl in a skirt turns him on."

"A gaze against which no girl can protect herself."

"He says the cloth swaying in the wind is almost too much for him."

"It doesn't even need to get flipped…"

He really was on a different level.

Or rather…

Yeah…

"Okay, let's get in there and have fun washing each other's chest."

"Don't you mean back?"

"Um, Miss Hankeawa?"

I'd started to peel off my clothes, concerned about this conversation getting dragged out any longer, when Miss Senjogahara abruptly asked me a question, her expression somewhere between smiling and serious.

"Do you still love Araragi?"

"Yes. I still do."

I answered immediately.

012

I think this is a good time for me to discuss Araragi a bit.

To discuss Koyomi Araragi.

Koyomi Araragi, Miss Senjogahara's boyfriend and my friend.

I actually knew about him from before spring break—I don't know everything, but I did know about him.

He doesn't realize it himself, but he's quite the celebrity at Naoetsu High.

He stood out, you might say.

Like a sore thumb, to be honest.

He loves to treat me like a celebrity, but we could go toe-to-toe as far as that goes.

Though it's more correct to say he's feared.

Yes, people are afraid of him.

Just as I hated being treated like a model student, he hates being treated like a delinquent, but really, if you're skipping school whenever you feel like it, not taking classes and tests seriously—or not even taking them at all—then I'm not the only one who'll start thinking of you that way.

When I asked him after we became friends for details about what he did when he was skipping school and not caring about classes and tests, which is to say when I casually dug deeper into the matter, it all sounded close to the same as what happened during spring break and Golden Week.

All in all, it wasn't as if turning into a vampire over spring break or becoming involved with aberrations had transformed his life; at the root, that had been Koyomi Araragi all along.

While his face turns sour and he begins to grumble whenever Karen and Tsukihi's activities as the Fire Sisters come up, what they're doing, likewise, is nothing more than a rehash of Araragi's middle-school days.

No, according to his sisters, Araragi's time in middle school was far more precarious. Extracurricular activities that barely toed the line of legality—nay, fighting on the opposite side of the law wouldn't be too great of an exaggeration. Beyond being taken aback, I'm impressed by the fact that he managed to make it to high school alive.

Of course, while he might be doing the same thing in high school that he was in middle school, there does seem to be a major difference in his motivation.

He adamantly refuses to talk about it, even more than about spring break, and none of his current friends, myself included, know the details, but he appears to have experienced some psychological turning point around the time he was a freshman.

I guess it was why he became a "washout," to use his word?

…I'm making it sound like a big deal, but maybe he couldn't keep up academically, and that's all it was. There's no rule stating that changes in a person's mindset have to be the outcome of some huge incident.

And either way, whether he changes or not, Araragi is Araragi.

He's still him, even though he's changed completely from the cool person he was when we first met.

No matter how much he changes, he's Koyomi Araragi.

So these are nothing more than memories of his middle-school days, when his disposition was more hi-tension, upper, hotblooded—memories that Araragi, himself, has forgotten. In that sense, it could be a very normal event called settling down once you start high school.

Normal.

Mundane.

This event of his.

Or.

Spring break. And Golden Week too.

And maybe everything with Miss Senjogahara, with Hachikuji, with Miss Kanbaru, with Sengoku, and with Karen, too, was no match for all the things he experienced in middle school.

As for today, he was on the move again for some reason.

At some point down the line, I fell in love with him—but I'll talk about when that happened a little later.

014

...?

Did we skip another section number?

What's going on here?

We couldn't have skipped 13 just because it's an unlucky number. Once, Araragi complained that while it made a certain amount of sense to skip over 13, whoever first thought to skip 4 in parts of Asia because it sounds like the word for "death" had to have been incredibly influential to spread a pun so far (that perspective is very him), but it's not like we need to skip 13 just because it makes a certain amount of sense.

???

Well, it doesn't inconvenience me in any particular way, so I'll keep going—I got up after noon.

No one woke me up.

Miss Senjogahara had been right. Unable to get a good night's sleep in those ruins after all, I'd fallen into a deep slumber that cleanly removed the dull fatigue entangled somewhere inside my body.

I was a bit on the surprised end to find Miss Senjogahara's sleeping face in front of me when I woke up, though.

No, not a bit. I was pretty seriously shocked.

I can only describe it as a feast for the eyes.

What a handsome face it was—something about a beauty with her eyes shut offers up a different flavor from when she's awake.

Miss Senjogahara's sleeping face, in particular, was so well formed it almost appeared crafted. So smooth like it was made of porcelain, it also had an undeniable sensuality that only nature offered. I found my heart racing before I realized it.

Thump thump thump.

I wasn't tired anymore, and there was no way I could stay half-asleep anyway with my blood pressure rocketing the moment I woke up.

So Araragi was getting to hog her sleeping face these days?

I blushed at myself for my own adult-themed thought.

I felt like an idiot.

Actually, I was obviously an idiot.

…No, maybe not.

Even Araragi couldn't hog her sleeping face yet—because she was living with her dad.

Her father.

He'd seen more of his daughter's sleeping face than anyone else.

And watched over it.

"…Oh."

Miss Senjogahara opened her eyes all of a sudden.

She seemed to be less waking up than coming back to life.

Like maybe she was having her switch flipped on.

Booted up.

Apparently she wasn't the type to be very "still asleep" either—even though she came across as hypotensive.

There's actually no casual relationship between low blood pressure and rising and shining, they say.

If anything, it has more to do with low blood sugar?

"Good morning, Miss Hanekawa."

"Good morning, Miss Senjogahara."

"Though I doubt it's the time of day to be using that expression."

"You're right. Not at this hour."

"What time is it?"

"Um." I turned my neck to check the clock on top of the dresser again. "One-thirty."

"AM? PM?"

"PM, of course."

How long did she think she'd slept?

Time for a flashback—after that.

After that, the two of us really did take a shower—it was my first time ever doing so with anyone else, so I'll let you know that many embarrassing, clumsy moments were had.

Hence Miss Senjogahara took the lead entirely and ended up washing me all over. She had practiced hands and a veteran's moves.

She was used to flirting with other girls!

Or that's the impression I got.

I couldn't take it in silence, however, and washed her all over right back.

There we were, in the not-too-big shower, quite literally naked, and I'm not sure exactly how to put this, but I feel like we crossed some line.

I, who always set boundaries, crossed a line.

You might call it a turning point.

At least, maybe there was no longer any reason to act too reserved around Miss Senjogahara. While she'd forced me to come along with her, to tell the truth I'd still been reluctant about staying over at someone else's house.

Now I could think: I'd be a bother to her for just one day.

I was able to.

I honestly felt that way.

For a very long time, I hadn't done such a simple thing.

What do we mean by "honest"?

What do we mean by "feel"?

There was no end to it when you thought about it too deeply.

Come to think of it, Miss Senjogahara was also someone who'd built firm walls in her heart.

Back when she was called the "cloistered princess," she'd never have let me stay over or shower with her, let alone spent all night running around town searching for me.

Considering the weight of all she'd overcome in the past few months, I felt pathetic for having just as many experiences but not overcoming a thing.

Right.

I haven't overcome—a thing.

Not even after the commotion over Golden Week, not even after that day before the culture festival.

I haven't grown.

I haven't changed.

Which is why, I thought, I'm so jealous of Miss Senjogahara—and love her so much and can't bring myself to hate her.

I honestly felt that way.

Having frolicked in the shower for about thirty minutes (no one was around to stop us), we then exited into the bathroom, refreshed.

We wiped each other's bodies and put on underwear.

"I can understand having reservations about putting on my underwear, but could you at least borrow my pajamas?" begged Miss Senjogahara. "I'll throw out those sweats that I fear you bought at some kind of discount store. Their design would stupefy a stupa."

"Huh? You don't like them?"

"They're awful." As Miss Senjogahara shook her head, she seemed annoyed by her wet hair. It was also a blunt comment. "Those clothes weren't made with any human wearers in mind…and are exclusively for mannequins. Or maybe I should call them mock-ups created to test clothes hangers."

"……"

She was going to go that far?

With no mirrors in the abandoned cram school, I was never able to check how I looked in them, but…was Miss Senjogahara crying when she woke me from my sleep on my handmade bed because of what I was wearing?

Hmm.

Well gosh.

"Really?" I asked. "I can borrow your pajamas?"

"Go ahead. I'm well-stocked when it comes to clothes."

"Then I think I will."

For my underwear, I'd broken out what I'd bought at the hundred-yen shop.

I put my arms through the sleeves of the pajamas that Miss Senjogahara went to get from the dresser.

It was a strange feeling, wearing another person's clothes—despite being clothed, I felt incredibly liberated.

Like I'd allowed something.

Miss Senjogahara was tall, which meant she wore larger-sized clothing than me, so they did feel unnecessarily baggy.

"And yet it looks tight around your chest," she noted. "It's wonderful, you never let me down."

"Um, it doesn't feel tight..."

They felt normal for pajamas.

And when had I gotten her hopes up in the first place?

I waited for her to get into her pajamas, and then we took turns blow-drying each other's hair. It didn't take much time at all—both of us had worn our hair pretty long during first term but basically had short bobs now.

Soon they were dry.

I felt a bit dissatisfied by the fact.

"Say, Miss Hanekawa, you've been growing your hair out ever since you cut it after the culture festival, haven't you?"

"Hm? Oh, I guess. I might not have gone to a hairdresser yet."

"Are you going to wear it long again?"

"Huh—I'm not sure. I only noticed once it was short, but long hair can actually take less work to keep up in some ways—don't you think?"

"Hmm. Perhaps I don't entirely disagree."

"Right?"

"Like getting bedhead."

"Right..." She was really dragging that one out. "So maybe I should just grow it out again, considering what I'll be doing after graduation—you know?"

"Ah. After graduation," Miss Senjogahara repeated my words as if to imply something. "To be honest, I don't know about it. I certainly don't think you're in any need of a university education, of course, but college isn't just a place to study. The way I see it, traveling around the world and going to college are like the same thing."

"……"

The topic was one that had come up many times before, but the reason I liked her so much was that she was willing to say these kinds of things out loud.

That's right, I'm not going to college.

It was why I didn't have to worry about my attendance record or my report card.

I intend to spend two years or so traveling the world after I graduate—and my plans for it are close to finished. Of course, they're pretty slapdash since scheduling every little thing out would make it feel like I'm on a package tour or something.

At this moment in time, the only people who know about my post-graduation wishes are Araragi and Miss Senjogahara.

Araragi, being the person that he is, didn't try to stop me.

Miss Senjogahara, being the person that she is, gently opposed it unequivocally.

"And I only feel more against it given how careless you must be to stay over in those ruins like there was nothing wrong with it. You could even say my position has hardened. Not every country in the world is as safe as Japan, right? If something terrible happens, it'll be too late, okay? You should act under the assumption that every boy in the world is after that skin of yours."

"Specifically my skin?"

"Picturing it getting burned as you walk through the tropics is enough to make me despair," she said, her face really betraying despair. How much did she care about my skin? "Maybe it'd be best if I put a collar on you and locked you up in a cage…"

"Miss Senjogahara, Miss Senjogahara, you're trying to do something awful to me here in a country as safe as Japan."

"Don't you think you're just being difficult?" she asked, ignoring my repartee. It reminded me of Araragi's complaint that she ignored his quips all the time. Maybe hers wasn't a funny-woman routine, and she was just funny. "Though I don't know if it's toward Araragi, or toward Mister Oshino, or toward me—or maybe someone else, like those parents of yours."

"……"

She made me fall silent for a minute.

She made me think.

Maybe she was right—no.

"I'm not being difficult. I wouldn't decide on a path just to be difficult."

"I see. I hope not."

"I just want to make up for what I'm lacking, that's all—oh, I know what you'd call it these days. A journey of self-discovery."

"Self-discovery."

"Though I did already meet my 'self' over Golden Week—so maybe it'd be more accurate to say I'm going on a new journey of self-creation."

"Hm. Well, I doubt I could overturn any firmly sworn resolve of yours anyway. If I'm being hard about this, then you're a rock. But," she said.

Quietly.

"If you start to feel like you don't want to, you don't have to. You can even turn back mid-trip. We won't find that embarrassing. Yes, we. Down deep, Araragi must want to stop you, too."

"He must?"

"Like a wall of steel," she swore.

But I wondered.

I still wasn't quite sure how Araragi felt about me—but in any case, that was the kind of girl talk about not very girl-talky subjects we had as we finished drying each other's hair.

Miss Senjogahara proceeded to take a futon set out of the closet.

"There's another pair, my dad's, but I don't know about making a high school girl sleep in bedding that a middle-aged man past forty is always using. All right, I guess there's no way around it. Miss

Hanekawa, let's sleep together in mine."

"……"

That conclusion didn't take long to come to.

"It's okay, it's okay, it's okay! Don't worry! I won't do anything to you! We'll just be sleeping on the same futon! I won't lay a finger on you!"

She was pulling off an impressive feat, losing my trust by emphasizing how trustworthy she was.

"I won't use you as a hug pillow, Miss Hanekawa!"

"I feel like I'm learning why you're able to go out with Araragi."

The possibility that it wasn't me but Miss Senjogahara who'd made him that way was rapidly rearing its head, too.

And when I really thought about it, I recalled that he was already pretty bad by the time we met during spring break.

Okay, so it wasn't my fault.

"All right, sure, sure. No need to say all that, I wasn't even worried."

"Really? Thank you," Miss Senjogahara expressed her gratitude for some reason. It made her a highly suspicious girl, in fact. "Please go ahead and use my pillow, then. I'll use my dad's."

"Hm? Wait. Right, wouldn't you sleeping on your father's futon be another option here?" Even if they were family, or precisely because they were family, girls of a tender age began to feel repulsed by their dads—which I took to be the logic behind not using his futon, but if she was willing to use his pillow, maybe that wasn't it.

"What? I wouldn't be able to sleep with you if I used my dad's."

"I see."

A very logical point. Hard to argue against.

"Also," she said, "I'm actually a daddy's girl, so I'd be too excited to get any sleep if I used his futon."

"You're being too open about this, Miss Senjogahara."

What a family.

Then again—it absolutely wasn't the kind of quip I was allowed to make as someone who didn't have the first idea of that whole concept.

"Well," responded Miss Senjogahara, "every home has its own family relationships—and there's clearly something abnormal about

Araragi and his sisters."

"Yeah, abnormal!" I agreed breathlessly without meaning to.

I won't mince words. Their sibling dynamic is hazardous.

In constant battle with ethics, it's been winning a string of crushing victories lately. The balance of that war is in extreme peril.

"I only met them the other day," remarked Miss Senjogahara, "but compared to the level of respect that Karen and Tsukihi pay to their brother…the way I feel about my dad easily counts as commonplace."

"Hmm."

While you couldn't deny that she was offering an even worse example in order to normalize herself, let's not pursue the topic.

It just isn't for me to pursue, when I never became a family with those two after living in the same house with them and spending fifteen years under the same roof.

Even the house—was gone now.

How could you be a family—with no place to call home?

"Well, why don't we go to bed, Miss Hungarian Goose Down Quilt—er, Miss Hanekawa."

"Who accidentally says 'Hungarian goose down quilt' instead of 'Hanekawa'?"

"Hungarian" and "Hanekawa" both had four syllables and started with the same letter, but that was it. Not to mention all the words that came after. It had to be intentional, but even with her now-expressive face, it was hard to tell just how serious she was being.

It was eight in the morning at that point.

We could still make it to school if we sprinted there, but meekly notifying my teacher that I'd be missing class—

I went to bed with Miss Senjogahara.

"Good night."

"Good night."

Those words, too.

I hadn't spoken them in so long that it felt like my first time. You might say good morning to a Roomba, but you wouldn't say good night.

015

End of flashback.

"Half past one in the afternoon... Seems like we got a lot of sleep. Did you just wake up too, Miss Hanekawa?"

"Yeah, more or less."

"Ah. I never imagined I'd get to wake up on the same futon as you."

"Could you not say things that sound like they could be pillow talk?"

"I'm such a high-strung person that I can't sleep very deeply, but it feels like I was knocked right out. Could it have been the pillow?"

"When you say that, are you talking about your dad's pillow? Or are you talking about your hug pillow?" I asked, though neither would be appropriate.

Then again, I was in no position to talk. I slept so soundly myself that I didn't have any dreams at all. I don't know if it was thanks to Miss Senjogahara's pillow, or the futon, or the hug...

No, stop.

There really wasn't any hugging going on.

"All right, then. Aren't you hungry? I was thinking of making us breakfa—no, lunch," offered Miss Senjogahara.

"Oh, that sounds good. I'd love to join you."

"Is there anything you can't eat?"

"No."

"'Kay," she said, crawling out of bed toward the bathroom. Her plan must have been to wash her face to wake up fully before wielding a knife.

Returning, she headed straight to the kitchen.

Of course, while I call it a kitchen, this was a single, hundred-square-foot room, so we were basically in the same space.

"Hmm, hmm, hmm..."

Miss Senjogahara hummed as she donned an apron.

She seemed excited for some reason.

Maybe she liked cooking?

I recalled Araragi complaining to me that it was hard to get her to cook him anything, but I also realized I hadn't heard anything about that lately. Did it mean he'd finally savored a home-cooked meal prepared by his lover?

"Miss Hanekawa?"

"Yes?"

"Would you get turned on if I suddenly stripped down to nothing but this apron?"

"I'd get pissed off."

I see, she nodded, pulling ingredients out from the refrigerator.

It looked like I wouldn't have to get pissed off. I felt relieved, because I didn't know how to.

"By the way, Miss Hanekawa, did you know 'bean sprout' uses the same character as for *moé*? I've found them delicious ever since I learned that."

"Well, I think they kept tasting the same to me..."

"In which case..." Miss Senjogahara turned around with a dashing look—the tip of her knife pointed my way. "Maybe calling a kid a 'bean sprout' wouldn't be as insulting as calling them a beanpole."

"Bean sprout..."

To be honest, it wasn't a very funny or smart observation, but she did have a knife pointed my way. I had to pick my reaction wisely.

Though blades really did suit her, I had to admit.

"Do you like your toast with butter or cream cheese?" she continued.

"Oh, so you've already decided we're having bread, not rice?"

"Of course we are. I'm preparing you a real spread here. Why else would people talk about eating three square meals a day? If we were supposed to eat rice, wouldn't it be three round meals?"

"I think they make round bread too…"

And you could always just say breakfast, lunch, and dinner like a normal person.

There seemed to be a lot of holes in Miss Senjogahara's logic.

"Hmm, you're right about that," she admitted. "It's a logical hole that 'three round meals' sounds like something you'd eat while watching a short fight."

"No, there are bigger holes here than that. Anyway, do you really keep both butter and cream cheese here?"

"Of course not. We just have a mysterious blended product."

"Mysterious, you say…"

"You know, that stuff that comes in a tub."

"What's your point?"

"The first time I tried it, I couldn't believe it wasn't butter."

"You're about fifteen years late for that joke to be funny."

Yes, there really was a time when such statements about margarine were in fashion.

"Don't worry, my dad is really picky when it comes to bread. We even have our own bread machine. This thing's expensive, you know. Doesn't it look out of place in this kitchen?"

"Hmm."

She was right, it did. If I may, it looked more expensive than any of the furniture there. We didn't have one at our house, so I secretly began to get my hopes up.

"Miss Hanekawa, do you cook often?"

"Yes, I do."

I didn't know how much I wanted to go into the topic because giving too straight an answer always got people creeped out by the Hanekawa family situation. But she was looking after me, so it seemed only right to give her at least a few details. Not to mention that she'd met the two who should be called my parents. There was no point in awkwardly trying to keep up appearances here. I'd even told her about sleeping in the hallway—

No.

This wasn't about things "seeming only right" or having "no point."

I simply wanted to tell her.

I didn't want to hide much from someone who'd been so worried for me.

"Everything I ate, I made for myself."

"Oh. There was a time in my life like that, too. My mom and I weren't on good terms."

"...They got divorced, right?"

"Yes. I haven't met her since then—but I do wonder where that woman is now, and what she's doing. I just hope she's happy." Despite her words, her tone didn't sound particularly concerned—her knife continued to chop vegetables the entire time. I don't know if that was natural or unnatural. "There's a lot that happens in any home, really."

"Yeah, you're right."

Cutting the heat on the pot just as the bread maker let us know that our bread was ready, she began plating our food. She probably had this routine calculated out.

While I did ask her if there was anything I could do to help, she refused to the end, insisting that I let her handle it all. She disliked people getting in the way of her rhythm. Soon, the low dining table featured a full lineup of plates—I did at least help her carry over the dishes.

"Thank you for this meal."

"Thank you for this meal."

Bread, tea, and vegetables with chicken.

I was a bit happy for whatever reason that she'd made such basic home-cooked food instead of anything too fancy. Explaining the feeling would take quite a bit of work, though, so I decided not to convey it to her.

We ate.

"Oh, this is good."

"Really? It is?" She looked surprised. "Araragi didn't seem very happy. To be honest, I was prepared for you to bash it."

"Bash…"

And wait, Araragi didn't seem very happy…

Hmm.

He needed to work on being better boyfriend material.

Even if the food wasn't to his taste, he should at least pretend to enjoy it.

Though it was very like him not to.

"Well, I think it tastes good," I said. "Then again, taste is a personal thing."

"So in other words, you and I have similar tastes. In food and in men."

I spit out my tea.

It was a horrible display of manners on my part.

"Miss Senjogahara…you're sometimes too open about—"

"Well, no, I thought if we really want to be honest with each other, it might be best to go ahead and talk about this with you."

"It feels like one wrong move could drive a wedge between us, but okay…"

She never backed down from a challenge, did she?

Then again, I was also glad that she broached the subject—because it was a hard one for me to broach, even if I tried.

"So, Miss Senjogahara, how about we just put it out there and say what each of us love about Araragi?"

"No, we shouldn't put it out there, in case this conversation leaks somehow. It'd give him a big head."

"I see…"

She was very stern when it came to her boyfriend.

It seemed like she was no carrot and all stick.

"What should we talk about, then?" I asked.

"Well, why don't we tell each other what we hate about Araragi?"

"Sounds good!"

The next three hours were a whirlwind of our truest feelings.

I'd let myself get excited over badmouthing someone...

016

"I know it's already late enough to start getting ready for dinner, but why don't we talk about the future?" Miss Senjogahara cut our conversation short with the kind of regret in her voice you'd expect from someone announcing that the party was over.

We both felt rejuvenated for some reason. Supple. What exactly was this sense of solidarity?

"What do you mean, the future?"

"Your future. Okay, you'll stay over at my house tonight. What will you do starting tomorrow? Do you have some kind of lead?"

"Well, I—"

If I said, "I'll just go back to that abandoned cram school, I guess," even as a joke, she'd probably smack me. Actually, I could even see her kicking me.

"—don't."

"I see." She gave a solemn nod. She looked so serious, I found it hard to believe that just moments ago, she'd been criticizing the wicked deeds of her boyfriend with all her body and soul. Sure, she was expressive now, but it was almost two-faced. "To tell you the truth, I'd like you to continue to stay here after tomorrow... I'd like to keep you under my control."

"Your control?"

"Under my watch."

"I'm not sure if that correction helped much…"

It felt like the same thing.

It must have been the truth, though. She was trying to say that she was worried about me.

"But you can see for yourself just how cramped my home is—and I'm not going to ask you to go to sleep, wake up, and change clothes in the same room as my dad after he gets back tomorrow."

"Yeah, that's a little…"

It definitely gave me pause.

Plus, it would probably be a pretty massive annoyance as a father to have your daughter's classmate staying over in the same room.

"I mean, whatever would I do if my dad fell in love with you?"

"That's what you're worried about?"

"The day may come when I'll have to call you mom."

"No. It won't."

"Excuse me? Are you saying my dad isn't good enough for you?"

She glared at me for real.

What a bothersome character trait.

It seemed like she wasn't lying about being a daddy's girl.

Hm.

When I considered that, or even if I didn't, I wasn't going to be able to stay at her place for much longer.

So, what to do?

"I think he could take it for a day or two, though," Miss Senjogahara said. "We could just have him stand outside while you change or something."

"There's no way I could ever ask someone's dad to do that, you realize…"

What kind of guest would that make me?

"By the way, Miss Hanekawa, what's your read on what'll happen next with the Hanekawa family?"

"Those people," I began.

I didn't have to force myself to call them my "father" and "mother" in front of Miss Senjogahara anymore, so I deliberately chose the term "those people."

"Those people won't be able to live out of a hotel forever, so they'll look for a place to rent soon. It has to be the cheaper option. They're going to be getting a fire insurance payout, so I assume we'll live out of that rented place while they use the money to rebuild a house."

"Rebuild a house, huh? I wonder what that takes?"

"If it's the same size as the old one, probably around thirty million yen?"

"Oh, no. I was talking about time, not money."

"Oh."

What an embarrassing mistake.

I'd gone straight to how much.

"Hmm. It depends on how they make it, but when you factor in all the paperwork, maybe half a year?"

"Half a year..."

In other words, Miss Senjogahara said.

"You'll have graduated high school by then and will be off to travel the world."

"—I guess so."

It wouldn't be ready—in time.

No, I didn't know what was supposed to be ready in time or not for what here. The house I had lived in for fifteen years was burned to the ground now—it would be a different house, rebuilt.

Everything had been lost.

That was all.

There was no making it in time or not—it was simply the wrong time to make anything of it.

"Well, let's forget about six months from now. You'll have somewhere you can stay if they hurry to find a place to rent, right?"

"Yes, a hallway."

"A hallway? Oh, right," she reacted, seemingly having forgotten what I'd told her. That was the only reaction, though. "Well, a lot of things happen—in every house."

"Yes. In every house."

"Which means..." Extending her arm to snatch her phone off the charging station, Miss Senjogahara opened its calendar. "You'll need a place to stay until that rental gets figured out—did your textbooks and notebooks go up in flames, too?"

"Up in flames," I nodded. "The only things that made it out were what I'd brought to school that day, my writing tools and my wallet. But I think our teachers will let me borrow a textbook if I asked."

"I see. So there's no need for me to worry about that, either."

As she said this, Miss Senjogahara operated her cell phone with one hand—I couldn't see what she was doing from my angle, but she didn't seem to be using the calendar anymore judging by how fast she was hitting its keys.

Was she writing an email?

"Miss Hanekawa. I just had a good idea, would you like to hear it?"

"A good idea?"

"You could even call it a scheme. Call me Hitagi the Schemer. A series-spanning collaboration that readers could only dream of."

"……" Seems more recycled than collaborative to me.

"So it should take a week at the very longest until your parents find somewhere to rent—and if that's all, I think I could make something happen."

"Hmm."

To be honest, this idea, scheme, or whatever it was didn't feel particularly enticing—in the worst case, I just had to go to the hotel where those two were staying. In other words, this was about me being selfish, not something worth having Miss Senjogahara fret and ponder over.

So it wasn't the idea itself.

Rather, the fact that she'd thought one up made me so happy that I said:

"I'd like to hear it. Would you please tell me?"

"Oh, I'm not so sure. Should I, or shouldn't I?"

"……"

Over the course of her rehabilitation, Miss Senjogahara's once-subdued personality had grown the slightest bit obnoxious.

017

After that, the two of us had dinner (for your reference, we cooked rice. Not only did the kitchen have a bread maker, it had a very nice rice cooker. "Square meals are important, but so are rounded diets," apparently) before taking another shower together and washing each other. From there, Hitagi Senjogahara and Tsubasa Hanekawa went to bed before the clock struck ten, in part to help foster our bravery for the coming day.

And nyow it was my turn to wake up.

By "my," I of course mean the nyew aberration based off of the Afflicting Cat that you all nyoh, "Black Hanekawa" as that Hawaiian-shirted jerk nyamed me.

I snyuck out of the sheets without making a nyoise (unlike vacuum cleaners, cats specialize in moving around silently), and then—

"Mmh, myow!"

I stretched my paws.

I think this goes without saying, but the reason we've been skipping chapters when my myaster, Tsubasa Hanekwa, goes to sleep, is that I've been showing up like this. I'm a nyaberration, so it's nyot something I'm familiar with, but according to my myaster's knowledge, sleep is important to rest nyot just the body but the psyche, too—I don't think much about anything, and I don't have anything close to a psyche, so it really doesn't make a whole lot of sense to me, but it sounds like thinking can be a pretty big burden.

And that's why humans have to spend thirty-three purrcent of their time sleeping, a third of their lives.

Everyone sleeps.

Even my myaster sleeps.

But you see, with all that happened, what would be called nyormal "sleep" is nyo longer enough rest for my myaster. I don't nyoh how much of this my myaster realizes—nyo, actually, even an idiot like me realized this one. But my myaster is just so dull to her own pain that she doesn't realize the incredible shock dealt to her psyche, which is to say her heart, when the house she lived in for fifteen years burned down.

Which is why I came out.

Black Hanekawa, nyow here for a third appearance.

There was Golden Week, then before the culture festival (what's that, anyway?), and nyow this, which makes three.

Of course, you could say that the me that showed up during Golden Week, the me that showed up before the culture festival, and the current me are all different cases—or different people, if you want to say it like a human.

Or different cats?

Of course, every change in pattern of a Black Hanekawa would seem so mewniscule to a human that there'd be no nyeed to identify each one—just like how I can't tell humans apart.

In other words, if you were going to use a nyarticle to talk about me, it would be "a," not "the." Maybe it'd be easier to understand if I said there's nyo plural form for "Black Hanekawa"?

If a human saw three Yeti, they wouldn't say "Yeti A," "Yeti B," and "Yeti C." Nyo, they'd just call them all "Yeti."

So it's the same with me. Nyot Black Hanekawa C, and nyot Black Hanekawa Three—just Black Hanekawa.

Nyice to meetcha.

"Meow, meow, meow," I said as I went to the bathroom.

I took a look at the mirror.

My hair had turned bright white.

Ears had grown from my head.

I had the piercing eyes of a cat.

I nyever had a mirror or anything nyear me when I first woke up at the abandoned cram school, and I was so busy figuring out my situation anyway (in case you're wondering, even as someone purrsonally devoted to my myaster, it didn't take a mirror to think there was something weird about her taste in sweats). And when I "woke up" this morning, I was too sleepy to do anything. I'm nyocturnal, so my brain doesn't work that good when the sun is out.

So this was my furst time seeing myself in a mirror.

"Hmm. The ears are charming in an all-nyew way nyow that my hair's short," I checked out the important stuff as I washed my face.

I nyoh humans say rain's on the way if you see a cat wash its face, but this didn't have anything to do with the weather.

I left the bathroom and grabbed the key sitting on top of the dresser. I think it goes without saying that it was the key to the room.

That annyoying little human they were calling Koyomi Araragi seems to have thought I was such an idiot that I couldn't even use a key. Gimme a break! I can at least use a key. Don't you underestimate human-based aberrations.

I snyuck around—so that I wouldn't wake up Hitagi Senjogahara, this woman who seems to be my myaster's friend, and silently opened the door before locking it just as silently.

Well, I say friend, but I think she was supposed to be my myaster's enyamy, too. It seemed silly to move around so carefully when I thought about that, but I was just going to do as my myaster wanted here.

Because my myaster, at least, nyever once resented this woman.

Nyot once.

Meow.

I didn't wear shoes.

They're so hard to prowl around in.

Why would you ever wear something that keeps you from using your fingers?

"Meow, meow, meow, meow."

Nyow, I'm sure some of you are worried that my myaster isn't getting any rest at all if I'm nyout and abyout while she's asleep.

Thank you for your concern.

But nyot to worry.

It's all okay.

Because, as I'd put it, I balance out my myaster's mental state—if anything, my myaster's psyche is soothed merely by me coming out. Physical fatigue isn't a problem, because I'm a nyaberration. Even when I'm in a human body, I mewve it using a different set of rules than a human. So my myaster's body should actually be getting even more rested than if she was just sleeping.

Really, just think about it.

Nyo myatter how good of a bedmaker my myaster is, nyo one can get a good nyight's rest and wake up ache-free after sleeping on cardboard boxes wrapped around a desk—that's nyo bed, it's a bedhead generator. And even if sleeping on the same futon with a friend who'd cry for you is better beyond comparison, even if it would be moving if you got a good nyight's sleep that way, you nyormally don't sleep as well when you use an unfamiliar pillow and bedding.

But nyo, she slept soundly and got a nyice and healthy rest. Nyot to brag, but that was because I came out like this.

I'm an embodiment of my myaster's stress, which is to say a symbol of her fatigue. Just being *cut loose* like this is enough to give my myaster peace of mind.

So I may nyot be able to take all the credit, but you can at least say that it's partially thanks to me that my myaster doesn't know what it means to be "still asleep."

I'm sure it was a coincidence, but whatever dirty little human compared me to a nyightmare made a keen-eyed point—because I'm like sleep itself to my myaster.

A dream.

Sure, I went around draining the enyergy of every human I could get my paws on over Golden Week because I couldn't do enough to relax my myaster—but nyo need to worry.

I wasn't planning on doing anything that meowtrageous this time around.

There'd be no point, anyway.

To put it like that annyoying little human, I only appear like this as a nyaftereffect of a nyaberration, as something like a nyecho—just a phenyomenyon in the end.

Like El Niño. Or La Niña?

There's basically nyothing I can do.

I can keep her from being terrorized by her nyightmares by coming out like this. That's it.

It's all I can do to care for my myaster's mental health—which is to say, I'm as good as nyothing.

But then again, "There's a reason for every aberration," according to that Hawaiian-shirted jerk—so even if there is nyothing I can do, I think there's meaning in me being here like this, like a nyecho, like a simple illusion.

I can't do the things that I can't do.

So I just have to do the things I can, meow.

As much as I can.

…Hrmph.

Nyow that I say this, this me and the previous me really were different cases—I harbored nyo feeling whatsoever of wanting to force things forward, of wanting to solve things with violence.

I was warmer now, if I do say so myself.

I guess it's nyormal for a cat to be warm, though.

Nyo, maybe nyot.

Maybe it was my myaster who grew warmer.

We can talk about humans and aberrations all day, but in the end, my myaster and I are one and the same. So if she gets softer, I do too.

Nyo need to wait for the sun to come out.

Nyo need for a foot warmer.

I nyoh my myaster has doubts about that Hitagi Senjogahara woman's rehabilitation, and I nyoh she's wild about rehabilitating that annyoying little human Koyomi Araragi (he even makes fun of the fact and calls it a rehab program), but I think my myaster has also been pretty rehabilitated compared to nyot too long ago.

Rehabilitated, or maybe restructured?

I can observe my myaster from inside her heart, from her inner mind—so I feel like I nyoh what I'm talking about.

Her family situation was her family situation, after all.

It would be a miracle if she nyever went off the rails.

Becoming a model student as a way of going off the rails is so very much my myaster—but she stopped acting too much like one ever since she cut her hair and took off her glasses.

I'm sure lots of people think lots of things about that, but if you ask me, I'd say it's nyothing short of great.

That's one place where I agree with Hitagi Senjogahara.

I'm sure I'll disappear some day, too.

I'll fade away into nyothingness.

This was a transition—so that my myaster can fully become who she is.

Me, I'm just like a nyadolescent fantasy.

At the latest, by the time she comes back from traveling the world.

I'm sure she'll have forgotten me and left me behind, like the imyaginary friend that anyone dreams up when they're little.

I'd be lying if I said that doesn't make me feel sad, but it was my role from the start. I'm nyot planning on defying that.

There are partings just as there are meetings.

It's the same with aberrations.

So I just have to do the things I can—

"Meow, meow, meo—ver here?"

Instead of going down the stairs, I leapt onto the roof of the Tamikura Apartments and looked all around me, three hundred and sixty degrees.

"Nyo—maybe here?"

So.

If you're curious why I slipped out of the futon and left the room— if you want to know what I wanted to do if nyot drain someone's enyurgy, it of course wasn't to go on a walk at nyight or anything.

I nyoh I shoulda gone straight to "work" like this when I came out at the ruins and when I came out in the morning, but I had to make prepurrations, okay?

Nyow.

"Mm. Mmh? There you are."

Nyot long after, I found my *target*—and flew into the air without a sound as soon as I did.

Cats can fly, you see.

Okay, I nyoh that's supposed to be birds.

But Black Hanekawa can jump higher than a meowntain—careful nyot to make a sound, though, I wasn't going to be leaping quite that high this time.

And if I really tried to jump, it'd destroy the apartment under me.

It was still enyough to jump about five hundred yards. I was far enyough away that I didn't have to be silent anymore, and I landed with a thump, hard enyough to make you think my feet might get stuck in the nyasphalt.

It was purrfectly dark on this street. Nyot a single car drove through at nyight.

And in front of me.

There stood a tiger.

018

<Afflicting Cat... No, you are no Afflicting Cat. But nor are you anything else. Explain yourself. What are you?>

The tiger—too impossibly big to be a real tiger, so enyormous it threw off your perspective—tilted its head at me, confused as it said this.

A tiger tilting its head in confusion was a pretty rare sight.

I wanted to snyap a photo and post it to my blog.

"Afflicting Cat is close enough—nyot quite if you went into the details, or if you went into the fundamentals, but well, you're nyot too wrong," I replied with the biggest smile I could make to show my friendly intentions, but—

<Is that so? You seem to be something else entirely to me.>

The tiger nyarrowed its eyes and didn't even grin.

Hrmm.

I nyow you shouldn't judge aberrations by appearances, but my furst impression was that we weren't going to get along.

<—The aberration I know as the Afflicting Cat is a slight one, one with so little presence it may as well not be there. But you—>

"Well—cat argue with that."

Nyothing I could say there.

Afflicting Cats have so little there there it might be better to call them nyarrations than aberrations—and even if they didn't, I got the feeling that in *this thing's* view, most aberrations may as well nyot be there.

Because as I assume you nyoh, tigers are sacred beasts.

"We've all got a lot going on. Even someone like me."

<I see,> the tiger nodded.

Looking unyinterested.

Like it couldn't care less about a nyaberration like me.

<Well, I don't really care about you.>

It really said it.

Nyow that was annyoying.

<But I must ask what it is you want of me. I am a tiger. You, as a kindred aberration, must know what it means to block my way.>

"A kindred aberration?"

Nyow it was my turn to tilt my head.

This one and me shoulda come from completely different places—nyo, maybe that's nyot what it meant.

Kindred as animals, simply.

Cats and tigers—is what it musta meant. Nyow I understood.

"Well," I said, "of course I nyoh—but I'm nyot here to block your way or anything. Nyot one teeny-tiny bit. I'm nyot very smart, but I at least nyoh where I stand here."

<Indeed you must not be—but I am not so sure you truly know where you stand,> the tiger said. How rude.

It really did like to talk for a nyaberration that wasn't even humanyoid, though.

That actually made me worry more.

<So, then. Why do you stand there?>

"Well, I'm just here to announce something—I don't care one bit what you came to this town for or why you're still here. Go ahead and do whatever you nyeed to do. I'm nyot interested one bit in what you really are, either. Because that's how aberrations are. But—" I said.

Maybe I wasn't making an announcement.

Nyow that I think about it, I should have called it a declaration of war.

"—if you do *anything more* to harm my myaster—I'll kill you."

<...I see.>

The tiger took in my words.

And then—it silently nyodded, like it understood.

Like it was chewing it over.

Like it was chewing—a piece of meat between its teeth.

It nodded.

<I thought I had seen you somewhere before... So you're *that girl*. That girl—has been possessed by you.>

"Nyo, I wouldn't say possessed—maybe if I was a nyormal Afflicting Cat. But I'm, like, her," I helpfully explained to the tiger who finally remembered me, or rather, my myaster. It's nyot something you'd be able to understand without an explanation—even that Hawaiian-shirted expurrt didn't understand it all.

Nyo one can understand the truth of a nyaberration.

"It'd be closer to call it assimyalation, or no, mewnification. I am my myaster, and my myaster is me—my myaster's personality is the dominant one, of course, but I might actually have more control over our actions. Because I'm the fundamental, primitive core of my myaster's psyche."

<Hm. I don't care.>

It went and said it again.

It's nyot like I purrticularly wanted this thing to like me, but it woulda been nyice if it had a little more interest in me.

<An aberration who assists a human, then. Remarkable—you are not. But then you ought to know better than any other aberration. An aberration's traits cannot be suppressed. *The problem lies with the seer, not the seen.*>

"......"

<I am a tiger, and this master of yours saw me—that is all that matters.>

Saying so, the tiger—glared at me hard.

That very instant, I leapt.

Nyuh oh, I thought—like we were just about to get into a fight.

This tiger was awfully violent—awfully simplistic—

And so I leapt.

I flew.

Nyot a step backward, much more than that. I took off with everything I had—like I really wanted to soar, to fly over a meowntain.

But.

Once I tumbled onto the ground somewhere on the outskirts of town after more than five minutes of airtime, I have no idea how it got there first, but in front of me—

There stood a tiger.

<Futile.>

"……"

<It is all futile. I am a tiger—and that woman has seen me. That alone is essential, and that alone is of import. I am a tiger—and have already begun.>

If I'd made a declaration of war.

The tiger's words were an ultimatum.

019

"Could you please wipe your feet before you come in?"

Waiting for me when I returned to the apartment was Hitagi Senjogahara, nyow holding a wet towel.

I thought I'd nyopened the door without alerting anyone to my presence, and of course without making a sound, but it seemed like the woman had already arisen.

"It's easy for me to wake up in the morning. It's because I'm high-strung. Didn't I tell you?"

"Well, nyot to me."

"But you're Miss Hanekawa, aren't you?"

Here, Hitagi Senjogahara held out the wet towel like it was a nyormal thing to do. I just took it.

I wiped my feet, just like she told me to. I wasn't paying much attention, but it made sense to me when I saw the towel turn black. I must've been pretty dirty.

"I guess it is the first time I'm meeting you... Black Hanekawa, right?"

"Sure, that's good enyough."

"I see," she said, nyow holding out her other, empty hand.

"...? What's the idea?"

"Oh, I just thought we'd shake hands because we're meeting for the first time."

"Do you nyot listen to a word anyone says to you?" She seemed hopeless, but I educated her. "My special trait as an Afflicting Cat is my always-active enyergy drain. Touch me and I'll suck up your vitality—I'm nyot giving anyone a handshake."

"Energy drain. Yes, I've heard," Hitagi Senjogahara stated plainly, "but it's not like you suck it all up in a single moment, right? I should at least be able to shake your hand."

"……"

I started to say something—but decided nyot to.

It didn't seem like saying anything would make a difference with her.

So I silently took her hand—but only for a meowment.

"Ugh—" she groaned for that one meowment—and that was all.

Enyough lassitude to make a lot of people fall to their nyees should have been assaulting her whole body, but she didn't even show any sign of distress. True, my enyergy drain wasn't enough to make someone pass out after a single meowment, but most people couldn't take it—and I'd shaken her hand nyowing that.

I guess my plan had failed.

Still, and while I'm sure these were my myaster's feelings—some part of me went, *Nyaturally.*

Nyaturally.

Nyaturally, this woman.

"……"

Well.

I—and of course, my myaster, too.

It's nyot like either of us wanted to see her in pain.

But something about that nyon-reaction of hers tore into my heart.

"Nice to meet you. And please, take care," she continued as if to pile it on, with a smile, even. "Please, take care of Miss Hanekawa."

020

......

How did that happen?

We skipped three sections at once this time.

What happened while I was asleep?

Everything's okay, right?

Nothing weird happened, did it?

"Good morning, Miss Hanekawa," called out Miss Senjogahara, sitting in front of me as I lay too confused even to begin stirring on the futon.

Hm?

Something about her expression seemed absentminded, in complete contrast to the day before—no, maybe not absentminded or sleepy, it was like she was just plain exhausted—

But what kind of condition was she in to be tired as soon as she woke up?

It's not as if she could've had her energy drained by an Afflicting Cat.

"You're up early, Miss Hanekawa... It's only six."

"Yup."

Today I had really relied on my circadian rhythm—though I could have slept in a little later because Miss Senjogahara's home was closer to Naoetsu High than mine.

But it's not like waking up early ever hurt anybody.

"Well, you're up, too, Miss Senjogahara."

"I go on a little run in the mornings," she said, standing up slowly. "It's not easy for me to keep this figure, you know... I've got the kind of body that turns anything I eat straight into flesh."

"Straight into flesh..."

Was that her roundabout way of saying she put on weight easily?

Then again, she once had some special circumstances relating to her weight, so maybe she was particularly fussy about managing it. It wasn't as if she was a model, though, and she'd look more charming if she were a little thicker, in my humble opinion.

Was there really a need for her arms and legs to be that skinny?

Looking at them, I got scared that they might snap.

"I'm jealous of you, Miss Hanekawa. You've got the kind of body that turns whatever you eat straight into chest..."

"Straight into chest..."

What kind of a body was that?

Listen, it's not exactly easy for me, either.

It's tough being a girl.

After washing her face, Miss Senjogahara changed into shorts and a T-shirt and began stretching for her run.

Wow...

She was flexible!

I was doubting my own eyes.

Her body had wobbled around like it was an overdone 3D animation.

It was incredible. Like she was a mollusk.

"Sorry. Can I try touching you?" I requested.

"Hm? Do you mean my right breast? Or my left one?"

"No, I mean your back..."

"My right shoulder blade? Or my left one?"

"I don't have whatever kind of ultra-specific fetish you're talking about..."

She was really quick.

That was a skill I didn't have.

I walked behind her as I thought this and pushed her back as she did a perfect split.

Her torso was now flat on the floor.

Zero resistance, zero friction.

Like there'd been no need to push at all.

"Why is your body this flexible? Should joints have this much motion? Actually, I don't even know if your joints are connected to begin with…"

"Um, stretching can be addictive… And I mean that in a masochistic way."

"Did you really need to add that clarification?"

"I can't get enough of the feeling of everything inside my body creaking and straining."

"You don't seem to be straining very much, though."

"There's no strain left in it any longer. Stretching is so boring now."

It was boring for her…

True, you only get more flexible the more you stretch.

The fruits of her training during her time on the track team—or maybe the traces of it.

"Miss Hanekawa, would you like to run with me?"

"No, but I'll make breakfast in the meantime. We can eat together once you get back."

"Do you not like to run?"

"That's not it."

If anything, I'm someone who likes exercise.

I even have a little habit of running in the mornings, though I don't do it every day.

It was just that I could imagine the scene after getting back being yet another shower with Miss Senjogahara, and I thought we might not need that much fanservice crammed in.

It'd be indecent, and in more ways than one.

"Actually," I suggested, "why don't you also take a break from running today? You look tired to me."

"I want to run the most when I'm feeling tired."

"I guess you are a jock, after all."

A former member of the track team. Her spirit had been tempered, too.

It didn't seem worth it to try and stop her, so after helping her with her stretches (though I didn't do anything you could call "helping" in the end), I saw her off and went to the kitchen.

021

"Mgh."

Miss Senjogahara made an indescribable face as soon as she put a cucumber from her salad into her mouth.

I thought it would be wrong to tamper with someone else's kitchen too much, so I'd prepared a very simple breakfast. Leftover bread from the day before with hot milk. A simple salad and a fried egg on top of bacon. When I laid it out on the table, though, she did comment on how good it looked.

Everything was fine as she chugged down her milk, but her demeanor changed when she put the first bite of salad into her mouth.

Like a switch had been flicked.

"Could I ask you a question, Miss Hanekawa?"

"What is it?"

"Oh, no, hold on. First let me be sure that this unbelievable situation really is happening."

She continued to fill her cheeks with more salad. She kept going, silently eating her eggs and bread.

The grave expression stuck to her face the entire time.

I'm not a dull person. I could tell pretty much what she was thinking, based on her reaction, but...hmm?

Had I messed something up?

I started to think, and then I took my own fearful bite of the food I'd prepared—nothing seemed particularly strange. At least, it didn't seem like I'd done something like burn the eggs or get dish detergent in the food.

Then what could have been bothering her so?

"Hmm," she said suggestively, noticing that I was now the one with suspicion in my eyes.

"Uh, Miss Senjogahara—"

"Miss Hanekawa. Do you know what dressing is?"

"Huh?" The question caught me by surprise. "Well, of course I know what it is. The stuff that people *sometimes put* on salads."

"I see, I see." She gave a deep, understanding nod. "There are three competing factions in Japan when it comes to fried eggs. People who put Worcestershire sauce on them, people who put soy sauce on them, and people who put salt and pepper on them. What's your stance there?"

"Oh, I've heard of those people before. Yes, apparently some people put things on fried eggs."

"Yup, yup." She nodded again like she was conducting an experiment and was pleased with the results. "Did you notice the spread and the jam in the fridge?"

"I saw them, but…we had those just yesterday. Oh, oops—did you want to use them?"

"Hm."

But rather than get up to grab butter or anything else from the refrigerator, she tore off another piece of bread, put it in her mouth, and silently chewed.

Silently.

"I have a few more questions."

"Please, go ahead."

"They're about your culinary lifestyle."

"My culinary lifestyle? I think my eating habits are very ordinary, but okay."

"How much soy sauce do you use on sushi?"

"None."

"How many times do you dip your tempura in sauce?"

"None."

"Spoons of sugar in your yogurt?"

"Zero."

"What do you write on your meals with ketchup?"

"A blank."

"Any sauce on your *okonomiyaki*?"

"Plain."

"Do you salt your rice balls?"

"Just rice."

"What syrup do you get on your shaved ice?"

"Simple."

"How many sugar cubes in your after-meal coffee?"

"I take mine black, thank you."

Okay, she said, ending her questions.

It felt like I had just undergone some sort of psychological test, but I did understand now what was making her so upset.

"Oh, I get it, I get it. I'm sorry, Miss Senjogahara, you're one of those people who puts dressing on their salads. And that's why you were making such a funny face."

"No, it's that I didn't know there was a no-dressing faction. And it's my first time seeing a plain fried egg, and it's also my first time being served just a piece of bread. Are you, let's say, someone who rejects the idea of seasoning food? Perhaps you want to savor the ingredients as they are?"

"Hunh?"

It took a moment for me to understand what she was saying, and then it took a few more for me to think it through before I replied, *Ah, no.*

"It isn't like that at all. I think salad tastes *just as good* with dressing on it, and I can eat fried eggs *all the same* even if they do have Worcestershire sauce, soy sauce, or salt and pepper on them, and I love pizza just the same with or without pineapple on it."

"We're not talking about pizza toppings," she shot back.

Aw, I was so happy.

My setup hadn't been for nothing.

"But doesn't food taste good even if it doesn't have any flavor?" I asked.

"And there we have it. The clincher."

"What? But all I said is that food's the same whether or not it has flavor."

"So this is why they say the best way to get a secret out of someone is to ask them how their day went."

Though I guess all I did was ask you directly, she added, putting down her chopsticks.

She hadn't given up on her meal, though. It was very much like her to have cleaned her plate.

"Thank you for the meal," she made sure to say, before continuing, "I take back every word I said about the two of us having similar tastes."

They'd been annulled.

"You're like the opposite of a picky eater, aren't you? But it's not that you don't have dislikes, either."

"I'm sorry, I still don't understand what you're trying to say."

"The taste of home cooking, huh?" she ignored my query, as if lost in thought. "But no, it's not like that. Maybe you're someone who accepts the taste of anything… It might be an exaggeration, but you only care that your food provides you with nutrition. No, maybe nutrition doesn't even matter so long as you've filled your stomach…"

"Don't make it sound like I'm a warrior or something."

"In that case, your sense of taste is only a burden. If you aren't enjoying the flavor of the ingredients—then, in the end, you aren't bothered by trivial details? When I think about it, being fixated on how something is seasoned might be a luxury."

Still, you did manage to smash straight through what I believed to be common sense, she said, staring straight at me as my portions sat on my plate. "But you know…I'm not so sure about living that way. It's not just how you deal with food. You, well—"

She seemed to be choosing her words carefully.

That was rare.

"—you accept everything that comes to you, don't you?" she went with the same verb she used earlier. "It's important to have things you love, but isn't it just about as important to have things you hate? But you accept it all. And I wonder if that's what you're doing with me, and with Araragi, too."

"Huh?"

Did our conversation change subjects?

Did our conversation get derailed?

Did our conversation just turn into something bigger?

No—it hadn't.

We were on the same subject, and we hadn't been derailed.

The scale of our conversation was the same, too.

We were talking about how I lived my life.

Tsubasa Hanekawa's lifestyle.

"It wasn't that we have similar tastes, my tastes are simply subsumed by yours—no, maybe I shouldn't call what you have tastes, Miss Hanekawa. It's probably better that I don't. After all, if you like everything that's out there, it's like everything is all the same to you."

"......"

"Miss Hanekawa?" she asked, still looking into my eyes.

And it was just a hint.

But something in her tone sounded flat—the way it used to.

"Did you really love Araragi?"

And then another question.

"Are you still able to say, now, that you love Araragi?"

022

Miss Senjogahara and I both actually meant to attend school that day, but just before we left, we realized that she wouldn't be able to for a whole week thanks to the unnecessarily big lie she'd told the day before, namely that she had the flu.

"This is what they call being hoist by your own petard," she lamented, but it seemed more comical to me than that, like she'd tried to shoot a Roman candle at someone but held it the wrong way around. "Now I have to stay here at home like a good girl for a whole week… I can't believe it. I've been grounded when I haven't done anything wrong."

However funny this turn of events seemed to me, it seemed to be a grave situation for our perpetrator who now had her hands to her head. Of course, lying absolutely counts as doing something wrong, so this could safely be classified as chickens coming home to roost.

Or maybe the fowler getting caught in her own net.

"My dad's going to be so mad at me…"

"……"

She, a girl in her last year of high school, appeared to be afraid of her father being upset with her.

It was so cute.

"But it seems Araragi won't be able to come to school for a while, either, so maybe it works out just right," I reminded her, not particularly to comfort her but in the way of a little sarcasm.

"You've got a point," she responded, quickly putting her hands back to her sides.

What a pair of lovebirds.

And so I went to school all alone—where a whirlwind of questions awaited me, though I'd expected it. They had a bit of a curious, gawking bent to them, but that couldn't be helped. I was happy that my classmates were concerned about me.

Classes had now started for me.

As I flipped through the textbooks I'd borrowed from Miss Senjogahara, who'd lent them to me saying, "It's not like I can use them for a week," I thought back to something else she'd said that morning.

"You know, I'd always thought that the world must look so bland to people as smart as you—that because you *understand* so much of it, nothing's exciting or thrilling. But I might have been only half-right about that and wrong about the other half. There was never any guarantee that you and I interpreted what it means to be bland in the same way. Yes, my very premise was faulty."

I didn't imagine anyone could be fine with tediousness, and even crappiness—said Miss Senjogahara.

How could I not give a panicked reply to that?

"No, I've never thought that the world is bland. And I don't like tediousness, and I think crappiness is bad."

"I wonder. Something makes me suspect that you're just saying so—or rather just thinking so." She wouldn't accept my defense. "Actually, I've been wondering for a while. What the difference is between you and Araragi—both of you are willing to do anything for the sake of others, even putting yourselves at risk, but from where I stand, the two of you seem completely different—you don't even seem to resemble each other. To put it simply, Araragi looks fake, while you look like the real deal. It made me wonder why, especially because your behavior is the same—but I think I understand now after eating this meal you cooked."

"What do you mean, you think you understand…"

"Of course, claiming that I understand someone's temperament because I ate their food makes it sound like I'm in a cooking manga that will go unnamed," she said. "It sounds like I'm in *Oishinbo*."

"Why go back and provide the title you just censored?"

"You and Araragi understand danger in different ways. For example, if there's a cat that's been run over in the middle of the street—giving it a proper burial is probably the right thing to do. I think *you* would, and while he'd moan and groan about it, Araragi might too at the end of the day."

"……"

"And I think the difference here is that moaning and groaning—the reason so many people would ignore a dead cat run over in the middle of the street, passing by as if they didn't see it at all, is that it's 'dangerous' to bury it. It's extremely risky in our society for people around you to know that you're a 'good' or 'virtuous' person—it becomes extremely likely that people will start to take advantage of you."

At some point, children intentionally start to act bad because they think it's "embarrassing" to do good, but it's not really because they're embarrassed. It's because such goodness is nothing more than a weak point, a liability amidst "the malice" out there in the world—Miss Senjogahara thought out loud.

She continued to lay out her unique theory.

"Araragi probably knows it's safer to act bad—he knows just how much of a risk he's taking by being a 'good person.' Again and again he's acted like some defender of justice knowing there's a chance he could die in the process, or at least fall by the wayside. When he was in middle school, and now that he's in high school, too. That's the reason he ended up washing out, but I think he always understood the risk that he might. He's doing it even though he knows. Well, maybe not the risk of dying and then coming back to life like during spring break, but that aside."

"Spring break…"

That time—he did regret it.

He definitely regretted his actions then—but.

He definitely faced those regrets.

There was no mistaking it, and Miss Senjogahara was exactly right.

Me, on the other hand.

"You, on the other hand, don't understand any of that—no, that's not it. Even you must be aware of those risks. But *you don't think they're anything to be worried about*—that must be what it is. You don't regret anything. It's like you don't find the malice and crappiness daunting. No, actually, you accept it. This all sounds like I'm describing just how incredible you are, but that's not it at all. I had an incredible amount of respect for you until today—but it's as if those feelings just vanished into thin air."

Indeed, the sense I got from Miss Senjogahara as she spoke—was that she wasn't praising me at all.

It wasn't high praise in the least.

If anything—

She was mad.

Just like when she discovered me sleeping in those ruins yesterday morning—or possibly madder.

"I'm pretty hurt you said my cooking tasted good if that's how you feel. Araragi didn't show any signs of enjoying it, but you're even worse."

"Miss Senjogahara…"

"For example, what do you think about the way I live?" With that question, she spread her arms to present Room 201 of the Tamikura Apartments. "My shaky single-father household, my single-room apartment of a hundred-or-so square feet, no bathtub but saved so fortunately by my shower that sometimes has no hot water, my truly meager kitchen with only a single gas burner, my circuit breaker that trips if you use a hair dryer while running the washing machine— what do you think about my lifestyle?"

"What do I think about it?"

"*You don't think anything about it, do you?* You don't sympathize with the way I live or recoil from it, do you? And I'm sure that's a wonderful thing. If we were in a novel or a manga or something, that is—or if we were talking about great historical figures, yes, that would be incredible. I might even find myself moved. But, Miss Hanekawa, you're a real human being, aren't you?" she put to me.

While her tone remained flat—she seemed to be holding herself back with all she had so it wouldn't get away from her and turn rough.

"After all, even I think this way of living is the worst, and this is about me. I don't believe, like some enlightened person, that this is a far more human life than the one in the mansion prior to my parents' divorce. There's no way I could. I don't think for a second there's anything more human about living in poverty. In fact, I agree with the saying—poverty dulls the wit. My father is working himself to the bone to repay our debts and get us out of this life. He's working so frantically that I wouldn't be surprised if his health failed any day now—and it's all because we know how dangerous it is for us to continue living this way."

But you don't feel that kind of danger, she said.

"You realize that the danger is there, but you don't feel a shred of it. That's why you're able to spend a whole night in those ruins."

"When you put it that way…"

I was cornered.

I couldn't argue back even if I wanted to.

"I think it's that you're too white—too pure and white. You must not understand how heartless it is to tell foolish people it's okay to be foolish, how cruel it is to tell crappy people it's okay to be crappy— and you don't even attempt to understand why seeing defects and calling them virtues is sheer malice. You don't have a clue about how irreversibly damaging it is to affirm something that's negative. You can't accept everything. If you did, no one would bother trying anymore. They'd lose the will to improve—but you aren't the least bit wary of foolishness or crappiness. You always run straight off to do the right thing knowing that people are going to try to take advantage of you because you don't pay the fact any mind, and you try to act ethically even though you know it makes you stick out like a sore thumb. What could be more frightening than that? I'm impressed that you've managed to live your life on such a razor's edge and still be in sound

127

health, I'll give you that. So in conclusion, you're not a good person, you're not a saint, you're not a holy mother—you're just dull when it comes to darkness. That just makes you...a failure as a creature."

A failure.

It was the first time anyone had called me that, and it was a little depressing to hear.

We cut the conversation short there because it was almost time for me to go to school, but her words continued to swirl around in my head while I was on my way and all during class, too.

You're not a good person, just dull when it comes to darkness.

Just dull when it comes to darkness.

A failure, a failure, a failure, a failure—in other words.

White.

Too white.

Pure and white.

Transparently—white.

"......"

But now that I was in class and distracted by the doodles in the margins of Miss Senjogahara's textbooks, I couldn't deny feeling that those words felt a bit in vain.

There were *FMA* drawings on every single page.

They were ridiculously good, too.

And she was preparing for college?

023

Miss Senjogahara probably felt frustrated.

I ended up not understanding half of what she'd said and what she'd wanted to say, but that was still the impression I got.

It really was just an impression.

It was nothing more.

Lunch came around, and I left the classroom and headed to the cafeteria—I usually pack my own lunch, but I wasn't going to use someone else's kitchen for that.

No, I probably wouldn't feel like making lunch in any kitchen, even the one in my own house, after being told all of those things by Miss Senjogahara.

My own house.

Would I, too, have made flavorful food if I *actually* had one—or so I wondered.

When.

"…Oh."

I saw a familiar figure in front of me after I'd walked a ways down the halls—it was Suruga Kanbaru.

She was walking from there to here, in the opposite direction as me (she really did seem like a cheerful person, just from the way she walked. Even from my distance I could tell she was humming some kind of tune), and she noticed me at the same time.

"Ohh!" she exclaimed louder than you'd ever expect in a hallway, then dashed over to my side faster than you'd ever expect in a hallway.

She moved so fast it was like she'd teleported.

Two tassels of hair arrived a moment later.

"Well, look who it is! It's been a while, glad to see you're doing well!"

"...Yeah."

She was awfully excited.

This was more than being upbeat.

I could only nod, not sure how to react.

Judging from her demeanor, the news of the Hanekawa residence burning down had somehow yet to reach her. Then again, given her personality, there was a chance that she could be this excited even if it had.

Good manners, zero consideration.

That was her personality.

"I was actually on my way to go see my dear senior Senjogahara," she said, with good manners and zero consideration, "but is she in her classroom right now?"

"Umm."

It was hardly surprising.

It went without saying.

At least, I hadn't thought that dashing over my way the way she did meant that she had some kind of urgent business with me—generally speaking, she was only interested in Miss Senjogahara.

It was to the point that she applied to our school, Naoetsu High, in order to follow Miss Senjogahara here.

Araragi seemed to have somehow broadened her frighteningly narrow horizons, but—

Well.

I envied how straightforward she could be.

Or maybe I should say single-minded?

At the very least, I doubted Miss Senjogahara would look at her and feel frustrated.

130

She was strong.

Reliable—that would be the impression.

Suruga Kanbaru, a second-year student at Naoetsu High.

Miss Senjogahara's junior since middle school (which meant that she also went to the same middle school as me, but I never met her then. I'd only heard stories about her), the two together are called the Valhalla Duo.

The Valhalla Duo, from the character for "god" in Kanbaru, the characters for "battleground" in Senjogahara, and the character for "field" in both of their names, which could be read both "baru" and "hara." I later learned that Miss Kanbaru was apparently the one to come up with the moniker herself. While I did think it was a cool name, there was something sad about it when I learned the title was self-assigned.

Also, she's the best-known student in all of Naoetsu High. At a private prep school that places no focus whatsoever on sports and club activities, she led its girls' basketball team to the national tournament. She's an awe-inspiring superstar (while they'd never admit it, the faculty seems a little annoyed, as in: won't she read the room?).

Of course, as you could tell by the bandage wrapped around her left arm, she'd retired early.

A monkey.

For Miss Kanbaru, it was a monkey—I want to say.

But even so, I think.

While she'd sported an athlete's short, boyish haircut as an active player, the girl in front of me had hair almost as long as mine used to be, though she didn't braid it.

Putting aside the fact that her hair grew at a supernatural speed—Miss Kanbaru.

Looked girlish, you could say?

She looked cute now.

And what got her to do that—like with the way Miss Senjogahara was now—must have been Araragi.

Broadened horizons, huh?

"She's taking the day off from school… She's sick with the flu."

I'd become a party to her lie.

But what else could I do?

If we looked back at the circumstances, she'd lied for my sake—I had to make sure our stories were straight. Even if it was fine to tell Miss Kanbaru, she struck me as someone with loose lips.

She was so candid that it felt like whatever she wasn't supposed to say could slip out of her mouth at any moment. And I couldn't see her feeling bad about it afterwards, either.

She wouldn't even try to defend herself because she couldn't see anyone taking offense.

"Ah, the flu," she said, mildly surprised. "That's like the devil getting sunstroke."

"......"

It was an awful way to talk about her "dear" senior, an excellent example of her showing good manners and zero consideration—in fact, of her being "politely rude" as Araragi put it. She was probably just using a phrase she'd heard somewhere, though, and I doubted she ever stopped to consider its meaning.

I'm sure Araragi would interrupt the conversation with a quip here to correct her, but I wasn't that close to her. All I could do was reply with silence and a vague smile.

Grin.

"...Wait, maybe that means something else."

She'd understood.

That made me honestly happy.

Hmm. I still had to admit, it was difficult to figure out where I stood with people who were friends of friends (whether via Miss Senjogahara or Araragi).

A big part of it was that I was dealing with Miss Kanbaru, though.

"Hmm, I see. So she's not here. What should I do."

I was sure she'd turn around and go back to her classroom once she learned Miss Senjogahara was absent, but instead she stood there with her arms folded like she was at a real loss. The cafeteria was going to get crowded with our school's cafeterians if I didn't hurry, but I couldn't leave her in that state.

"Did you have something you needed to tell her? I'd be happy to listen if I could be of any help."

"Hmm." She thought for a brief moment. "Well, I guess you'd do."

Now she was just being rude.

Not even politely so.

This, I thought, was something I ought to warn her about, but she said, "I just got a message from my dear senior Araragi," and silenced me by shoving her phone's screen in front of my face.

We weren't allowed to use our phones on school grounds, they were supposed to be off while at school, the words "just got a message" implied that she received his e-mail during class—all of these were more words I found suppressed.

By the message I was seeing.

—come to second floor classroom tonight at 9 alone i need to ask you something

"What do you think this means?" asked Miss Kanbaru.

"What else could it mean?"

Such a short message didn't leave any room for interpretation—it didn't even seem possible that it was in some sort of code. Yes, the text was a bit sloppy (the "alone" was misplaced), but that only meant he was in a rush—

"It means that Araragi has a question for you, and that he wants you to come alone to the second-floor classroom tonight at nine in the evening, no?"

"So my hunch was right. Hrm," she grunted. She looked serious. "I presume—he isn't at school today either?"

"Yup," I nodded. She was sharp in unexpected ways—or rather, she had the uncanny ability to pin down the gist of a conversation, and wasn't to be underestimated. "In his case, it's not like he has the flu, but…he hasn't come to school ever since the new term started."

I'd asked our teacher just to be sure, but it seemed that he hadn't attended the day before, either. Miss Senjogahara, Araragi, and I had all missed school on the same day, which apparently sparked a bunch of groundless speculation.

Groundless speculation…I wish they'd stop.

Please, don't spark anything.

Hrm, Miss Kanbaru grunted again.

"I know he's my senior, but sometimes I don't know what to do with him. The second-floor classroom? That's way too vague to be a meeting spot. How many buildings does he think Naoetsu High has?"

"Well, I don't think he means our school. It has to be that abandoned cram school, right?"

"Oh, I see," she agreed as if she'd just realized.

She was dull in unexpected ways.

"But if that's the case, why doesn't he just call me? I tried calling him several times just now, but he wouldn't pick up."

"……"

Miss Kanbaru had made these calls at school, and my silence here was of course—not to scold her for that. It was because this new info made it absolutely impossible for me to imagine the kind of situation Araragi was in.

I thought it had something to do with Mayoi, but…why would he summon Miss Kanbaru?

It seemed unlike him…

It didn't make sense.

"So…he's inviting me on a date! And he must not be picking up the phone because he has some kind of surprise ready!"

"Um," I objected, "doesn't the way it's written make it sound more serious?"

A surprise… How happy-go-lucky was she? And she wasn't kidding, either.

Just talking to her was exhausting!

"Okay, all right, now I understand," she said. "I had a book I wanted to read tonight, but if he's inviting me out, there's only one thing for me to do: answer his call, come hell or high water!"

"Hell or high water…"

She just wanted to read a book, right?

She was blowing everything far out of proportion, and her old-timey phrases made her more likely to sound like she was joking the more serious she got. She was losing out thanks to that quirk.

Perhaps it didn't make her frustrating, but her earnestness really was concerning.

"Uh, Miss Kanbaru…"

"Hm? What is it?"

"Uhm…"

I thought about what to say, but I couldn't find the right words in the end and settled on nothing but:

"Be careful."

And.

"Say hi to Araragi for me."

"Okay. Thank you for everything!"

"No, not at all… You're welcome."

"When I heard that your house caught on fire, I thought you might be feeling down, but I'm glad that doesn't seem to be the case! There's the senior I know!"

"Oh."

So she actually did know.

She knew, and that was how she approached me? For reals…

No.

But still, I wasn't feeling down?

"May fortune be with you on the battlefield!"

Raising a hand, Miss Kanbaru returned the way she came.

Not running, but walking.

I was planning on warning her if she started running down the hallways again, but it wasn't as if she always ran everywhere she went.

She was annoyingly random.

"……"

Now that Miss Kanbaru had left, I needed to hurry to the cafeteria—in part to make up for lost time, if I were actually doing so—but was unable to move a step.

Not—because her last line still echoed inside me.

What was gripping my mind instead was Araragi's present situation.

He had to be in some sort of trouble—that much was already a definite fact. But he wanted Miss Kanbaru to come see him, which probably meant that whatever he "needed to ask her" was necessary to escaping the crisis.

Only, it didn't feel like he was simply seeking assistance.

It felt far, far more serious.

"……"

That's why it seemed misguided.

Araragi had texted her out of some necessity and was requesting her help rather than mine—so dwelling on that fact was misguided.

But I wondered.

Although understanding this perfectly and being satisfied was what Miss Senjogahara found so "frustrating" about me—it still didn't sit well with me to be called pure and white for it.

I did envy Miss Kanbaru for getting that message from Araragi.

I was properly mad, too.

Araragi hadn't texted me—and I was mad at him.

024

I headed home while being assaulted by a powerful sense of self-hatred.

I considered asking Miss Kanbaru if I could go with her, but if Araragi's message said "alone," it seemed best that I didn't—I understood that much.

What did give me pause was whether or not I should tell Miss Senjogahara about this. The honest way to look at it was that I should, Araragi being her boyfriend, but I knew I'd absolutely cause her worry—and on her part, she'd get unreservedly angry at him.

I arrived at the Tamikura Apartments still unable to reach a conclusion—

"Oh, welcome back, Miss Hanekawa. That took a while."

"Yeah, I went to the supermarket to buy ingredients to replace what I used this morning...hm?"

Then, as I opened the door, I noticed that there was another individual in the room other than Miss Senjogahara.

A man with long, salt-and-pepper hair tied neatly in the back.

He looked striking in his suit, and as serious as could be—to use a bit of an old phrase, he was like a corporate warrior.

His appearance suggested professions like lawyer or bureaucrat, but I knew that wasn't the case.

I'd heard from Miss Senjogahara.

That *her father* works as a consultant at a foreign company—

"Nice to meet you," he greeted me first. He was seated at the low table but got up for me and bowed his head. "I'm Hitagi's father."

"Ah… Um."

I was at a loss.

Now that this was happening, I realized she'd said her father was coming home today. I just didn't think he'd be returning at such an early hour.

He doesn't work at a foreign company for nothing and won't let himself be bound by time, I thought, weirdly impressed.

"I'm Tsubasa Hanekawa. I apologize, I stayed the night yesterday."

"M-hm," Mister Senjogahara nodded.

And then he was silent again—he seemed reserved.

He struck me as the type of man who stayed extremely quiet as I stood there in the entrance, my shoes still on, when he glanced my way.

Saying, "I'll make some tea," he headed to the kitchen.

From there, he put a kettle on the gas burner.

His words, along with his actions, freed me from my nerves in an instant, and I could take my shoes off at least.

A pause.

I sat next to Miss Senjogahara, making sure to keep her dad in my line of sight.

"I'm sorry, Miss Hanekawa. He seems to have taken care of his work earlier than expected, and so he also came back earlier than expected," she whispered.

"Oh, no. It's not a problem or anything," I whispered back. I was the one barging into their apartment, after all. "But in that case, you could've sent me a message or called me to let me know."

"Well, I was curious to see if you'd be surprised."

"……"

Yes, I was. Of course I was.

When I began to wonder whether these kinds of surprises awaited Araragi daily, his life started to seem like a lot of trouble in spite of its sunny appearance.

"You have a very cool dad," I said.

And not as flattery.

It made a little more sense now. Putting aside how serious she was being when she said it, I could see why Miss Senjogahara might be a self-described daddy's girl—living with a father like that would surely make every boy in your class look like a kid.

I had mixed feelings about the thought, but it was impressive that Araragi managed to win over her trained eye.

You often hear that women fall in love with a man who resembles her father, but in that sense, the person preparing tea leaves at the moment was nothing like Araragi. Forget about them being different types of people, they nearly seemed to be made of different stuff.

Araragi could play at being cool and collected, he could even be called the "unmoving silence," but the truth is that he rather likes talking—you could almost call him the polar opposite of Miss Senjogahara's dad, an actual reserved individual.

And—though this is an incredibly tautological way to put it— while Mister Senjogahara was indeed cool, there was something so fatherly about him, like he was more cool as a dad than cool as a man.

And what that indicates—

…Oops.

Why am I even trying to analyze my friend's dad?

I thought I already stopped doing that kind of thing.

Yes.

It seemed that I, of all people, was slightly shaken by a "dad" appearing out of the blue.

Not that anything about me is special enough to warrant the "of all people."

An ordinary girl—I may not be, but even then.

There was nothing to be shaken by to begin with—it's not as if I had any mental image of what a "father" or "dad" is.

I may know a person who should be called my father.

But what I didn't know—was a person I ought to call my father.

I didn't know anything.

"Anything interesting happen at school?" asked Miss Senjogahara, moving along to a regular line of conversation as if to conclude the topic of her father's presence.

I could certainly learn from the audacity she showed at times like this. "What do you mean by that?"

"Was Araragi there?"

So that's what she wanted to ask.

I hesitated for a moment, but it felt wrong to hide it. I decided to tell her what happened at school.

"He texted Kanbaru?"

"Yes. He seems to need her help with whatever's keeping him occupied at the moment... But it was so short that we couldn't figure out why he was summoning her..."

"How unbearably unpleasant."

Her words, surprisingly direct, were mirrored by her expression.

"Direct" was actually an understatement. She was furious.

What's more, she was angry at Miss Kanbaru, not Araragi.

Her ire was pointed at her junior, not her boyfriend.

I immediately found myself regretting telling her.

Was it going to create a rift between the Valhalla Duo?

"That woman got Araragi to ignore me and seek her help instead? What should I do to her? Starting with her organs—"

"Miss Senjogahara, you've gone back to being your pre-rehabilitated self."

"Uh oh," she noticed, pulling her own cheeks until her face formed a smile.

It was such a forced smile that it hurt to look at...

"I'm sure there's a reason—for why that happened," I said. "Especially because he wants to ask her something. And unlike the two of us, there's still an aberration remaining in her left arm."

"I suppose—there is."

The Monkey's Paw.

Miss Senjogahara continued, "So could that mean it's not Kanbaru he needs—but her left arm?"

"It's just a guess, of course." I doubted it was that simple, but broadly speaking, it seemed likely.

"So if it's Kanbaru's fighting abilities he's after—does that mean even more fight scenes down the line?"

"It's hard to say. But as far as combat, Araragi has Shinobu now—so I doubt he's necessarily looking for more people to help him in a fight."

All of this was based on conjecture.

Miss Senjogahara and I didn't know what kind of situation Araragi was in. We could talk all day and never arrive at a conclusion.

"So, Miss Hanekawa. What are you going to do?"

"What am I going to do?"

"Are you going to their meeting spot? Or are you not? Whatever the situation, you'd be able to meet him there, yes?"

"...I considered it, but I don't think I will. I feel like I'd only get in his way if I did—"

"Oh," she nodded at my reply. "Then I won't go either."

"Really?"

I'd assumed she'd insist on going and was ready for a heated argument, but instead I was fooled, or maybe tripped up.

I'd been wondering what I could possibly do to stop a determined Miss Senjogahara who insisted on imposing upon him.

"I'll take his lack of correspondence as proof that he's doing well—it doesn't seem like he's trying to hide anything the way he did with Kanbaru's monkey," she said. "If anything, he's being out in the open with it. He has to know that any message he sends to Kanbaru is going to make its way to us."

That was true.

But still.

"You're not going?" I asked as if in confirmation.

"I'm not," she replied. "I feel the same as you. I could go, but all I'd do is get in his way—and it also feels like there are other things I might be able to do."

I didn't have a clue what her suggestive addition was supposed to mean—but that's how things stood.

His lack of correspondence was proof that he was doing well.

A sign of trust.

Yes, I was going to accept that convenient interpretation—

"But it does seem like Araragi and Kanbaru aren't the only ones with lingering aberrations in their bodies."

"What? There's someone else?" I tilted my head at her remark. "Araragi's demon and Miss Kanbaru's monkey are the only aberrations around us left, aren't they?"

"Purrcisely," she responded, making for some reason what sounded like a cat pun.

I wanted to press her, but just then Mister Senjogahara brought tea and teacakes for three, and our whispered conversation was cut short.

No, it probably would have been at that point even if he'd taken a little longer to make tea.

I say this because at that moment, there was a knock at the door of Room 201, Tamikura Apartments—it didn't have an intercom, if you were wondering.

"Oh. Looks like they're here," Miss Senjogahara said, getting up, so she must have been expecting the guests.

Expected or not, I was on guard, in the dark as to who could be visiting. But when she opened the door and I saw who was standing there, I understood everything.

Including the nature of the "scheme" she'd mentioned the day before.

I didn't need any explanation.

And I didn't need any introduction.

Outside the door were Araragi's little sisters, Karen Araragi and Tsukihi Araragi. The Fire Sisters.

025

There was apparently a conversation that went like so.

"My goodness, look at what we have here. If it isn't Karen. What a surprise, meeting you in a place like this."

"Oh wow, look at that. It's you, Miss Senjogahara! What a coincidence, meeting you like this in front of my home."

"Yes, it's almost as if I used my phone's map to figure out your exact route back from school and was waiting here to ambush you, heheh."

"Ahaha. Well, maybe some people might be stupid enough to get that mistaken impression. The world is full of idiots, after all. It's too bad there are so few clever kids like me out there. Wait, but what about school, Miss Senjogahara?"

"School? What's that?"

"Er, I guess it's fine if you don't know…"

"No, I'm just kidding. Of course I know. That was just a 'Gahara Joke. I took the day off due to somewhat unavoidable circumstances. Your middle school has half-days until today, right?"

"Yep. But you've got some bad timing. I'm sure you wanted to meet my brother while you just so happened to be here, but he's actually out right now—he went off somewhere as soon as the new term got started. My guess is that this is his journey of self-discovery part two. He'll probably be able to shoot a *Kamehameha* by the time he gets back."

"Journeys of self-discovery aren't about that sort of training...no, never mind."

"He might even be able to shoot an *Evangelion*."

"I don't think Araragi has the talent... Oh, but I just happened to think of something. You know, completely out of nowhere. Did you hear that Miss Hanekawa's house caught on fire?"

"What?"

"Oh, I'm sorry. That was a stupid question. How could Karen Araragi, the enforcer of those two defenders of justice the Fire Sisters, she who singlehandedly upholds peace in this town, not know about an incident of that magnitude?"

"Hm? Oh, yeah, of course. I know all about that, real rough stuff. I was planning on visiting a visit on her."

"She wasn't hurt, fortunately, because it happened while she was at school. But her home did go up in flames, and she doesn't have a place to stay tonight."

"Huh? Really?"

"You didn't know?"

"Well, I did know. I was just thinking of bringing that exact topic up. Why'd you have to go and say it first?"

"I'm sorry, okay? But it really is strange, isn't it? To think that a good girl like Miss Hanekawa doesn't have a bed in the world she can sleep tight in. It feels like the most unjust thing imaginable. Like if justice really did exist in this world, what's it doing not helping her?"

"......"

"So, since that hollow so-called justice won't do a thing for her, I'm actually taking the day off school looking for a place where she can sleep. Oh, speaking of which, you went to school today like it was any other day? Did you have fun? While Miss Hanekawa was in trouble?"

"......"

"Oops, sorry, sorry. There's no point in telling you, is there? You're just Koyomi Araragi's little sister after all, nothing but a middle schooler. I'd be expecting far too much of you if I started treating you

144

like him. Your big brother is your big brother, and you, Karen, are you."

"......!"

"This really is some rotten timing. If only Araragi was around. I know he would never abandon Miss Hanekawa. The Fire Sisters (lol), on the other hand."

"(lol)?!?"

"I'm so sorry, I must only be a nuisance talking to you here when you can't do a thing without that big brother you love so very much. I didn't mean to worry you, not when, unlike Miss Hanekawa, you're enjoying your life. It's enough that she's in distress. We've been standing here and talking for quite some time now, so I think it's about time for me to go. After all, I understand now that justice is like a bed for Miss Hanekawa—nowhere to be found in this world."

"Hold on just a second!"

"Hm? Does something seem to be the matter?"

"A bed for Miss Hanekawa does exist...and so does justice!"

......

Thus, deftly leading Karen along, Miss Senjogahara pulled off what she called her scheme—well, describing it as "deft" might not be right.

It was more like watching a bird fly straight into a window. I suppose that if you really wanted to, you could call it a scheme that she went after Karen and not Tsukihi, the strategist.

So with that.

I had come to the Araragi residence.

To its living room...

"Just make yourself right at home, Tsubasa."

"Mm-hmm! Treat it like it's your own home. Just like your own, Miss Hanekawa."

With those words, Karen and Tsukihi poured me some tea.

While the older sister dexterously took the chilled barley tea out of the refrigerator, the younger sister took glasses from the cupboard. They'd split up these duties without so much as a single advance meeting.

I was getting a first-hand look at how well the Fire Sisters (lol)...
sorry, the Fire Sisters worked as a team.

They were communicating silently.

Your own home, huh?

This wasn't actually the first time I'd entered into this house—I'd
already gone in a number of times. I did work as Araragi's home tutor,
after all (though I held classes at the library, not here), and I'd stayed
late into the night in the past, like the time that Karen had collapsed
with a fever.

But it was a little different on this occasion. This was my first time
(at this late date) being invited to the home as "a guest."

It made me weirdly nervous. Or maybe it's better to say that it
made me feel oddly uncomfortable.

"......"

Karen Araragi and Tsukihi Araragi.

Araragi's little sisters.

The more I looked at them, the more they resembled him.

You could even say they were his spitting image.

I know it's a strange way to describe them, but they were like
triplets who weren't the same age.

Of course, their personalities, or rather their character traits, were
quite different—Karen was a martial arts-obsessed, handsome girl,
and while there was something calm about Tsukihi, you could tell she
had a firm core.

It did surprise me that both of them had changed their hairstyles
from when we'd last met... Karen had chopped off her distinctive
ponytail to give herself bobbed hair (her bangs were straight, just like
me and Miss Senjogahara in the past), while Tsukihi had a thick braid
wrapped around her neck like a scarf (Wasn't she hot? It was summer).

"You know, Tsubasa, you're too standonish," Karen said, sitting
down on the sofa with just her own glass of barley tea in hand.

She must have meant "standoffish."

"You shoulda come straight to me if you didn't have a place to
sleep. I was really just waiting for you to say something. But I did
think it might be hard for you, which is why I went and made the

proposal on my own."

She had yet to realize that she'd been manipulated by Miss Senjogahara. Even the lie that she knew about the Hanekawa residence burning down—she seemed to believe it more than anyone else. I'd have worried about her future if I weren't so concerned for our middle-school girl's dangerous here and now.

"Mm-hm. You proposed it, Karen. All on your own!" Tsukihi said, trailing behind her sister with both her tea and mine in hand. This girl who sat smiling next to Karen seemed to have made a conscious decision to go along with Miss Senjogahara's plan.

Yup.

The younger one was pretty black-hearted.

By the way, Karen was in her third year of middle school, while Tsukihi was in her second. When I saw the two of them seated there in the same clothes (Tsuganoki Second Middle School uniforms), they really did seem like twins (there's a height difference between the two, so they don't when they're standing).

"I was thinking. So, barley tea is a tea made out of barley, right?" Karen burst out about a random topic. "Does that mean that it can become beer if it tries really hard?"

She had such an incredible sense of closeness to others.

This wasn't a conversation you had with someone five minutes after inviting them into your home.

I wished she would start by calming my nerves.

I told her, "They do both start off as barley, but I guess the difference is that it's roasted for barley tea and fermented for beer. So, well."

Though I didn't know about "trying really hard," you could say they were like relatives in the beverage world. I'd intended to say that they were completely different, but I had to admit, her question actually did address the truth of the matter.

"Huh. No wonder I get all excited when I drink barley tea."

Her conclusion, on the other hand, was a disappointing one.

Karen chugged down an entire cup of barley tea in a succession of gulps—how stirring.

Actually... Upon closer inspection, these cups seemed really nice. Were they Baccarat crystal?

They were nice enough that it almost felt rude to call them cups.

What's more, judging by the way Karen and Tsukihi used them, they probably didn't know what these cost...

Was the Araragi family, in fact, affluent?

"Anyway, Miss Hanekawa," Tsukihi said, shooting Karen a sidelong glance. She gave me the feeling that as Karen's little sister, she'd gotten used to her wild ways. "If you don't have a place to stay, you're welcome at our home for as long as you'd like. Conveniently, our big brother isn't home right now. So use his room."

"Araragi's—room."

"Yeah. He has one of those pointlessly bouncy beds, pointlessly enough."

This was something—that I knew.

It was also what you might call the crux of Miss Senjogahara's scheme.

I couldn't help but feel more than a little guilty that it took advantage of Tsukihi and Karen's youthful earnestness and sense of justice as the Fire Sisters—but I couldn't stand on ceremony, either, not when their favor came from a place of benevolence.

Miss Senjogahara must have called it a "scheme" because she'd foreseen my own reaction to the situation too. That's probably why she didn't tell me.

So I didn't have to have known.

She'd let the villainy of it fall on her own shoulders, so to speak.

It was a complete mystery to me what kind of mental state you had to be in to place another woman (not just any, but me) in your boyfriend's house to stay the night, but maybe her old self-punishing streak was still alive and well.

She'd done it for me.

And put up with the pain.

Karen's earlier sentiment came back to make my heart ache when I considered that.

I was standonish—standoffish.

148

You shoulda come straight to me if you didn't have a place to sleep.
I was really just waiting for you to say something.

Just like when I stayed the night at Miss Senjogahara's, I never sought help for myself—and this seemed to be a totally different problem from what Mister Oshino liked to say about "people just going and getting saved on their own."

Yes.

I probably—stopped caring about me.

I wasn't even trying to get saved on my own.

I recalled what Miss Senjogahara had told me earlier in the morning.

I accepted blandness.

Dull when it comes to darkness.

A failure as a creature.

"Tsubasa? What's wrong, why are you all spaced out? Your face looks so stupid."

"......"

Karen didn't pull her punches when she spoke.

My face looked so stupid?

"Is it shock from your house burning down after all? The only other case I know of is what happened to Nagasawa's place in *Chibi Maruko*."

"Oh, no. I'm fine," I said. I'm fine, I found myself saying—though there was no way I could be. "But yes, I think I'll take you up on your very kind offer to put up with me—until Araragi gets back, then."

I didn't know when that would be, but it'd probably take about as long as it took the persons who should be called my father and my mother to find a rental home.

Without the slightest idea about either, there wasn't any point in thinking too deeply about it.

"Thank you very much."

"No prob!"

"You're welcome."

This somehow led to us shaking hands.

There were three of us too, which made it look more like we were in a huddle.

Were we about to start playing volleyball or what?

I didn't know what Miss Senjogahara had said about the Hanekawas' domestic situation (actually, she didn't know about the Hanekawas' domestic situation), but I was honestly grateful that neither of them asked about it.

"Let's have a pajama party and all, Tsubasa!"

"I think I'll pass."

"We could play pro wrestlers!"

"I think I'll refuse."

"Man, I've always wanted an older sister since I'm the eldest girl in our family. Can I call you Big Sis while you're staying over?"

Karen was saying things that made her sound a little like Sengoku. Tsukihi looked on with a smile—the picture made it hard to be sure which of the two was the older sister.

That's when I noticed.

Well, I guess I didn't notice anything. I'd known from the start.

"Right, if I'm going to be intruding here for a while, I'm going to have to say hello to your parents."

I'd never properly met their father or mother during my previous visits to the Araragi residence, in part because all three siblings wanted it that way—yet while the sisters could give me as much permission to stay over as they wanted, I'd have no choice but to leave if her parents said no.

Hmm. How would this go?

Faced with a high school girl walking around town from bed to bed like some kind of net café refugee, wouldn't any sensible adult's judgment be to simply lecture her and convince her to go back to her *parents' side*?

"I don't think you have to worry about that," Tsukihi said. "These are the people we and our big brother call Mommy and Daddy. I think that gives you an idea of their personalities."

"Really... Still—"

"They both have a hot-blooded sense of justice. They're not going to look at someone in trouble and tell them to get out."

For some reason, Tsukihi was brimming with confidence.

Now that I thought about it, I had no clue what kind of people Araragi's parents were. I suppose that's obvious since I'd never met them, but it was also in large part because Araragi didn't like to discuss the topic—I didn't pay this any particular mind, as it's natural high-school-boy behavior to be tight-lipped about one's parents, but...he seemed particularly gauche about them.

A sense of justice, though?

A hot-blooded sense of justice, at that?

Something about it sounded unnatural.

"Hey, Karen? Tsukihi? I just wanted to ask—you said that both of your parents work, right?"

"Yup."

They nodded in unison.

"I think they'll come back at around six today."

"What exactly is it that they do?"

The two answered in unison.

"They're police officers."

......

No wonder Araragi's been so guarded about it, I thought. And also: we must be living in the end times.

026

There was, of course, some trouble.

Though the grownups of the Araragi family had been appraised by their daughters as possessing a hot-blooded sense of justice, they also possessed the kind of good sense that adults (and police officers) had, so they had to wonder.

Still, they allowed me to stay over much faster than I imagined they would, albeit reluctantly, saying, "I guess we have to if that's your situation."

Karen and Tsukihi's desperate pleas were a factor as well—but this really did make them seem like Araragi's parents.

Both of them resembled him, too.

By the way, while the fact that family members resemble one another does of course have to do with genes, it seems that similar lifestyle cycles also play a major role. If you live under the same roof, live life at the same pace, and eat the same diet as someone, the materials that go into creating your bodies are the same. It makes sense, then, that the finished result of those materials will be similar, too.

Conversely, if family members live their lives at a different pace and eat different diets, the way the Hanekawas do, they won't resemble one another.

You could say that families with similar appearances and

personalities have some degree of unity to them—and in that regard, the Araragi family was a healthy one.

Having dinner with them, and watching, I likewise felt: *So this is what a family conversation looks like.*

I found it refreshing and joined in—though I did feel a bit hesitant when Araragi's mom asked me every little thing she could think of about her only son.

After that was bath time.

I realized three days had passed since my last time in a bathtub.

Maybe it's some rule for this installment because I ended up getting in together with Karen and Tsukihi—it got pretty cramped!

"You never put on airs, do you, Tsubasa?"

What follows is our conversation in that bathtub.

The three of us were crammed in like in some experiment where you tried to stuff as many people as possible into a phone booth. In other words, it was amidst a thoroughly unsexy lack of elbow room that Karen said, "I dunno, maybe I just think this because I'm stupid, but talking to the smart kids at school, I end up wondering all the time if they're really all that smart. They use weirdly hard words and quote stuff I don't care about. But even though you're smart, you talk to us eye-to-eye, and that makes me really happy."

"Yeah," Tsukihi chimed in. She had undone her braid in the bath, and her hair was quite long. It seemed to grow at an even faster pace than Miss Kanbaru's—like she was a monster or something. "That seems to be the way it is, actually. People who're truly smart…or not even that, people you'd call 'first-rate,' whether it's in sports or whatever, can be surprisingly normal when you talk to them. It's not like they exude auras or anything. Maybe that means they don't need to dress themselves up because they're the real deal."

"……"

While I felt a little uneasy about being praised like this, and while Tsukihi was right about just how surprisingly normal "first-rate" people can be, I thought my case was different.

I wasn't normal.

And—I wasn't smart, either.

154

I doubted there was anyone more vain and adorned than me—I knew it all too well from Golden Week and the eve of the culture festival.

Enough to make me sick of it.

Enough to make me hate it.

"A lot of times, I wonder what the world looks like to a smart person," Karen said. "I wonder if we look at the same things and just see them differently. I just see a bunch of numbers when I look at Pi, but maybe Einstein saw some kind of beautiful order."

"I wonder," I replied vaguely.

It was a difficult question to answer one way or another.

There were some geniuses with the kind of sensibility that allows them to look at Pi or the golden ratio or whatever and find some kind of value or meaning in its mathematically functional beauty—but I didn't think it was a prerequisite for being smart.

There had to be some smart people who saw Pi as nothing more than a bunch of numbers. And the opposite was probably true, too.

It was nothing more than a matter of individual differences, and not some kind of requirement.

I doubted the gap between the ways Karen and Einstein saw the world was that different from how Karen and Tsukihi saw it.

"I think if you took a novel with a first-person narration and recounted it from another point of view, you'd have a completely different book," I tried to explain. "Like how a case told by Doctor Watson and a case told by Holmes himself feel quite different from each other."

Now that I mentioned it, there were short stories in Sherlock Holmes's case files told from an omniscient perspective.

But you'd be wrong to call those objectively correct worlds.

There's no guarantee that God won't screw up.

For example.

Take the careless creation of man.

…But now that I was stuck to Karen's toned and firm beauty, along with Tsukihi's contrastingly cute and childish body, it made me think, "Araragi is always getting to hang out with little sisters like these"—and couldn't help but comprehend his eccentric behavior to a certain degree.

Or something.

We got out of the bath.

I'd run out of the underwear from the hundred-yen shop and was preparing to have to suck it up and re-wear something for just one night, but Karen let me borrow a brand-new pair of panties.

She even lent me some pajamas.

After enjoying all of their hospitality so far, it would have been strange to decline, so I simply accepted both.

"Hm? Wait, but aren't these men's pajamas?"

"Hmm? Oh, those are our big brother's."

Gurk.

I wore Araragi's pajamas...

I checked myself in the mirror.

Why did it feel like I'd just made a big mistake?

But taking them off now would only make me seem even more weirdly conscious about it, so—no, that's just an excuse.

Now that I'd worn them, I felt reluctant to take them off. So I just said, normally, "Huh, are they? They're the exact right size," which didn't even sound like I was hiding my embarrassment, and began brushing my teeth before bed.

There was no way I could tell Miss Senjogahara about this...

From there, I let the two sisters lead me to Araragi's room.

When I thought about it (or without really needing to), I'd invaded Araragi's home totally without his permission, borrowed his pajamas, and was about to borrow his bed—you wouldn't be wrong to say I was rampaging here.

I doubt he imagined permission from his family and his girlfriend could lead to all this.

Perhaps I needed to send him a message, but I hesitated to do that too since I didn't have a clue about his current circumstances.

Hey, I'm wearing your pajamas right now!

Even if I did send such a text and he was able to receive it, it might just ruin what was surely the very serious situation he found himself in.

Also, when I looked at the clock (I'd noticed this when I'd been in Araragi's room before, but for some reason it has four. He isn't that punctual of a person, though…), it was already past nine. He was probably meeting with Miss Kanbaru around now, and that would be a little, you know—well.

It made me hesitant.

"Okay, Tsubasa, good night. You're free to do whatever you want with anything in this room."

"Good night, Miss Hanekawa. I'll see you again tomorrow."

The Araragi sisters left me with those words, and I was alone in his room. I didn't know what to do.

Not that there was anything to do but sleep.

I could try to study for the day, but I only had my school textbooks—and even those were Miss Senjogahara's.

As I thought about how I might go to the library tomorrow and borrow some study aids, my eyes began to wander over Araragi's bookshelf.

Time to check it over.

While Karen had said I could "do whatever I wanted" with this room, it was Araragi's, so I couldn't really. But it seemed all right for me to peruse the books lining his shelf.

The lineup had changed quite a bit from the last time I was there— he'd told me he never threw books away, so he had to be one of those people who stocked his bookshelf with unread titles, storing the read ones in a closet.

I was surprised by how many novels there were.

I'd imagined he read nothing but manga based on the way he talked and acted.

I plucked a foreign novel from the shelf at random, sat in his chair, faced his desk, and read for about an hour. Of course, the *feeling of Araragi* I got from the desk and chair made it impossible for any of the sentences to make their way into my head.

It was a little past eleven by the time I turned off the lights and lay in bed.

Even then, thinking about how I was wearing Araragi's pajamas, how I was tucked into Araragi's bed, and how my head lay on Araragi's pillow made it impossible for me to fall asleep. His clocks' hands must have been pointing straight up by the time I actually did.

I could hardly criticize Araragi.

Thinking about all of that was lewd of me.

027

A little after midnight, my myaster finally went to sleep, so it was time again for me to make my appearance.

I do have to admit, back during Golden Week, I nyever would have imagined that I'd wake up in that annyoying little human's room.

Meowsery acquaints a man with strange bedfellows, and nyow I was in a strange fellow's bed.

What was I going to do about my myaster, too?

I had nyo idea what Hitagi Senjogahara's intentions were when she set this all up, and maybe I was wrong about her, but I at least was frustrated by all of this.

Nyot that there was anything I could do about it.

In the end, I'm nyothing more than my myaster. I can't go beyond her—and the thought makes me feel powerless.

"All right…"

I got out of bed and onto all fours, then stretched my back—mewving like a cat does—then spoke to myself as if to make sure.

"I dunnyo, though. If I'm out here like this, it has to mean that my myaster is feeling some kind of stress again…but nyow I can't even guess what it is. I'd gone and pinned it on her house burning down, but it seems like it myight be more than the fire if I keep showing up—"

That's how it seemed to be for *me this time.*

I was basically my myaster during Golden Week, and I was so closely connyected to my myaster before the culture festival that you could say I was like a mirror personyality—but this time my personyality seemed to have been completely cut loose and divorced from hers.

Was I developing independence as a nyaberration nyow after all of these appearances? I'm nyot smart so I don't know, and I'm sure that Hawaiian-shirted jerk would interpurrt it anyother way.

"But things really are getting more convenient every time I show up—appearing only while my myaster is asleep really gives me more room to breathe. They were all doing everything they could to make me go back into hiding the last two times. Myaahaha, they even got help from that pipsqueak vampire."

"Who are ye calling a pipsqueak vampire?"

"Mrow?!"

I was speaking to myself but got an answer.

I don't nyoh when, but when I looked around—wait, I didn't nyoh when? Well, she was sitting there in the room, nyo, above the room, on the ceiling, with her hands around her knees like she had always been there, from before the dawn of time.

A young blond girl.

Shinyobu Oshinyo was there.

She was wearing a helmet with goggles on it the last time I saw her, but it looked like she'd nyocked that off.

Also.

She was expressionless the last time I saw her, and during Golden Week, too. But nyow—I don't nyoh exactly how to explain it, but she wore a gruesome smile as she looked down on me.

I dunnyo, she myight have been managing a smile now, but for some reason she seemed cuter back when she was expressionless.

"Hmph," the vampire snorted confidently.

She was making light of me, wasn't she?

True, it was nyatural for her to feel confident since we'd fought twice and I'd lost twice—as Black Hanekawa, as an Afflicting Cat, or as a nyaberration, I was as good as nyothing compared to her, couldn't hold a candle to her.

"It's been quite some time, cat—I've not a clue why ye are here in the room of my lord and master, but I suppose only a boor would demand an aberration to account for its appearance."

It's not as if I'm that Hawaiian-shirted boy, the vampire added.

Hmm.

I was planning to ask her what she was doing here, but nyow I realized she would be wondering the same thing about me.

"Wait, nyow hold on a second. Weren't you trapped in that annyoying little human's shadow?"

That should have been the case.

According to my myaster's memories.

So it didn't make sense for the vampire to be here unless that little human was around, too—but he wasn't clinging onto the ceiling or anything.

Nyothing that scary was going on.

"Aye, 'tis true—but a bit of an irregularity has occurred," the vampire divulged, still sitting on the ceiling. "At the moment, the pairing between my lord and master and I—in other words, between Shinobu Oshino and Koyomi Araragi—has been severed."

"Severed?"

Mrow? I tilted my head.

I didn't understand.

"In other words, we've reverted to the state that existed before the Hawaiian-shirted boy disappeared—no, 'tis even worse than those days. For I do not so much as know where my lord and master is, nor the state he is in. Honestly..." she said before looking at me, snyorting, and concluding with, "Telling ye would do me no good."

She was giving up on me.

It was probably the right mewve, though.

I can't understand any dialogue that goes on for more than three lines.

But in any case, it seems like that little human really was in trouble—I mean, being cut loose from this vampire made it a pretty serious situation, right?

There was the monkey, too.

What could have happened to him, anyway?

I'm nyot the kind of aberration to get worried about others (if anything, I hate him), but nyohing my myaster, this would worry her—so in that sense, you could say it was good timing that she had showed up while I was out, which is to say while my myaster was sleeping.

"I had thought that perhaps my lord and master had returned to his home, but I now see what a fleeting hope that was. What's more, I find thee here instead. It's as though I've missed the forest and found the trees."

"……"

Even I nyew she was using that idiom wrong.

But I did get what she wanted to say.

Again, it wasn't like me, but I decided I'd let her nyoh.

Nyot about the idiom, but about her human.

"Your lord and myaster should have been in that abyandoned cram school at nine last nyight. He had an appointment with the monkey girl."

"An appointment? But why meet the monkey now—ah, I see. Indeed, that is a clever plan by my lord and master's standards. It was not the aberration so much as that girl's lineage he was thinking of."

"Her lineage?"

"Never mind—but this is a superb piece of information. Now my trip has not been in vain. Allow me to praise thee. I had thoughts of sucking thy blood to calm myself, but I shall refrain from as much, as a show of gratitude."

I couldn't believe it. She was really thinking of doing that?

Nyow that was a close one.

"Or perhaps thou would prefer me to suck thy blood as a form of thanks? Thou art that woman's stress, so sucking thee up would bring her some relief—or so it should go."

"Hm. Nyo thanks, I think I'll pass."

Nyow that she mentioned it, though, she was right. The last two times, my myaster did get "saved" by her sucking my blood—but things were a little different this time around.

What was different about me compared to before?

I probably had a clear mission nyow—nyot the kind of reason that's behind every aberration, but an unyusual mission. Of course, I didn't nyoh exactly what that was.

But I bet I had one.

"Hmm. I see. Thou art akin to a new breed of aberration, and thus there are things about thee that both I and that Hawaiian-shirted boy are unfamiliar with—it would be wrong for me to make careless decisions about such matters. One could even compare thy previous appearances and thy current one to *Terminator* and *Terminator 2*."

"Nyow that's an easy example for me to get, but should a vampire really be using it?"

She was alarmingly mainstream.

Did that annyoying little human show her those?

"Of course, in any case, sucking thy blood would only be a palliative treatment of sorts, nothing more than a stopgap measure. 'Tis not a method that should be repeated too many times."

"Yep," I agreed.

I nyew better than anyone how pointless "palliative treatments," or solutions through brute strength, were.

Also—I couldn't forget.

I may be making grand appearances, but at the end of the day, I was just my myaster's personyality's flip side. I shouldn't be grandstanding.

I nyeeded to lay low.

I nyeeded to sneak around.

"The front, the back… They are two sides of the same coin, after all. Perhaps that is an overstatement, but it does at least seem to be reversible. While my lord and master excels at spinning his wheels, or perhaps going in circles, I must say I get a similar impression from thee."

"Hm?"

"Well, this may strike thee as a commonplace tale as it is surely in thy master's databank, but 'tis a meaningful recollection from my five hundred years alive, so sit quiet and listen. An anecdote regarding the emperor Napoleon—it seems he slept but three hours each day."

"Oh."

She was right. That was part of my myaster's nyowledge.

Actually, it was really well nyown. Wouldn't anybody nyoh that one? Even that ignyorant little human might have heard it.

Of course, it seemed purrposterous to call it a recollection.

"And what about it? Does that have something to do with me being awake while my myaster is asleep?"

"No, I've no intention of relating it to that. Just listen."

"Nyohkay, I'm listening."

"Meanwhile, this emperor was renowned for his love of baths. They say he bathed for over six hours each day. To compare him to a contemporary figure, think of Shizuka-chan."

"……"

First it was *Terminator*, and nyow it was *Doraemon*…

She needed to do something about her lopsided nyowledge.

"They are saying many things these days about the subject, but perhaps, in the end, even Shizuka-chan will be censored… Though practically speaking, she in fact already is. On that note, the good old ending theme of *Perman* now seems crazy risky. To think that Per-ko is just sitting there with her panties out… In fact, those words 'now seems' suggest that even before any regulations are enacted, wherever you look, self-censorship must be setting in. What a sad state of affairs."

"I hate to burst your bubble while you're talking about this like it's someone else's problem, but if any regulations do get ennyacted, you're gonna be the first one getting censored."

With all due respect, she shouldn't be worrying about the late creator of *Doraemon* and *Perman*.

"Indeed. Oh, we've strayed from the topic."

"Yeah. If that's what you quieted me down to say, this is definitely getting cut from the manyuscript."

But in that case, I still had nyo idea what this vampire was trying to tell me.

Meow??? Meow.

How little that empurror slept and how long he bathed for was famous—certainly more so than your average anyecdote.

"And. When I learned those two things, I came upon a thought," the vampire stated.

In a dramyatic voice.

"He absolutely must have been sleeping in the bath, then!"

"……"

Oh.

Nyow it made sense. That's what you got if you connected her two anyecdotes—putting aside the truth of the myatter (according to my myaster's knowledge, he attended to government affairs while in the bath), it was one way to look at it.

"So there are situations in which we're able to take two idiosyncrasies that, in a sense, could be called abnormal and connect them in our minds to arrive at an utterly sensible conclusion. Perhaps we could say that the way that a negative multiplied by a negative results in a positive, crossing one mystery with another creates a stable, proper result. In other words, what I'm trying to get across here is that matters that may appear to be unrelated may, contrary to expectations, be connected—it is pointless to separate two related sides, the front and the back, when considering them. Thou may indeed be Black Hanekawa, a personality cut loose from Tsubasa Hanekawa—but there are no clear differences between ye two."

Or so I think, the vampire said—and let out a gruesome laugh.

"Aberrations and humans look alike to my eyes, after all."

"…Do they."

Nyow that I heard her say that.

I felt like a little weight had been taken off my shoulders—and that a ton of bricks had been placed in my heart.

Me and my myaster—the same?

I nyew it, I recognized it, I even said it myself—but nyow that she was saying it to me.

"I really mustn't let you suck my blood, in that case."

"I suppose not. Yes, natural extinction is in fact the best course of action. From an expert's point of view, of course, but from an aberration's point of view as well."

"So, vampire?" I asked, having thought of something—the vampire's remarks had made me think it. "If you want to thank me, do you think you could answer a question I have?"

"Hm? Well, that'd be quite fine with me—but please, I ask thee to be quick. I must hasten to my lord and master's side. If this meeting was to take place at nine, then he may not be in the same location—that hapless fool will get himself killed this time, if I do tarry."

She myight have acted carefree, but it seemed like she was in a tight spot, too.

So, as requested, I asked her point-blank.

"Do you nyoh about a tiger aberration?"

"A tiger?"

"Yep, a tiger—"

A tiger.

A mammal belonging to Carnivora Felidae.

"—It's wandering around this town right nyow."

"There are countless tiger aberrations. A significant number that I myself am familiar with, and if thou were to add that Hawaiian-shirted boy's knowledge—"

The tally would easily break fifty, the vampire informed me.

Meow.

Nyow that was a problem.

I couldn't even grasp such a number as fifty.

"Well, for my part, I have my myaster's knowledge—but it isn't enough to pin it down. I nyoh it's a terrible aberration, but I don't have a clue what it really is—"

"Indeed, to name a thing is to fix its identity—whether 'tis my Shinobu Oshino or thy Black Hanekawa. Not knowing the name of a thing, and thus not seeing its true form, makes it dreadfully frightening—that is how it works. One who is no one is more terrifying than anyone. The fears of an anonymous society are nothing new. Have ye any clues aside from it being a tiger?"

"It was a big tiger."

"Tigers are, in general, big. Now if it were a small tiger."

"Hmm. It was super fast. It got to where I was going before me in nyo time at all."

"Tigers are, in general, fast. Now if it were an immobile tiger."

"Hmm. And it talks."

"It talks?"

That one made the vampire react.

Purrty openly, too.

"An aberration that takes the form of an animal yet speaks—that is, I might say, quite uncommon. But I feel as though hearing that has further obscured its identity," the vampire said, standing up.

Though that sounds wrong because her feet were on the ceiling.

She skillfully held the hem of her dress between her thighs to keep it in place—should we call that prim?

On the nyother hand, her blond hair was all upside down.

"'Tis impossible for me not to have noticed an unknown aberration prowling around this town."

"Hm?"

Nyow that she said it, I realized she was right.

A little sardine like me could do whatever I wanted, but there was no way this king of aberrations, of un-life, wouldn't have spotted a nyaberration as powerful as that crawling around.

An iron-blooded, hot-blooded, yet cold-blooded vampire.

Nyo aberration can say they aren't food to her.

"But that's nyot something you'd be paying attention to nyow, right? I don't nyoh exactly what's happening, but that annyoying little human's in trouble, and your pairing's been severed, and—"

"No, that's precisely why. How could I possibly let an aberration escape my notice in my situation—'twould be a bolt from the blue. Um, and so ye saw this tiger?"

"That's right."

Nyo, nyot exactly.

I saw it, but before that—

"My myaster saw it. So I saw it too."

"Which would mean—perhaps that is where we ought to focus. In other words, *an aberration only visible to the two of thee*—a tiger only visible to the two of thee."

"……"

"'Tis a possibility. Sorry that I cannot be of help."

I shall think of another way to show my gratitude, promised the vampire, calmly walking along the ceiling so she could leave the room from the window. She must have been headed to that abyandoned cram school.

…Hmph, I thought.

There wasn't any reason to show any more kindness to her since she didn't even let me nyoh the identity of this aberration, but—it was true that I'd wasted her time.

I might as well give that back to her.

Nyot that I was doing it for that little human.

"Hey, vampire."

"What is it, cat."

"Lemme take you there. I could get to those ruins in one leap."

"……"

"Nyo need to be cautious. You can't fly right nyow, I bet—nor leap so high you look like you're flying. It's nyot a big deal for me. But it'd save you thirty minutes."

"…Hmph."

The vampire—looked indecisive (or really, like she didn't wanna) for just a moment, but then hopped from ceiling to floor, or actually down onto the bed. It had powerful springs, so she ended up bouncing back up and doing a pointless roll in the air, though I gotta admit I was impressed by her clean landing.

"Then would ye be so kind?"

I'd feared that there was a slight, nyo, high chance that this proud vampire would reject my purrposal, but she practically decided on the spot.

So that's how serious the situation was.

Yeah.

Come to think of it—while she didn't make it sound like a big deal, her pairing with that annyoying little human getting severed wasn't just bad, it could be catastrophic.

After all, that meant he'd lost his immortality, right?

On the other paw, since the vampire had been sitting and standing on the ceiling, she myight've regained some of her vampirism—but it was really bad news if he was deprived of his immortality.

He was only able to survive this long thanks to it.

Yet nyow.

"Of course I would," I nodded. "But I'm only taking you close by—because that's what my myaster wants. She doesn't want to get in that little human's way when he's in a fix."

"Ah—well, it may be unlike her, but 'tis wise. True, she did have a nasty experience or two over spring break—where her rash, self-righteous deeds only served to plunge my lord and master into ever-greater suffering."

"Mmgh…"

I had those memories too.

I didn't exist as me back then, but—I had those memories.

If you asked me, there was myore than that to her deeds, but the vampire was right for the myost part.

"'Tis pointless to argue if the lesson has been learned. Very well, then. That would be of great assistance on its own."

"Nyoh-kay!"

I picked up the vampire.

Right in my arms, like we'd just gotten myarried.

My enyergy drain activated from the myoment I touched the vampire, but she didn't seem to mind.

Nyow that's what I call tough nyerves.

I opened the lock on the window and stepped onto the frame. I was barefoot, like I always am, but I could just wipe off after I got back. I was lucky, too—the room had wet tissues that the little human seemed to use to clean (he sure liked cleaning, meow).

Speaking of which, I wanted to nyoh—how did the vampire get into this room? While the thought occurred to me, there was no point in asking that kind of question about a nyaberration. So, without a thought, I just jumped.

I flew.

Toward Eikow Cram School—but.

The vampire and I couldn't head toward the building—well, we were able to head to its location.

After all, I had set my heading, aimed for it, and jumped.

But.

But—we couldn't arrive there.

Because where we landed, and arrived—lacked the building that shoulda been there, the abyandoned cram school.

What was there was cinders.

The ruins of the abyandoned cram school, a refuge for Koyomi Araragi and Shinyobu Oshinyo, a home to Myèmè Oshinyo for months, a place filled with memories for my myaster, for Hitagi Senjogahara, for Suruga Kanbaru, for Nyadeko Sengoku—had been incinyerated.

052

What happened?!?!

052?!

The section number got double-point scored in one night!

I don't know about the other times, but this I can't ignore!

No, no, no! I'm not overlooking this!

What the heck happened while I was asleep?!

What kind of grand adventures took place for us to skip twenty-five sections?!

An entire novel's worth of tales weren't told just now!

"......"

You get the idea.

Putting aside silly meta-commentary—I really couldn't help but feel that something was off now that we'd gone this far.

The bed in those ruins, I supposed I could understand.

Rather attached to the lovingly handmade cot I'd worked so hard to put together, I'd been able to get a good night's sleep, my feelings helping to make up for any of its shortcomings. At least, part of me felt that way—and also that the good night's sleep I got at Miss Senjogahara's house was assisted by a reaction to the adverse conditions from the previous day when I'd camped out in an abandoned building.

The two cases may appear to contradict one another, but they could both make sense if you thought of them together.

Just like those two anecdotes about Napoleon.

Let's also put aside the question of when I thought of the imperial episodes (it didn't seem like my kind of idea), and ask…

Getting a sound night of sleep in Araragi's bed?

Me?

I'd woken up feeling completely refreshed.

And emotionally calm, too?

How could that—be?

I don't know if I should say this, but I was nervous from the moment I got under his sheets—if I were to put it in shameless terms, I was so exhilarated that I was in no shape to sleep.

It was as if I'd experienced firsthand what Miss Senjogahara said about not being able to sleep using her father's bedding, and in that sense Araragi's sheets couldn't have been more uncomfortable—not to mention that I also had his pajamas on.

It was like feeling Araragi with my whole body.

If I'd gotten a good night's sleep in that situation, I might as well rest in peace as a girl.

Not being able to get a wink of sleep would be going too far, but it ought to have been shallow.

And yet—I felt reenergized.

What an invigorating morning.

It was clearly—abnormal.

It was clearly aberrant, clearly an alteration.

An aberration.

"…Hmm."

I rose slowly and examined my body—there would have to be marks left behind if *something* had happened to me.

Maybe it was my imagination.

But there had to be proof—something that would let me know if my nerves were tougher than I imagined, or if they weren't.

There had to be something left behind.

And I found it right away.

First, there were the pajamas I'd borrowed from Araragi—apart from the night sweats I'd soaked it with, I noticed they had the slight smell of dirt to them.

If "smell of dirt" is too vague, maybe I should say *an outdoors smell.*

"I went outside while I was sleeping?"

Like a somnambulist?

I sat cross-legged as I mumbled to myself and bent over like I was stretching before a run to check my feet next—primarily my soles.

But there was nothing there.

Size 7 1/2 feet.

Very clean.

"But," I said, my eyes resting on the box of wet tissues on top of Araragi's study desk (or so I call it, but I'm sure it wasn't until very recently that it started being used for that purpose).

I was right. It wasn't in the same place as yesterday.

By about an eighth of an inch.

I got out of bed and peeked inside the wastebasket by the desk. Just as I expected, there were a number of used wipes—and they were stained with dirt and gravel.

That would mean, I thought as I looked at my hands.

Just like my soles, my hands were clean too—but not under my fingernails.

A slight bit of dirt was present.

Some very rugged nail art.

"I've heard of catching a criminal thanks to the grit under their fingernails, but…this is no joke."

Muttering, I looked to the window next.

Nothing said that I must have left through the window—*but when I considered Golden Week*, it was hard to imagine that I'd bothered to walk out into the hall, descend the stairs, and open the front door to leave. The window was the closest exit and the rational route to pick—and though it was a lucky shot, my prediction hit its mark. The window's sliding lock had been left undone.

I had of course made sure that everything was locked before heading to bed last night.

That degree of caution was inevitable after Miss Senjogahara had gotten as mad at me as she had—and yet.

In other words, someone had opened the lock to this window while I was sleeping, and since I was the only person in this room, that someone had to be me.

"I don't know about criminal, but I do feel like a culprit getting pinned down by a great detective."

Of course, culprits in detective novels wouldn't leave so much evidence—what great detective would be inspired to work on such a case? It would get tossed wholesale to the men and women of Scotland Yard—but then again.

A case with a Changing Cat as the culprit might be fit for a good, old-fashioned great detective—or so I thought.

Then, as if to strike the finishing blow, I went back to the bed and grabbed the pillow.

Araragi's pillow—it may have been, but that didn't matter right now.

If I'd spent even a moment lying in bed while in *that* state—

"…There it is. Our conclusive evidence."

I picked a single hair from the pillow.

Male or female, any human's hair is constantly replacing itself. It's normal for some strands to fall from your head while you're sleeping—that much is natural, but the question was why this hair was white.

White hair.

No—maybe I should call it white fur?

Because it looked less like human hair and more like body hair from an animal—

"Oh…so it's happening again. I'm turning into the Afflicting Cat…into Black Hanekawa."

I didn't want to believe it—or even think about it, but there was no point in running from reality when the situation was so certain.

I wasn't going to continue denying the facts until cat ears actually grew out of my head the way they did the day before the culture festival—or so I thought before I had my doubts and checked the mirror on top of the desk.

It was fine, they hadn't sprouted.

Not yet.

But, and I realize this is a completely unrelated digression, it struck me that Araragi might actually be a bit of a narcissist if he had a mirror sitting on top of his desk at all times.

What a weird kid.

Okay, anyway.

"But when I step back and think through it all—it's not just the cat ears. There seem to be a lot of differences from last time, and the time before that. There was no headache signaling what was going to happen, and given how I've been able to return to normal without Araragi..."

Anything past that was going to be pure conjecture, but I had probably "Black Hanekawafied" when I spent the night in the ruins, and when I stayed over at Miss Senjogahara's home, too—pure conjecture, but I was almost sure I was right.

I say that because it finally explained why I felt so refreshed.

Yet—I'd turned back.

I'd turned back into me.

"Could that mean I've *gotten used to becoming* Black Hanekawa? Just like how Araragi is able to make good use of his immortality?"

Immortality...

It was strange. That word, too, seemed to snag against something somewhere in my brain—hmm, but what?

Really, now—what happened while I was asleep?

Something must have happened.

Something very significant...

"Of course, I do have an idea why I became Black Hanekawa again..."

The house fire.

It couldn't be anything else.

Black Hanekawa is a manifestation of my stress—a flip-side personality who shoulders feelings that are too much for me.

"It's probably not going wild to relieve my stress again... There'd

175

be more obvious marks left behind in that case."

But it also felt like wishful thinking.

Either way, having a blank space in my memories was discomfiting.

"Deary me... I wonder if Black Hanekawa will whisk this stress right away for me too," I said in jest as I began changing clothes.

If there was no point in running from reality, then I faced another unshakable truth: even though I'd discovered that I was turning into Black Hanekawa, there was nothing I could do about it, and I had to go to school.

I needed to talk to Araragi or Mister Oshino about it, but I didn't have them, either.

I could be absent again and say it was due to psychological exhaustion from that house burning down—the thought occurred to me, but it felt hard to do so now that I realized I was offloading the exhaustion to *someone other than myself.*

And, to be completely honest, I also wanted to ask Miss Kanbaru if she'd been able to meet Araragi yesterday and if he was okay—I didn't know her phone number or email address, so direct contact was the only option.

"I suppose there's another way, which is to go through Miss Senjogahara...but she's so sharp that she might get a hint that I've been turning into Black Hanekawa."

No.

This was her we were talking about. Maybe she'd gotten that hint already.

I seemed to recall her suggesting as much...

Then.

Just as I finished changing into my school uniform.

"Miss Hanekawaaa."

Tsukihi's voice came from the other side of the door and made me jump.

Oh no.

Was I talking to myself too loudly at someone else's home?

Did she hear me?

Fortunately, that didn't seem to be the case.

"Hey, are you up? If you aren't, wake up, okay? It's time to eat, okay?" continued Tsukihi. "The Araragi family has a rule where we always have breakfast together."

"Thanks, I got it!" I replied. "Don't worry, I'm awake. I'll be right there."

"Okaaay," the cute voice said, and I heard the sound of footsteps going the other way down the hall.

Oh.

Was I feeling let down?

Araragi described his sisters "rousing him from bed" every morning like they were a pretty big nuisance, but what could possibly be annoying about this adorable wake-up call?

Really. He shouldn't.

The way he described it, he was liable to give people the wrong impression, as if they practically attacked him in his sleep with a crowbar.

Thinking this, taking one last look in the mirror, and with my contact lenses in hand, meaning to drop by the bathroom before heading to the living room, I left Araragi's den.

Meow.

053

A rule about always eating together.

As far as I could tell, Araragi was constantly breaking this rule, but now wasn't the time to be asking about that.

He probably wouldn't want to hear it from me, and I didn't want to say it either, but Araragi seemed to have trouble maintaining a comfortable distance between himself and his family—that obviously included Karen and Tsukihi, but also his father and mother.

Then again, the nuance seemed to shift a bit when I took into account that both of his parents were police officers.

And so, to this mom of his.

I said "I'll be on my way" at the entrance before heading out— Karen and Tsukihi had left about half an hour earlier since their middle school was farther away—and put my hand on the doorknob when she called out:

"Hanekawa-chan."

To me.

"I don't know what your family situation is, and I don't plan on asking you about it at the moment, but please don't think it's normal to be away from your parents and leaving our home with an 'I'll be on my way.' That's the one thing I don't want you thinking."

"……"

"While we can host you, it's not as if we can bring you into our family. No matter how much Karen and Tsukihi adore you like an older sister. Oh, I don't want you to get the wrong idea—I'm not saying you're a bother. Karen and Tsukihi are delighted you're here— and you're Koyomi's friend, so we want to treat you as well as we can. And I've heard that you're to thank for his newfound motivation to study."

"No…"

Not at all, I replied.

How do I explain it? Araragi's mother—resembled him, but there was a kind of satori in her eyes.

Like she saw things for what they are.

I felt like I understood why Araragi didn't like dealing with his mother, even if you took away the fact that she was a police officer.

"I'm sorry. I seem to have worried you unnecessarily—but there isn't anything really worth mentioning about my family situation. I don't know, I guess you could say we're not on the best terms…" Or that we were on bad terms. Or that it was warped. "…That's all."

"You know that parents being on bad terms with their child is a kind of abuse on its own." *So,* Mrs. Araragi said. "You need to ask for help if you're ever in trouble. That could be a public agency, or you could ask Koyomi. He can be surprisingly reliable."

"Yes…"

I—knew that.

I knew very well just how reliable Araragi was.

I'd always known—and yet.

I tried my best not to rely on him.

I was unable to rely on him.

"A family isn't something that you need to have, but it should be a happy one if it exists. That's what I think. As a mother."

"As—a mother."

"Hanekawa-chan. It's okay for people to go ahead and run from bad things, but just looking away doesn't count as running. No one on the outside can lend you a hand while you're consenting to the way things are—so maybe you could start by 'speaking up' about it."

Mrs. Araragi saw me off with those words—a rather long "be safe" in reply to my "I'll be on my way."

My goodness.

Mothers really are strong—was my dumb impression.

I felt totally owned.

But it wasn't the worst feeling.

…Mother, huh?

That was another thing—that I didn't know of until now.

What in the world, I wondered, had I been doing all this time?

Not just at night—during afternoons and mornings, too.

"Just looking away doesn't count as running? Those are some weighty words."

I was overcome with admiration.

That was closer to something that Mister Oshino might say, rather than Araragi.

And so, chewing over the words, I headed to school—but en route, I ended up face-to-face with something that I wished I could indeed "look away" from.

No, really. I wanted to turn around on the spot and go back the way I came.

A boy with golden eyes and hair came walking down my path— his physique made him seem my age, but describing his face as "young" would be an understatement. His babyface, with its clear signs of immaturity, made him look like a middle schooler.

But for a middle-school boy—the look in his golden eyes, fixed straight forward in a glare, couldn't be any worse.

Of course—unlike spring break.

He didn't have a gigantic silver cross resting on his back, which may have softened his image.

"…Um."

I really was thinking about changing course, but he noticed me a moment before I was able to make that decision.

Mm. Hm.

His golden eyes with that terrible look acquired me.

My eyes met his.

Head-on.

"Oh, ohh, you—oh, what were you called again—you're that girl who nearly got herself slaughtered by me the other day. Keheheh—gotta love it."

Him.

The half-vampire and vampire hunter—Episode pointed at me, looking truly amused as he spoke.

"Hello…" I dipped my head. "Long time no see…Mister Episode."

He didn't seem very troubled by this meeting—but I was finding it as awkward as could be, and it was coming through in my speech.

But it made sense.

Just as he'd said, the other day—during spring break—I nearly got myself slaughtered by him.

No, it wouldn't be an exaggeration to say that he actually *killed me*—after all, he sent more than half of the organs in my torso flying.

He'd originally come to this town chasing after Shinobu, a legendary vampire. Then, in order to defeat her, he ended up having to fight Araragi, her thrall—and that's when my painful experience took place.

It was my fault for sticking my nose into a duel between two guys, but still, didn't he feel bad at all?

"I heard that you went straight back to your home country afterwards… Why have you returned to this town, Mister Episode?" I asked timidly.

I did so wondering if he might have in order to try and "defeat" Araragi and Shinobu again—he could be the source of the trouble Araragi seemed to be in.

As an expert in the field, Mister Oshino would have settled all of that with flair—but he wasn't omnipotent. Perhaps Araragi and Shinobu had been exposed through some oversight—but the half-vampire (he was fine being in the sun, so he could get to work first thing in the morning) only smiled a wicked grin at my question.

"Gotta love it," he said. "What are you doing, calling me Mister Episode—I'm not old enough for anyone to be calling me mister yet, and why would anyone want to be polite to me?"

"What?"

But he was a vampire, half-so as he may have been… Didn't that mean he had a pretty long lifespan?

"Gotta love it—having a long lifespan doesn't necessarily mean that I'm old. This is supposed to be a secret, but I'll tell you for kicks. You're way older than I am—right now, this very day? I'm six years old."

"Six?!"

I couldn't hide my shock.

Maybe that was the reaction Mister Episode…er, li'l Episode wanted, as he looked delighted.

"It's my birthday next month, so I'll be seven then—but my parent on the vampire side of my family seems to have been a fast-maturing aberration, and I show some traces of that."

"……"

"Hey, don't judge people by their appearances—not that I'm a human, of course."

Li'l Episode put an end to the topic, leaving me with no way to figure out the truth of anything he'd said.

It seemed possible that he was just making fun of me.

If he was going to talk about judging others by appearances, though, there was something I wanted him to explain even more than his age: it was a blazing-hot August morning, so why was he wearing the same white traditional school uniform he had on over spring break?

Maybe he didn't feel hot because he was a half-vampire.

So…

He wasn't a high schooler or a middle schooler, age-wise he was a grade schooler and even younger than Shinobu and Mayoi…

Forget li'l Episode, you could even call him widdle Episode. He didn't have a babyface; in fact, he looked old for his age.

I couldn't deny feeling that it was a little late to be learning this kind of hidden backstory.

I mean, talk about a non-existent youth.

"And also, do you not have that cross with you?"

"Hm? Oh. 'Course not. I'd stand out if I walked around with that thing, duh."

Huh.

So he was at least conscious about that kind of thing.

"...Are you going to answer my question about why you came back to this town?"

"Wha? Man, you really want to know, don't you? Well, I owe you one, and I'd love to tell you," Episode said.

He seemed to think of nearly killing me as some sort of debt, at least.

I felt a little relieved.

"But I don't know why I came to this town yet, myself. I got summoned down here out of nowhere and just arrived this morning on a night bus—"

"Night bus..."

How oddly proletarian.

Or was he some sort of tourist?

"And what do you mean, you were summoned?"

"People summon me places. For the most part, I'm a freelance vampire hunter. I'm not like Dramaturgy and Guillotine Cutter. I'm a mercenary. I do what I want, and I'll work for anyone as long as the money is good."

"So you accept jobs without even hearing what they are?"

"Well, I got paid up front. And I had my reasons for taking this one. Who cares what the job is, though. Put me on it and I'll kill anyone so hard that there won't even be after-effects to deal with."

"...Then, is there a chance that you'd accept a tiger extermination job?"

"Tiger extermination?" Episode asked back with a simple, puzzled face. "Umm... Well, I'm a hunter who specializes in vampires. Tigers are a little... What, did the Shogun make a ridiculous request or something?"

"The Shogun..."

Why did he know the old tale about the Zen monk Ikkyu?

Was the Ministry of Education-approved anime about him an international hit?

Hmm.

I ended up with no reply to my question (I did want to get an answer out of him, but there was nothing I could do if he didn't know), but I was surprised by how much of a normal conversation we were having.

I had a lot of other, bigger ideas about li'l Episode in my head even though we'd only had contact with each other for a few hours in total during spring break with everything between him and Araragi—but this is what he was like if you got to meet him while the sun was out, huh?

It was almost like the saying goes, behind every ghost is a silver tongue.

He was such a normal kid it was almost a letdown.

While he definitely didn't look six or seven, it absolutely felt like I was talking to a younger boy now that we were here on the side of the street.

The white school uniform was nothing more than his self-conscious idea of fashion—

"But you know. Was it Tsubasa Hanekawa?"

However.

Something almost identical to the impression that I got of him—he had as well.

"Compared to the last time we met—you've gotten real normal."

"...What?"

He said it directly and without embellishment, so the words rang heavy in my heart.

"I mean, just now—I have the sight of a vampire but couldn't tell who you were for a second. And no, I'm not talking about how you cut your hair or how you don't have glasses. It's something more essential—that, what would you call it, overwhelming presence I felt coming from you last time? It's clean gone. Almost like it's been cut loose from you, without a trace—"

"......"

I understood what he was trying to say.

It wasn't something I understood until he said it—but the me that

Episode knew was the me during spring break.

Me before Black Hanekawa was born inside of me—me before I took everything black about me and set it loose as an aberration.

Which is why—no.

But hold on a second.

Saying I was normal, or that I'd lost whatever presence, was almost like—

It made me think back to what Karen said the day before in the bath.

You never put on airs, Tsubasa—but.

It's not that I don't put on airs, it was that I *couldn't put on airs* now—of course there'd be no way for me to put on any airs after I'd taken my individuality and set it loose—

No, no.

That wasn't right. That was even less right.

This line of thought—probably *didn't end well*.

Probably—some truth that I didn't want to behold—lay beyond—

"Oh."

What to me was a shocking statement seemed to be nothing more to Episode than a thought he happened to voice. He already seemed uninterested in the topic as he spotted something to my back.

Using his self-professed vampire sight.

He'd spotted someone behind me.

"There you go, over there—that's who summoned me out here without even saying why. I started asking questions, and it seems like she was that Hawaiian-shirted asshole Mèmè Oshino's senior back in college—which is why I had to take this job, it meant this had some kind of connection to me—"

I—turned around.

054

She introduced herself as Izuko Gaen.

A young dame whose large clothes looked quite casual on her small frame—but of course, while I call her a "young dame," this was just after I had been completely unable to figure out how old Episode was, so I didn't have much confidence in my ability to guess ages. I would believe you if you told me she was in her twenties, but if she really was Mister Oshino's senior, she had to be over thirty at least. To be honest with you, though, I could see her as being in her teens, too.

Actually, though I say this after all of that speculation, she was composed in a way that made it seem a little pointless to try to pin down her age—something about her seemed to stand apart. Just as it's boorish and meaningless to look at a masterful work of art and immediately start thinking about the year and age of its production, its origin, or who its creator is—she shut down such questions.

In that sense, her casual dress looked just right on her—a regular person wearing XL-sized clothes on an S-sized physique risked giving the impression of only being slovenly, but to be frank, she looked refined.

She wore a baseball cap tilted to the side and the heels of her sneakers were crushed, but it didn't strike you as improper or inelegant. It all fit perfectly in her brand of fashion.

"Hey, 'Sode—you were taking forever to show up at our meeting spot, so I decided to come get you. Now that I'm here, it looks like you were in the middle of hitting on a girl? Sorry if I got in your way."

That was her greeting.

She spoke with an amiable smile.

There was something odd about the way she talked—like she was providing a running commentary on her actions.

It felt like she was using her smile to cover up that oddness.

"Hmm? My, isn't the young lady..."

And then she looked at me.

"Tsubasa...Hanekawa—is it?"

"Oh, yes—"

Hearing my name before I'd given it—I was confused.

In part, I was already astonished because Episode said she was Mister Oshino's senior—but even if she'd heard about me from li'l Episode or Mister Oshino, unless she also had this "vampire sight" thing, there was no way she could recognize me as Tsubasa Hanekawa with my cut hair.

"—Yes, that's me?"

"Well, what a surprise. I'm glad I decided to act on a whim and come here because it meant getting to meet you, Tsubasa. Mèmè probably didn't tell you, but I was ahead of him in college, and my name is Izuko Gaen. He used to call me his senior. There are a lot of situations in my life where people call me that."

So she said.

She really did speak in an odd way.

And it was a strange self-introduction.

"Please don't call this hitting on her, Miss Gaen—I just happened to meet a familiar face, and the two of us were reminiscing, that's all," complained Episode (though I was taken aback to hear him say "that's all" about our conversation), to which Miss Gaen replied, "Well, that doesn't matter either way."

It really didn't seem to matter to her.

"So if you're done with your reminiscing or whatever it is, why don't we go—time is wasting and we're racing against the clock.

Yotsugi will probably be coming too, but we can't wait around for that to happen."

"Yotsugi? Who's that?"

"It doesn't matter who, not to you, 'Sode. But there are some folks for whom that isn't true, and for example, it's not true for me. Well, to tell you the truth, I wish either Mèmè or Deishu were here. But the two of them are such drifters. By the way, I don't want Yotsugi to be here, not at all."

"You're really only able to think about yourself when you talk, huh? It's like you assume whoever you're talking to knows everything you know."

Episode didn't even try to hide that he was appalled, but paying this no heed, Miss Gaen spoke to me.

"Hey, Tsubasa," she said. Her speech was way too free. "I know that normally I should edge my way into this conversation between you and 'Sode, and maybe go to a vending machine and buy you two sodas as the adult in this situation, but the circumstances are like I just gave. Sorry, but I'm taking 'Sode with me."

"Oh… Okay."

That was fine with me.

In fact, I would be breathing a sigh if she took him and left—he was still scary to me despite everything (I'd actually lost all my memories about the time he nearly killed me, but my body must still remember. My stomach was swirling), and I needed to complete my trip and get to school.

Being treated to a soda would only complicate things.

"So I can't help you with this tiger problem that you're having, either. Figure out how to take care of it on your own, okay?"

"What?"

My tiger—problem?

Wait… How did she know?

Could she have heard me mentioning it in passing to Episode earlier? No, that seemed unnatural given the distance.

Compared to getting my name right, this was almost another dimension—of unnaturalness.

It wasn't like she had read my mind.

I hadn't thought about the topic a single time while I was speaking to her.

"Hm? Why the strange expression? You can't be that shocked just because I knew about the tiger. There's nothing that I don't know."

"There's nothing—that you don't know."

"Yep," she said, "I know everything."

Full of confidence.

Like she really did know everything—

Like she had a grasp of the entire tale.

"Anyway, you'll probably end up facing the tiger some time today or tomorrow. You're about to name this peerless and all-powerful aberration the *Kako*, the Tyrannical Tiger, but no one is going to be able to help you with it. No one is going to save you. Because this problem is your own. It isn't my problem, and it of course isn't the problem of the boy you're in love with."

"Wh—"

What do you, I began to say before losing the words.

The boy I'm in love with?

"I'm talking about Koyomi Araragi. Don't tell me you don't know that?" said Miss Gaen like it was the most natural thing, like it was common sense—like it was something known by every human other than me.

And in fact—

"You don't know a thing, Tsubasa, do you," she accused, like she was deriding me, like she despised me.

Like she pitied me—like she sympathized with me.

Like she was looking at a poor little child.

So she said.

"You don't even know that you don't know anything. Not the wisdom of being simple, but the simplicity of being simple—you're thick and naïve. Ahaha, 'thick and naïve' sounds a bit naughty, like I'm talking about how full-figured you are. As a slender person, I'm quite jealous."

"......"

"Then again, maybe you're better off without the wisdom of being simple—remember how the brainless scarecrow always lamented the unbearable fact of his stupidity?"

"What…" I said.

My voice shaking.

I didn't know why my voice was shaking.

Even when I faced Episode over spring break—my voice, my body never shook so badly.

"What—do you know about me?"

"I know everything. And that's why."

I know everything, repeated Miss Gaen.

Again and again.

Like she'd repeated it time after time in the past.

Like "good morning" or "good night" or "thank you" or "you're welcome."

She repeated it.

And repeated it.

Then repeated it.

"I even know that you don't know anything. But that's nothing to be ashamed of since no human in this world knows anything. People try to make do unknowingly in living. You're not an exception, you're not special."

"I'm not an exception—I'm not special."

"It makes you happy to hear that, doesn't it?" Miss Gaen said, still as if she derided me. "I know."

"……"

"And of course, I also know quite well that the ruins of that abandoned cram school, a spot that should have a place in all of your hearts, including Mèmè's, burned down last night… Oh, is that another piece of information that you don't know yet? My cute little Tsubasa who doesn't know a thing."

055

Miss Kanbaru was absent.

Having dashed into class just before the late bell (this is, of course, a figure of speech. I would never run in the hallways. I walked how a competitive walker might, which was sort of suspicious—well, nothing short of suspicious), I only visited Miss Kanbaru's second-year classroom during our break after first period.

"Oh, it's Miss Hanekawa." "The senior?" "It is, it's really her." "Miss Kanbaru is always talking to her." "That's Miss Hanekawa, she's classmates with Miss Senjogahara." "No, we should be calling her Mister Araragi's savior."

…For some reason, I was extraordinarily famous there.

I wanted to hide my face and run away but stood firm and asked about Miss Kanbaru—and received the aforementioned answer.

She hadn't contacted anyone, not her homeroom teacher, not her friends in class (and while it may be obvious when you think about it, I was relieved that she had friends among her classmates).

"She's an incredibly serious girl, so it's really rare for her to have an unexcused absence. We're all worried about her."

"……"

While I knew this was a case of the same person having different reputations in different communities, there seemed to be a particularly steep gap in the way Miss Kanbaru appeared to our eyes and her classmates'.

No.

Maybe that was as it should be.

People like me—who appeared the same to everyone, like a carbon copy, were the strange ones.

It wasn't to be expected.

It wasn't normal.

Someone that everyone saw as a model student—would be abnormal.

"Do you know something, Miss Hanekawa?" I was asked.

I could only reply, "No. I'm sorry, I don't know anything."

The words must have rung cold, and the girl I was talking to gave me the most dubious look she could manage. Embarrassed, I left the classroom as if I was running away.

After that experience, I couldn't put myself into any of my classes from second period onward, and I want to give my sincerest apologies to all of the teachers who took the time to conduct them—but how could I not be worried?

Unsurprisingly, Araragi had taken today off as well. What could have happened last night?

No, if I'm being honest about it, I couldn't put myself into my first-period class either—I couldn't calm down after hearing from Miss Gaen that Eikow Cram School had burned to the ground.

Not only did it have a place in all of our hearts, it was where Araragi and Miss Kanbaru were going to meet. And it caught on fire?

I of course had searched for the news online using my cell phone after parting ways with Miss Gaen and Episode and discovered that she wasn't lying.

There was even an image attached to the story.

I saw the photo of a plain concrete building that had literally turned into a pathetic pile of rubble—the place in my heart where so many things had happened.

It had up and vanished from this world.

Wondering what Miss Senjogahara would think once she found

out, and at the same time struck with an indescribable feeling of the transience of life, I also understood that this was no time for sentimentality.

Last night—really, what could have happened?

Were Araragi and Miss Kanbaru okay?

I was so worried that, whether I was in class or on break, I couldn't sit still the whole day.

Even so—the fact that I was able to keep taking classes throughout the day and not leave early must have meant that some part of me was sure that the two were safe.

Somewhere inside me was a me who was certain that they hadn't been harmed in any way by the fire.

I thought these feelings were trust at first.

That this was Araragi and Miss Kanbaru, so I didn't need to worry. That I believed those two could get out of any situation, no matter how dire.

But it didn't take much for me to realize *that was wrong*.

I couldn't rest easy about Araragi in that sense at all. He was a boy who clung precariously to life, who could very well die at any moment, someone whose tendencies were more self-punishing than self-sacrificing. My familiarity with him was what made it all the harder for me to believe that he was okay in this situation.

And as for Miss Kanbaru, she and I were, unfortunately, not close enough that I could just decide to believe that she was safe (maybe she even saw me as an enemy given my relationship with Miss Senjogahara).

So why was I sure that the two were safe—or at least that they weren't harmed by the fire?

"It's because I know," I muttered.

I was on my way back from school.

No, I couldn't call it my way back—because I wasn't going straight back to the Araragi residence and was instead planning on taking a detour.

"Yes, *I know*—that the fire had nothing whatsoever to do with Araragi or Miss Kanbaru."

I knew.

I might not know.

But a me who wasn't me knew.

Probably last night, when I became Black Hanekawa—I saw it and knew. Knew that the two of them were safe. Knew that Araragi and Miss Kanbaru must have met and moved to a different location—knew that they and the fire were *mostly* separate problems.

So just like Miss Gaen said.

This case—was mine.

"To begin with, these fires must be—me."

The Hanekawa residence had burned down just three days ago.

And the Eikow ruins went up in flames a day ago.

In three short days—two buildings I was deeply involved with had burned to the ground.

There had to be something wrong with you if you didn't consider the two connected.

Plus, both incidents happened right after I saw the tiger—how could you not mind that?

They didn't know what caused the Hanekawa house fire, and as far as the online news articles said, the cause was also unknown for the abandoned cram school. Given that there didn't seem to be any potential for fire there, they did of course suspect arson, but—

"Arson..."

The worst of all possibilities crossed my mind.

I, as Black Hanekawa, am the culprit. In other words, the possibility that I'm the arsonist.

When I thought back to the outrageous spree that Black Hanekawa had perpetrated over Golden Week, it seemed like a very real scenario. And in fact, I couldn't deny having thought again and again about the Hanekawa residence, *I hope it just disappears*—and in a way, my wish had come true.

So you could say it was a strong possibility.

But this seemed wrong.

Not to say that the chain of events couldn't have happened—but that it was the worst thing that could happen.

I didn't know how to express it, but it felt like there was an even worse conclusion waiting for me at the end of this tale. A conclusion I was averting my eyes from—had its gaping mouth wide open and awaited me without mercy.

Yes, the truth.

The inconvenient truth—was waiting for me.

The path to it was the path I walked.

"If I want to turn back—now is probably the time."

Now.

If I just kept my eyes closed for a little longer—if I looked away.

If only I could hold on until tomorrow, it was unlikely that I would have to encounter the truth.

Like always.

I could continue being the Tsubasa Hanekawa I'd always been.

Still Tsubasa Hanekawa, Araragi's best friend—still me.

I could stay me.

Nothing had to change.

"...But."

But.

But, but.

I didn't know what Araragi was fighting this time.

I knew that he had to be fighting something, though—together with Mayoi or maybe Miss Kanbaru, probably with help from Shinobu too, and as always with his life on the line.

So I would fight too.

If it wasn't going to count as running away, then I wasn't going to look away either.

This time I was going to face—me.

My heart that I'd cut loose.

I had a feeling that *this*—was such a tale.

"Yes...the tiger."

That day, the day the new trimester began.

I saw it on my way to school—a gigantic tiger.

"This all started when I first saw that tiger."

That was the feeling I had.

I wasn't certain.

But I could tell *that's what it was*.
I knew.
"The Tyrannical Tiger… Is that what Miss Gaen called it?"
If I was going to approach it, that's where I would start.
I arrived at the library.

056

I realize I'm bragging about my own town when I say this, but we have an extremely extensive library. It boasts a significant collection despite its size, and though I'm unsure whether it's due to a long-standing tendency or the librarians' tastes, its shelves focus on fanatically niche titles rather than bestsellers.

It feels in some ways like a museum.

As a side note, when Mister Oshino was still here, I'd come to this library multiple times to borrow books on his request (he couldn't make a card since he wasn't a resident).

Its only notable flaw is that it's closed on Sundays, but I've gone to this library ever since I was a child. I've never attended a cram school or taken lessons in anything, but you might say that all the things I needed in life I learned here.

All the things my parents never taught me.

I learned them here in this library.

By myself.

Lately, I'd been using it a lot as a place to study with Araragi, but even when it was Miss Senjogahara's turn to be his tutor, I ended up visiting alone. To tell you the truth, I'd read most of the books in the collection by the time I was fifteen, but I liked the building's air, its atmosphere, and found myself coming here even when I didn't need to.

It was a perfect spot for studying.

While it may not have been home, it was at least a place where I felt at ease.

But of course, I hadn't come here today "when I didn't need to"—I was about to do research.

"Hello, Tsubasa. Welcome."

"Hello there."

I greeted a familiar employee before grabbing about five volumes that I already had in mind and sitting down in a window-side seat that was practically my reserved spot.

The full digitalization of collections that seems to be taking place all around wasn't being carried out here, which meant my only choice was to make my plodding way book by book. Although I'd read all of them before, it isn't as if my memory is perfect. More to the point, it couldn't be trusted on this issue.

Because anything that's inconvenient to me, I can cut loose.

I'm able to do so.

To draw on how Mrs. Araragi put it, I'm able to *look away* from anything I want.

I'd even forgotten all that happened over Golden Week, and I still couldn't remember it perfectly—no, I didn't want to remember.

I was forcing my painful memories and heartrending stress on someone else.

I was forcing them—onto Black Hanekawa.

Which is why my memories, my knowledge, and even my thoughts were of no use to me—if I still wanted to do something, if I wanted to struggle and flail to try to do something, I was going to have to go over and review everything like this.

Line by line, word by word.

Without looking away.

I was going to have to read as if I was burning it all into my eyes.

"...Hrmm."

But while I persisted until closing time—there was no book mentioning any aberration or supernatural creature that could be the Tyrannical Tiger, not only in those first five books, but in the fifteen in-depth tomes on the subject that I ended up digging through.

I was even careful to look for any creatures with a similar name, thinking that maybe I had misheard—maybe it was the Pyretical Tiger, for example, which could make sense given that it was manifesting itself through fires—but that was another swing and a miss (I did find an aberration called the "Water Tiger," but that was a kind of *kappa*, so it had to be unrelated).

Hm.

My intentions may have been good, but the results left much to be desired.

I thought I would be able to start rattling off facts and citations at this point in the story like I was Mister Oshino, but...things don't always go that smoothly.

Or was there actually some bit about the tiger, and had I failed to register it? The possibility that it was in those books, but that I had looked away, not wanting to know—

"I wouldn't be able to trust anything if I started to say that."

No.

I couldn't trust anything from the start so long as I was me. The question was what to do given that situation—what I could try to do.

If I couldn't trust anything, then there should be some way to use that unreliability to my advantage.

I'd have to use the internet for my research if the library had nothing, but honestly, I wasn't very interested in taking that approach. While the internet is an incredible medium for tapping into what's happening at the moment, it's far too full of misinformation when it comes to researching info from the past.

Frankly, it's a poor choice when it comes to aberration lore.

Still, there was a chance it could at least provide me with a clue. I couldn't afford to have some silly antipathy toward electronic information since I had no other choice—and it was an approach, a method unavailable to Mister Oshino, with his inability to figure out technology.

My phone was off because I was in the library, but I'd start searching once I got outside.

Having decided, I began placing each of the books I'd grabbed back in their original spots. I didn't know the extent to which my memory was accurate, but I seemed to remember at least where every book in the library went, so it was easy work.

"Are you alone today, Tsubasa?"

But as I did this, a different employee from the one who greeted me called to me. This one had seen me with Araragi multiple times, which explained the question. It seemed that some people thought that Araragi and I were a couple, and since he showed no signs of noticing this, I never went out of my way to correct them.

"Yes, I'm by myself today."

I still came to the library alone quite often, as I mentioned, but maybe I wasn't conspicuous (to this person) during those times.

"Hm. The library's about to close, are you all done with your research?"

"I am."

I'd come up empty but finished reading what I could.

"Looks heavy," the employee said, taking a glance at the stack of books I was re-shelving. "I wonder if that weight will be completely foreign to people once e-books become the norm. No, actually, there won't be much use left for libraries at all once that happens."

"Well, it's hard to say. I think you'll be quite all right so long as e-books are little more than digital photos. This weight is part of what makes a book a book… Books aren't flat, they have volume. Figurine collectors didn't start saying they were good with photos just because digital cameras took off. A book isn't a book without a spine."

Digitizing a book—was the wrong way to think about it.

Books and e-books ought to be seen as different things, like a book and a video—not a shift, not an evolution, but a new breed.

"I sure hope so." Apparently uninterested in having any kind of deep discussion with a high school girl, the employee let out a little laugh, looked at the titles of the books I held, and asked in puzzlement, "You're interested in ghosts?"

To be fair, none of the books were the kind that a girl in the flower of her youth would normally delve into, so I supposed I could understand the puzzlement. The more veteran employees knew about my tastes (as a voracious reader), but this one was still new.

"Yes, a bit—it's for schoolwork."

I wasn't actually going to explain the whole situation and chose a vague and nice-sounding answer to paper things over.

"In that case, we have a book like that in the New Reads section. Did you look at that one?"

"No—not yet." Now that I thought about it, I hadn't checked out their new acquisitions.

"I doubt there's any time left to read it now, but you can always borrow it."

"Yes, I think I'll do that."

I didn't get my hopes up.

It would be far too convenient a twist for this last, overlooked book to contain the info I needed about an aberration—but what did I have to lose?

I followed the employee's suggestion and borrowed the book before leaving the library.

"Hm? Wait a second. A New Read…"

New read—new breed.

A thought suddenly came to me as I placed the book in my bag— no, it would be strange to say it came to me.

After all, Miss Gaen had told me from the beginning.

An aberration that I was going to name.

"If I did all this research and couldn't come up with so much as a hint… If that tiger, like Black Hanekawa, is a *new breed of aberration*—"

057

Once I had a place to start, the rest fell into place.

They were quite literally keywords, and realizing this eliminated any need for a flashy display of references and quotations.

In fact, I should have thought of it as soon as Miss Gaen had spoken those words.

Yes, there was no need to go to the library, because this was a saying found in any Japanese middle schooler's language textbook—an idiom that any Japanese person has heard at least once.

"Tyranny is fiercer than any tiger."

A passage from the Tangong chapter in the *Book of Rites*.

While it might not be necessary, allow me to recount the story in the way of a review.

There was once a woman whose father-in-law and husband were devoured by a wicked, man-eating tiger, and later it even went on to eat her child. So then, she was asked, why do you not leave this place inhabited by a man-eating tiger? Her answer: "No matter what fierce beasts may live here, it is better than living in a nation led by tyrants"—tyranny in this case meaning a government focused on nothing but heavy taxation, conscription, and the like.

So if Miss Gaen is right and I'm going to name this tiger the Tyrannical Tiger—the saying would have to be the origin of its name. I say this because when I first learned the words in elementary school, I felt like some part of me just couldn't agree. I had a strong feeling that it wasn't true.

Any government had to be better than a man-eating tiger—that's what I thought.

It wasn't because I was a child who didn't understand the text's nuances. Her father-in-law and husband being eaten was one thing, but the issue I took with the story was the mindset of a woman, a mother, who'd impose such a philosophy even on her child. It was completely baffling to me.

Of course, now that I knew there were vicious forms of government that were worse than tigers, I couldn't claim not to understand her at all—but somewhere inside of me, it was still hard to swallow.

"My theory is that this means the Tyrannical Tiger isn't just an abbreviation of 'Tyranny is fiercer than any tiger,' but rather, 'a tiger that's *not at least better* than tyranny,' or a tiger that transcends tigers. What do you think?" I asked.

On the other side of the phone, Miss Senjogahara heard my hypothesis, paused for a bit, and disagreed.

"I don't buy it." She flatly disagreed, at that. "Part of me feels like she's leading you along. This Gaen person—from the sound of it, you didn't name this thing, it was clearly her."

"Yeah. I guess that's true."

It was hard for me to explain that part.

Words fell short of describing the temperament of this woman who called herself Mister Oshino's senior, Izuko Gaen—and in fact, even after seeing, meeting, and speaking to her directly, I didn't feel like I really understood her.

No wonder I couldn't describe her.

But there seemed to be no obvious reason for her to lead me along—for example, like the one Miss Senjogahara had when she manipulated the Fire Sisters.

Miss Gaen just pushed me away—saying she had nothing to do with me.

"You don't know that, do you? She could have been lying. She could have had some indescribable reason," argued Miss Senjogahara.

"Indescribable reason..."

"And by the way, that woman is probably Kanbaru's something."

"What?" I wasn't expecting that name to come up.

"I want to say her mother's maiden name was Gaen. I remember hearing it when I was in middle school—Kanbaru herself said that her name used to be Suruga Gaen. By the way, her mother's name was Toé. We can't know for sure until we ask the woman, but this feels a little too on-the-nose for them to be unrelated, or for it to be a coincidence, or for her to be just some distant relative."

"Yeah..." Suruga, Toé, and Izu—all three were names of old Japanese provinces. It would be stranger not to suspect that they were somehow related. The surname didn't seem that common, either. In other words...

"Kanbaru said that she received that Monkey's Paw from her mom—so this Gaen person seems fishy to me, personally."

"Yeah—and I wouldn't say otherwise, of course."

I truly meant that.

Not because she was able to boss around Episode, and not because of all the different things she got right about me.

—I know everything.

It was that line.

That line—pierced me to my heart.

Like a thorn.

Like a stake.

"Isn't 'Gaen' an old word for a firefighter? In that case, you can probably blame her for your house fire and the abandoned cram school's. You know, as in, it's the opposite?"

"Nope, nope."

As in, it's the opposite?

That wasn't a path we wanted to be going down.

"Speaking of which, Miss Senjogahara. Were you able to contact Miss Kanbaru?"

She didn't know that the cram school had burned down until I told her earlier, but she had to be concerned about the well-being of her dear junior. She had all the time in the world on her hands while she was out with the flu, so I could imagine her trying to call.

"Yes," she confirmed, as expected. She was a real woman of action. "But it didn't go through—and went to her voicemail, which makes me think either her phone is off or she's somewhere with no reception. And of course, I haven't heard anything from her—it's kids like those two who grow up to become college students who don't even go home over New Year's break."

"Well, they're not going to have to do that much more growing up before that."

What a raw, vivid prediction.

Were they really going to leave home, though?

Especially Araragi—I felt like his little sisters weren't going to let him. I could see them imprisoning him like in *Misery* if he said he was going to live in the dorms.

"Still, Miss Hanekawa, I don't think anything too terrible is going to happen if Kanbaru and Araragi were able to meet... But it also seems likely that Miss Gaen's reason for coming to our town has something to do with Kanbaru. In other words, Araragi and that half-vampire boy might meet again, then fight again..."

What is Araragi doing? sighed Miss Senjogahara.

Hm. I had trouble figuring out a way to console her.

I of course had my own thoughts about those two, but she seemed to be in a tougher spot, given their relationships.

"Well, it's fine," she said nonetheless, willing herself to endure the fact and swallowing the many things she surely wanted to say. Her ability to suffer these things was incredible, rivaling even her ability to act. Perhaps it was because she'd spent more than two years living with an aberration. "I hate giving up, but I'm good at waiting—so as an adult woman, I'm going to do the mature thing and wait for him to return."

"Whoa..."

"Because I can take it all out on him once he does."

"Wuh?"

Maybe she wasn't so mature after all?

It seemed as though once Araragi and Miss Kanbaru managed to escape the crisis they found themselves in, yet another would be in store for them.

"But let's put that aside and focus on this problem. Going back to what we were talking about," Miss Senjogahara reprised. "They might be in a tough situation, but so are we—the Tyrannical Tiger, was it? For argument's sake, let's say we do the brave thing and decide to believe this Miss Gaen." Her sense of caution, evident from the emphatic "for argument's sake," must have been supported by her experience of being tricked by five frauds. And speaking of them, Deishu Kaiki, one of those frauds, was also one of Miss Gaen's juniors, just like Mister Oshino— "Personally, I'd associate 'Tyrannical Tiger' with history. You know, like the past."

"The past?"

"Yes—more so than if it's the 'Pyretical Tiger,' written with the character for 'fire,' right? And you can also relate it to the idea of a trauma from the past."

"Trauma…" Transliterated into Japanese, it sounded like a pun on *tora* (tiger) and *uma* (horse).

"Oh dear. I guess that sounded like just another play on words."

Typical, she said in an embarrassed tone.

It seemed to me like she was usually unabashed about making those kinds of jokes, that she even loved them with all her being. But it sounded like she didn't want me to assume that one was on purpose.

I did get what she was trying to say.

History—and tyranny.

"We can't sit around just laughing it up," Miss Senjogahara declared in an excessively serious manner, though no one was laughing. "Let's put aside its name for now, and let's also put aside the question of whether or not it's a new breed. Doesn't this aberration pose a pretty realistic threat? What I mean is that its aims are pointed not inward like my crab or Mayoi's snail, but outward, just like Kanbaru's left hand—"

"Huh? What do you mean?"

"What do I mean? How could you possibly not see?"

Miss Senjogahara sounded exasperated, but I really didn't see.

What was she saying?

I had only called her to sound out a third person about my name for this thing taught to me by Miss Gaen (I know that structure is a little tangled), the Tyrannical Tiger—and her reaction was fairly negative, which actually helped to calm me down.

"Come on, Miss Hanekawa. There were serial fires at your house and then the abandoned cram school, okay?"

"Yes, right. Unfortunately, though, I don't have any proof at the moment linking that to my meeting with the tiger—"

"It doesn't matter if they're related or not. The only thing that matters is that in addition to the macro-sized, long-term factor they share in common, which is that they were places you know very well, there's one very micro-sized, very short-term factor they also share, yes?"

"Huh?"

She'd said so much—but I still didn't get it.

No, I probably did.

I was just—looking away from it.

"So you mean the fact that they caught on fire right after I saw the tiger on each of those days—"

"It's not that, it's—" interrupted Miss Senjogahara. It seemed hard for her to say—she must have wanted me to read between the lines and notice—but she came out and said it: *The fact that two places you had just slept in burned down in a row.*

"......!"

"In other words, unless we do something, aren't my apartment and Araragi's home going to burn down tragically some time around tonight?"

She'd said it coolly, but she was right.

There was no threat more realistic—than this.

058

I'd called Miss Senjogahara while sitting on a park bench—it was actually the same park where Araragi met Mayoi for the first time.

The thought also made me realize that it was where he and Miss Senjogahara decided to become boyfriend and girlfriend, giving it an even more important place in their hearts than the abandoned school building.

To me, of course, it was nothing more than a regular park close to where I lived, and I felt no special attachment. Part of the route I'd always taken on my walks, it bore no particularly deep meaning as the source point of my call. Thinking I would go see the remains of the burned-down Hanekawa residence, I'd headed to this spot from the library, but filled with dread as I got close, I decided to call Miss Senjogahara first.

It may have been more a way to avert my eyes than fear, but at this point I was starting to lose any idea of what it meant to look away from things.

I wasn't freaking out.

But I was fretting.

Indeed, Miss Senjogahara had pointed out something I wasn't expecting to hear—but even that, as she said, seemed like something I should have noticed without needing to be told.

Seeing the Hanekawa residence as "a place where I had just slept" required a bit of an imaginative leap (the obviousness of sleeping at one's house makes it rather hard to define it as such), but I should have at least thought of the abandoned cram school as "a place where I had stayed the night only yesterday."

It burned down because I stayed the night there—even if I couldn't believe such a thing, one day later and I might have died. That fear, I should have felt.

But I hadn't even come close, and it didn't seem like a lack of imagination so much as—

Looking away.

Turning my back on reality.

Maybe that was it.

That was probably it.

True, I couldn't unquestioningly agree with Miss Senjogahara's point—it wasn't a conclusion you could jump to, and there just wasn't enough data.

You couldn't draw a logical conclusion based on a two-building sample size.

At the same time, that didn't mean I could wait for a third and fourth sample.

After my call with Miss Senjogahara, I prepared myself once more and headed out to the charred remains of my house—but where I expected something, I saw nothing.

Once again.

There was so little there it was stunning.

Not a single rubbernecker now, it was a scorched field that looked like it could have been that way for the last fifteen years. No police tape or fences cordoning it off like the scene of some crime—it was what you'd call an empty lot.

There was nothing—I felt nothing.

I had trouble readily believing even this feeling of feeling nothing—but it wasn't as if I had lived on the plot, I had lived in a house. I thought I could at least half-believe the feeling.

Yes, indeed.

There was nothing here.

"……"

I stayed there for only about a minute, since I might attract attention if I stood still for too long, and quickly moved along.

"*Two places you had just slept in burned down in a row*—in other words, unless we do something, aren't my apartment and Araragi's home going to burn down tragically some time around tonight?"

Miss Senjogahara's fear seemed like a stretch even after I'd seen the scorched field, but it did bring to mind a relevant case: the story of Oshichi the Grocer.

Oshichi fell in love with a man whom she saw during a great fire, and to meet him again, she set her own fire, to her home—a dreadful idea that chills the spine rather than warms the heart. Yet her passion seems of a piece with ordinary romantic love.

Oshichi was born in *hinoe-uma*, the year of the fire horse, and women born under that zodiac sign have been said to be headstrong, which isn't even any aberration lore but just superstition, or rather, mere prejudice.

Because everyone alike has such feelings.

It's a fortune that could apply to anyone.

But—in this case, the term *hinoe-uma* seemed to carry special meaning.

Well, I knew it had no meaning.

Uma.

Horse.

Miss Senjogahara was embarrassed by how "trauma" sounded like a play on words, but puns seemed to form half of the basis of many a tale of an aberration. It certainly held true for *hinoe-uma*, about which they told that horses go mad when they see fire.

Tiger and horse, *tora* and *uma*—trauma.

Psychic wounds.

"I could come up with lots of possibilities—I'm not at a conclusion yet."

However, I did feel like one was on the horizon.

The question was if I could face it—even if it was a stretch, for example, the suggestion that Miss Senjogahara's apartment and Araragi's home might burn down was enough to make me fret.

Right.

It was time for me to settle this.

This tale about fires—this tale about me.

"...Um, pardon the intrusion."

Araragi's home was far enough from the (remains of the) Hanekawa residence that I could have taken a bus, but I ended up walking back instead of using public transportation.

I was able to enter without using the intercom because I'd been given a spare key (how trusting of them), but I still felt nervous. They could tell me to make myself at home, but I couldn't do that.

What did they mean—make myself at home?

I didn't know what it was to be at home.

In fact.

I didn't know myself.

Of course, I shouldn't be returning to Araragi's home if every place where I slept was going to go up in flames, but then, it was also too late now that I'd spent a night there, in which case it was fine to come back—I'd established a strange kind of logic for myself.

...Still.

My heart was so poor that I needed a logical reason just to go back to my bed for the night—and that made me want to die a little.

"Welcome back, Tsubasa. You're late, where'd you go?"

Karen emerged from the living room to greet me as I took off my shoes. She'd welcomed me back, but it wasn't like I could announce that I was home.

"I was at a park in the area for a bit. Just stopping by."

"Hm."

"Have you heard anything from Araragi?"

"Nope, we haven't. How prodigal does my brother think he can be? I'm kicking his ass once he gets back. As hard as I can," menaced Karen, showing me an actual kick.

A too-beautiful double jumping kick.

Even if he managed to get home safely after solving whatever case he was on, Araragi would be facing another predicament or two.

No, I shouldn't be talking about it like it was someone else's problem. Nope.

It made me really want to solve my own problem—so that I could chew him out too.

I wanted to be a predicament for him to come back to.

"Whatever, forget about that forgettable brother of mine. I was waiting for you, Tsubasa. You could even say I was on edge waiting for you. Or maybe that I was on pins and needles?"

"There's not much of a difference between those two phrases."

"Tsukihi's home too, so let's play a game or something. We already have cards lying ready on the living-room table."

"Cards?"

So she didn't mean a videogame.

I was somewhat surprised.

"Oh, I'm sorry, Karen. There's something I wanted to think about in Araragi's room—"

"C'mon, it's fine!"

As I tried to turn down Karen's invitation, she took my arm and started leading me into the living room.

"R-Really—"

"They say it's better for people not to think about things, you know."

"What?! What kind of logic is that?!"

"Logic, really? That stuff just makes your head hurt. I know they say that man is a thinking reed, but who decided it's wrong to be an unthinking reed?"

"What a bold opinion!"

But wasn't an unthinking reed just a plain reed?

Was she all right with being a plain reed?!

"C'mon, hurry up. You better not think you can put up a fight against me!"

"H-Hey. Okay, okay, just let me get these off, I need to take my shoes off! I'll do it, okay? I'll play cards with you!"

"Hooray!"

Karen threw up both arms.

She was such an innocent girl.

I really didn't have time to be enjoying card games when I had something that I didn't just want, but needed to think about—so no matter how forceful her invitation, perhaps I should have turned her down saying I didn't have the time.

But I didn't because I also knew full well how pointless it was to think about this alone—not to agree with Karen's opinion about there being nothing wrong with an unthinking reed, of course.

I didn't want to be a plain reed.

Yet—I was just as unwilling to be either a thinking me or an unthinking me.

I could think.

I could think and think, and no matter what I came to realize—if that realization was inconvenient to me, I would just look away, pry it loose from my mind, forget it, and perhaps ultimately be unable even to think about it.

So you could say what Miss Senjogahara had done for me earlier—in order to grab onto clues in the context of an exchange, a dialogue—was the smart way.

While my better judgment told me I shouldn't involve Karen and Tsukihi, middle schoolers, in this, I was already intruding on their lives. Weirdly standing on ceremony would only be counterproductive—and, above all, who better to talk to about fire than these girls?

They were Tsuganoki Second Middle School's Fire Sisters, after all.

A duo whose names both contained the character for fire.

059

"Fire? What do I think of when I hear the word? Isn't it obvious? The blazing heart that resides in my chest," Karen replied to my question with a somewhat dashing look. The certainty in her voice made me think she'd answered it often enough.

Quicker than I could've imagined.

It was like she'd answered before I even asked.

"So the short version would be passion," she said.

"Huh…"

I heard we'd be playing cards and expected poker, or blackjack, or sevens, or some other game like that, but to my surprise, Tsukihi proposed that we all build our own house of cards.

The rules were that we would share ten decks and that whoever built the highest house the quickest would win.

I'm sorry, but that's not fun.

It was like playing with building blocks, only with most of the creativity removed.

At the very least, it didn't seem like something to do in a group… but maybe that's what they call a generation gap speaking.

Still, this was a designated time and place for the three of us to play cards. I couldn't phone it in, and I'd build triangles out of cards as I asked the two questions disguised as small talk.

"In that case, what do you think of when you hear the word 'flames'?"

"Blazing passion that's even hotter," Karen declared. She really was certain about this. "Justice. To put it in a word, justice."

"Hmm. I see." I nodded vaguely, uncertain to the point of contrast. At least, it wasn't a definition that I could agree with given my current mental state. "So is that why the two of you call yourselves the Fire Sisters?"

"That's right!" affirmed Karen. "The Fire Sisters, or in other words, the siblings of justice!"

"If we're being precise about this, she's completely wrong."

Karen's affirmation was blithely negated by Tsukihi, who sat next to her.

Negated with a smile.

How merciless.

"We're called the Fire Sisters because both of us have the character for 'fire' in our names, that's all. I feel bad for how plain the reason is, though. People have been calling us that since we were in elementary school. Even before we began acting in the name of justice."

"Really?" asked Karen, tilting her head.

Her memory seemed to be cloudy.

I knew that was probably the case, but I supposed it was better than if they had named themselves the way the Valhalla Duo had.

"By the way, I personally associate words like 'fire' and 'flames' with romantic love," Tsukihi said.

"Love."

Indeed.

In fact, the story of Oshichi the Grocer referenced romantic love, too, though it deviated a bit from the theme—and it was also common to speak of someone's "burning love."

....

Then I was distracted from the thought by how incredibly fast Tsukihi was building her house of cards. She was outstanding when it came to tasks that required precision.

It seemed she possessed casually superb powers of concentration.

I had actually been playing this fire-based word association game by myself all the way back from the park—but had come up empty-handed on my own.

I'd only hit upon words that seemed to miss the mark, like "red," or "heat," or "civilization."

One person only being able to devise so many patterns, a lack of imagination—it couldn't have been because of any such generic-sounding reason that I'd come up empty-handed.

I was probably thinking in a way that intentionally avoided the word that would prove decisive.

My thoughts were proceeding in a way that avoided any hints.

So instead of continuing to deliberate further on my own, I'd transitioned to looking for an answer while playing with Karen and Tsukihi, but—

"Romantic love, huh?"

That was indeed something my mind wouldn't have associated with "fire"—not even while I was thinking of Oshichi's story—but as with "justice," it wasn't hitting home.

Somehow it felt—off the mark.

Tsukihi gave me a cute nod. "M-hm. You might not know, but the Fire Sisters don't just act in the name of justice, you see. We also give romantic advice."

"You do?"

That was indeed something I was hearing for the first time.

Araragi always emphasized how they were "defenders of justice," so I'd assumed that was their main field of activity. Now that I thought about it, they were something like the faces of our local girls' middle school (which really is an impressive feat), and it actually seemed to make more sense for that to be their focus.

"M-hm. We've even given our big brother advice about his love life."

"What? Araragi?"

Had they, now.

Araragi was asking his little sisters for romantic advice...

That was creepy.

"Oh. Yeah, I guess we did. Was it around May?" chimed in Karen, searching through her memories. "I want to say he asked us something naïve like what it meant to be in love."

"Huh… So I guess that means he went to you two for advice about Miss Senjogahara?"

Putting aside how reliable Karen's memory was, that's what it had to be if it was in May.

Those two first decided to go out on Mother's Day in the park I'd just visited—though, at the time, I'd mistakenly thought they were going out from before then.

…Hm?

What was this unnatural feeling?

Like I'd forgotten something—or rather, an easy feeling, like my thoughts had forcefully shut down and I'd leapt straight to the most convenient conclusion I could find.

Had I—looked away again?

"Hmm, I wonder. It was a while ago, and I forgot what he was talking about. I don't even remember what we told him," Tsukihi said dryly.

But her tone also made it feel more like she was glossing over something.

In fact, unlike Karen, Tsukihi seemed somehow suspicious about my line of questioning—or mystified by it.

Like she couldn't get a read.

That made sense, of course—if someone who'd been left without a place to stay after a house fire started asking about what you associated with the word "fire," you didn't have to be the strategist to find it unnatural.

"Anger also seems like a 'fire' word, but that connects to what Karen said about justice. For her, justice is anger."

"That's right!" Karen declared again.

So vigorously that her house of cards crumbled (though she was only up to a second floor).

Talk about flushing your progress down the drain.

"In other words, anger equals flames, and flames equal justice!"

"I guess in either case, you could say that Karen and I are thinking about heated emotions."

"Heated emotions…"

Hmm.

Then again, phrases like "frozen justice" and "cold feelings of romance" almost felt like you were talking about a sewing machine on an operating table, so Tsukihi's words made at least more sense than Karen's—

But were there any "heated emotions" in me?

Heated…hot…heat…no.

It felt off in some way.

"Actually, wait, Tsukihi. What do you mean? If anything equals justice, it's heated emotions," Karen clung to her sister's remark.

The older sister seemed to have the stronger attachment of the two to justice—I understood that it was Tsukihi, the younger sister, who was normally more passionate about their work, but to me it looked like she was just going along with what Karen did.

It was an easy arrangement to understand, though, the big sister having an influence on her little sister—but having no siblings, it was also difficult for me to understand the easily understood relationship.

"Mm, yes, you're right." And possibly for this reason, Tsukihi seconded her sister before continuing, "Still, Karen, your feelings for Mizudori aren't justice, but they're still heated, aren't they?"

"Hmm. I guess. Sorry, I was wrong."

Karen apologized.

How abnormally straightforward.

She was so amenable that I could understand Araragi's concern—of course someone like her would be deceived at will by someone like Mister Kaiki.

Wait, but who was Mizudori?

"Karen's boyfriend," Tsukihi replied openly when I asked. "By the way, my boyfriend's name is Rosokuzawa."

"Huh? What? Both of you have boyfriends?" Well, that was something I was hearing for the first time. Mark me surprised. "Araragi never told me."

"Oh, yeah. That's because he likes to act like they don't exist," Karen said.

Ah. Concise and easy to understand.

Too easy, in fact.

If you wanted to say it was something Araragi would do, it was— because at the end of the day, he doted on his little sisters.

I could feel it in every word he spoke about them, and there was also his explosive rage when Mister Kaiki duped Karen.

Really, what a big brother.

"So, out of curiosity. What's he like?"

Although it didn't feel like digging into the subject would help with my current problem, I asked anyway, simply interested in the Fire Sisters' boyfriends.

But then came their answers.

"Guy's like my big brother."

"Someone similar to my big brother."

I regretted having asked.

These siblings…

However, if what they were saying was true, maybe I couldn't blame Araragi for wanting to pretend they didn't exist—he'd be tormented by his hatred for people who were like him.

The same had to be true for his dim view of the Fire Sisters' activities, and you could even call it self-hatred.

Yes.

He fought while lost, while feeling regret.

"I don't know what to do with him." Karen shook her head like she really didn't know what to do. "I want to get his seal of approval somehow, but he won't even meet Mizudori or Rosokuzawa. He can be small when it comes to that kind of thing."

"You're right. But then he has the nerve to introduce us to Miss Senjogahara. The nerve!"

"Ahaha. That's cute, though." I felt bad, but Karen and Tsukihi sitting there looking legitimately troubled was a bit amusing. I even forgot the situation I was in and laughed. "At the end of the day, it's just that Araragi feels like his two cute little sisters were taken from him, and that's making him envy those guys, right? Like he's burning up inside, with jealousy—"

Gulp.

My own words—made me gulp in shock.

Burning up—with jealousy?

Burning?

Envy.

Ah, yes.

That was another one—another keyword so clearly related to fire that it should have been one of the first things to come to mind.

Burning—envy.

Even if Araragi was doing it as a joke, the fact that their boyfriends didn't exist to him was equivalent to looking away from the truth—just like with me.

It was the *one way* we were the same.

Looking away.

Turning away from reality.

And the cause was one of the most powerful human emotions, one of the seven deadly sins, even—envy.

Heated emotions—consuming envy.

Thus I was burning—with jealousy.

My hands, shaking from the truth thrust before me so abruptly that I didn't have the time to turn away—brought my fresh house of cards crashing down.

060

I'm sure there isn't a single person in modern-day society who hasn't thought of how great it would be if the human brain worked like a hard drive.

When I say that, I mean the ability to immediately erase any memories (records) that we want to forget as if they never happened, to overwrite any elements of reality that we want to avert our eyes from, and to never have to be brought down after suddenly recalling our traumas and fears—how wonderful would it be if you had such a brain?

And howsoever it came to be—that wonder seemed to be mine.

Cutting a memory loose, from the mind.

To take the most recent example, my morning conversation with Episode on the way to school was a good illustration—I, being me, in my own way recalled what happened over spring break and felt like I was speaking to him in fear, but any observer would have seen my actions as utterly bizarre.

I was having a nice chat with someone who had tried to kill me.

How abnormal can you get?

I was merely taken aback by how much of a normal conversation we were having? No, it might be one thing if we were characters in a manga or drama—but how could I do something that frighteningly eccentric as an actual human being?

There was something clearly abnormal about it.

The only person who didn't notice was the person doing it.

So—I'd forgotten.

While I naturally had forgotten the moment that my organs were sent flying (I thought the shock had caused those memories to disappear, but that wasn't it)—I'd also forgotten the fear, the terror I must have felt for him.

My body remembered.

But my mind had forgotten.

No, I'd go so far as to say that even my body had forgotten.

Which is why I was able to carry on with a healthy life even after *that* happened to me—I didn't live each day tormented by regret like Araragi.

I didn't know when it started.

I didn't know when I first learned to act like some kind of computer.

Judging from my current state, though, it was from *before I became Tsubasa Hanekawa*—it only made sense if I could do so unconsciously even before I was old enough to be myself.

I had no idea why I was able to acquire this supremely convenient ability that put an aberration to shame, this thing you could call a kind of skill.

I had a feeling—that the memory of whatever caused it was the very first thing I cut loose from myself.

So then—I'd been something of an aberration prior to my encounter with the aberration known as the Afflicting Cat. More than anyone else, I was close to being a monster, and at long last I began to feel the weight of Mister Oshino's remark that aberrations are nothing more than triggers.

No, maybe there was no Afflicting Cat at all.

Maybe Black Hanekawa—was always inside me.

And, or possibly.

The Tyrannical Tiger, too.

Just like the way the past always follows our lives—no matter how much we feel like we forgot it, how much we pretend it never happened.

Maybe it haunts us.

Maybe it never ends.

Mister Oshino had set a bar at twenty years old, but even that seemed unreliable to me—at least, so long as I wanted it that way.

So long as I continued to be me.

Forever—

Maybe I could continue to be me forever.

Just as Sherlock Holmes was forced to take the stage after he retired, not even allowed to die—like he continued.

Maybe I would continue.

I probably would continue.

…But this was it.

I was going to end it.

I had to end it—I was at my limit.

If anything, having been able to do it for all this time, fifteen years, maybe eighteen years, was bizarre.

Fooling myself so I could go on.

What was truly bizarre was being able to make such an absurd thing work for all this time—the only possible endpoint was bankruptcy.

I couldn't paper over it any longer.

I hadn't reached a limit—this was a terminus.

I continued to work on making a house of cards with the Araragi sisters (Tsukihi was the winner all the way. I'd make it pretty far but could never finish my tower. *So, Miss Hanekawa, there* are *things you can't do*, Tsukihi remarked), had dinner, together with Araragi's parents, after they got back from work, and shut myself in Araragi's second-floor room, alone.

It was only day two, but I already felt oddly used to the room. It must have been because it was Araragi's.

So first, in a show of bad manners, I collapsed on the bed with my uniform on and buried my face in a pillow.

"Phew…" I let out a lethargic voice.

Exhausted—I was not.

If anything, I felt on edge.

"We may never be able to meet again—Araragi."

But there was nothing I could do about that.

Because if my reasoning was correct—and it was correct—*the Tyrannical Tiger presented itself in this town precisely because Araragi was absent.*

I continued to roll around on the bed for another five minutes or so.

Not for no reason. There was a reason.

In animal terms, this was marking behavior—me leaving behind traces of myself on Araragi's bed.

The traces I didn't want to leave behind at the Hanekawa residence.

I was trying to leave them behind here—in Araragi's room.

Knowing him, he would notice.

Even if we never met again, some small part of him would probably remember me whenever he slept in this bed.

And I would content myself with that.

I'd be satisfied. Self-satisfied.

If my reasoning was correct, and if everything I was about to do went well—then no, I didn't think I would ever be able to meet Araragi again.

If he got back safely and I was able to be there, waiting for his return—that me would no longer be the me that he knew.

Episode had said the current me and the spring break me seemed like different people, and this would be even more dramatic—Araragi would meet a me that was practically a different person.

Because confronting my past.

Because defeating this tiger—meant that.

"Okay. That's enough."

By the end, I wasn't sure if I was leaving behind my scent or smelling Araragi's, but I finally decided to make my move around half past seven.

"Uh oh. I need to hurry a bit."

I had rolled around too much.

Of course, since the Hanekawa residence had burned down in

the afternoon, there didn't seem to be much proof that the tiger was nocturnal like the cat—but it was still a point of reference.

I started by taking off my uniform and putting it on hangers.

After that, rummaging through a clothes case for some of Araragi's casual wear that looked relatively easy to move around in, I wore those.

Pajamas were one thing, but I did have a few qualms about borrowing regular clothes without permission. Araragi, however, was the one who always wanted to see me in something other than my school uniform, so I hoped this would in fact be a dream come true.

A mischievous thought even popped into my head, and I considered taking a picture of myself and sending it to Araragi—though I still had no idea what kind of situation he was in.

It might annoy him, so I decided not to contact him—but when I thought about it, that was a convenient excuse. Me acting like I was being a sensible person. I'd have immediately tried to get in touch with him like Miss Senjogahara if I was really worried—wasn't that the human thing to do?

In that case, I'd be shameless. I'd send him a pic to cheer him on. I felt like I was still able to encourage him.

I took my cell phone out of the pocket of my now-hanging uniform—then held out my arm and snapped a photo of myself. I *am* a high school girl, so I'd been using a cell phone for a decently long amount of time, but it was my first time taking a selfie.

I messed up a few times but quickly got the hang of it and managed to take a pretty good picture, if I do say so myself. I attached the image to an email and sent it to Araragi without adding a word of text—then turned my phone off.

The next time it was on.

I'd no longer be of this world.

So it was closer to harassment than an innocent prank.

It was like I'd sent him a funeral portrait.

It was like bullying by a girl who'd always been called a model student.

A horrible thing to do, if I do say so myself.

Now there was nothing in my heart I would regret not having done.

There was nothing of my heart I would regret not leaving behind.

With a lightened heart—I could start getting ready.

I took a notebook and a pencil from my bag, sat in the chair, and faced Araragi's study desk. I wasn't reviewing my lessons for the day or preparing for tomorrow, though.

Yes, I was going to write a letter.

A proper letter.

I didn't know how to begin it at first, but then realized there was no point in being awkwardly formal. So I began with a regular opening line:

"Dear Miss Black Hanekawa"

Maybe it wasn't anything that I actually needed to do.

Maybe I was wasting my time.

Because while I had no memories as Black Hanekawa—Black Hanekawa would have memories as me.

Still, I wanted to express how I felt, and I wanted to do it as me, speaking to the now-independent me who wasn't me, to *her*.

In my place, she had taken on the burden of every dark part of me, every black part of me, and I wanted to convey to her—my feelings of gratitude and my final request.

Then.

061

—Dear Miss Black Hanekawa,

It's nice to meet you.

Well, I guess that's a strange thing to say. But this is Tsubasa Hanekawa.

Allow me to start by thanking you.

Thank you for all of the backbreaking work you did in my place, both during Golden Week and before the culture festival. I imagine that I've been forcing a lot of hardship on you this time, too.

I'm truly sorry for causing you nothing but trouble.

It's now finally begun to strike me how it may have been my ego that I buried you when you were there on the street that day, run over. My actions that day saddled me with a responsibility toward you that I doubt I am able to fully repay.

Maybe that's the kind of thing that Mister Oshino really meant by that line he used so much, "people just go and get saved on their own." Because if you're not thinking about whether you're ready to take on the connections, or honestly, the responsibilities that arise, you're going to have to get through the rest of your life relying on nothing more than one stopgap measure after the next.

Just as Shinobu was bound to Araragi because he saved her, I've shackled you, as Black Hanekawa, to me.

And on top of that, I barely let the fact bother me, unlike Araragi. I was living a carefree, peaceful life.

How sinful can one be?

And so I'm really not in a position where I can ask this of you, but I fear that I might end up hurting a very important friend if I don't do something.

I have no choice but to rely on you.

I have no one else I can rely on.

So I'm going to say it to someone for the first time in my life—save me.

Please save me.

I'll never bother you again, and I'll make sure you're never alone.

Please, I beg of you.

I know that you probably have to do as I say in order to protect me, and that saying this may not change a thing, but it is a sincere request.

I'm going to write down a few things I know about this situation, in case they can be of help. I know that you share my memories, but it seems that you have been completely severed from me this time (I have an idea why for that too, which I'll explain later), so I think it would be easier for you to understand if you read this in a letter. Unlike your memory, mine is full of holes, so while I can't be sure of anything, this is probably the truth.

I don't know everything, I only know what I know.

I've used those words with Araragi as a kind of excuse, but allow me to say them to you, too. I'm going to tell you everything I know.

So first, and while I think this goes without saying because it's something you, as an aberration, know quite well without being told, the true identity of that gigantic tiger, the Tyrannical Tiger, is that it is a new breed of aberration born from my heart, just like you.

Or to be even more precise, a new kind of aberration that my heart cut loose.

This I can state as a fact.

But one major point of difference between the two of you is that while you're based on an old aberration known as the Afflicting Cat, the Tyrannical Tiger has no base, nothing to which its spirit is bound.

If I had to say it was based on anything, it's you.

The Tyrannical Tiger is a tiger because you are a cat.

A more primordial creature.

A more primordial organism, a fiercer beast, and that is why after you, a cat, I came up with a tiger.

I guess you could call it a successor?

I should have realized it earlier, but I think that in these past few months, I'd gotten too used to aberrations, including you.

Knowing of aberrations draws one to aberrations.

That's something Mister Oshino said.

Just as Araragi became familiar with how to use his own immortality ever since spring break, I must have become used to prying loose pieces of my own heart as aberrations ever since Golden Week.

Like someone first starting to put in contact lenses or something— we can get accustomed to anything.

And the result of all my proficiency.

Is the Tyrannical Tiger.

I think the differences between you during Golden Week, you before the culture festival, and you this time aren't individual traits so much as a manifestation of this proficiency.

The fact that you appear only when I go to sleep, reduce my level of stress while I'm asleep, then turn back into me when I wake up without any need for Mister Oshino, Araragi, or Shinobu to "deal with you" makes you far too convenient an aberration, far too much of a blessing.

Then again, of course that's how it is.

Because you're an aberration brought forth by me for my own sake.

You're going to be convenient.

Naturally, and while you may have already noticed this too, though I had it wrong at first, I think you're here, I think I refused to learn my lesson and summoned you again so that I could do more than just relieve the stress of that house burning down. Yes, it had to be thanks to you that Miss Kanbaru saw me and thought that I wasn't feeling down the way she thought I'd be—but that's all incidental.

The fire itself had nothing to do with it—the cause of the fire was the cause.

I'm sorry that I have to say this like it doesn't involve me, but this is something that happened unconsciously, or actually I don't have any memory of it at all, but I think I must have relied on you as a way to fight against the Tyrannical Tiger I saw that day.

Just like I'd always been relying on you, even long before my life was ever affected by the Afflicting Cat.

And I relied on you again.

I know that modern medicine has a negative view on the condition popularly known as a split personality, more technically known as dissociative identity disorder, and I'm not a proponent of it either. But while the expression may not be correct, it would have to be the most understandable way to express who I am.

Araragi once told me that I was scary.

Mister Oshino once told me that it was creepy the way I acted like a saint.

But to tell you how I honestly felt when I heard them say those things, I had no clue what they meant.

I felt like there was never a time I was being anything less than my natural self.

Araragi would say that I was forcing myself to be a regular girl, that I was trying to be too ethical. And yes, that line of reasoning must have been pretty close to the truth, but it didn't serve as a reason why I was able to do something so outrageous.

It's not something you could simply will yourself to do.

So then why was I able to do it?

It's simple.

Because I'd looked away from any inconvenient reality ever since I was a child, constantly setting loose pieces of my heart.

Miss Senjogahara described this as being "dull when it comes to darkness" the day before yesterday, and she was exactly right. In fact, I don't look at the darkness at all.

I've averted my eyes from malice and misfortune.

Not as any kind of self-defense. If anything, I think it was self-sacrifice—I'd sever the parts of myself that were inconvenient to me in order to keep being me.

Like how I wasn't able to see that house from the classroom.

If there was ever anything I didn't like, I would say it had nothing to do with me and cut it off. No matter what horrible things happened to me, I would say they had nothing to do with me and cut them off.

So there was no way for my personality to become twisted.

There was no way for me to get bent over.

I couldn't even stop being naïve about the world.

Twistedness of that sort is something that any human needs in order to live, and I just skipped all of that.

Of course you'd feel scared, of course you'd be creeped out.

I know I'd rebutted Araragi by saying that he was going too far when he talked about miracles—but the way I am is the result of something more atrocious and blood-drenched than any miracle.

I understand that the most difficult step of the counseling process for children who were never loved by their parents, which is to say children who grew up abused, is getting them to recognize that they've suffered abuse.

How terribly they've been tyrannized.

It's no small feat to accept that you aren't loved by your parents.

In most cases, children act like the abuse itself "never happened." This shows itself in many ways, whether it's a twisted interpretation of the facts or pretending that it didn't happen at all, but one thing that all of these methods share in common is that they look away from reality.

So let me admit it now.

I grew up abused by my parents.

Every single parent I ever had treated me abusively.

I have never once been loved.

I have never for a moment been loved.

But I never recognized that.

I ignored my pain, saying that this kind of thing must happen in every home to some degree or another. I could be struck in the face, but I never thought that was abuse. I couldn't think it was. I set that stress loose before I knew it in the form of a cat and pretended that it never happened.

Of course, if you want to talk about what abuse really is, it's a very easy thing to understand and also a very hard thing.

Abuse can assume forms other than violence. As an extreme example—no, even this is still within the bounds of general opinion—abuse can exist in the form of spoiling a child.

Abuse that's called education. Abuse that's called discipline.

Abuse that's called an upbringing. Abuse that's called a parent-child relationship.

One can ultimately make a case for the view that abuse is anything a parent does to a child, and maybe we should listen to that case instead of rejecting it out of hand. Parts of it may bear merit depending on the way it's made. You wouldn't argue that it isn't abuse if the person in question is all right with what's happening to them—so while it's a vague conclusion, you simply have to judge every case as a whole.

Which is why I can make this assertion.

I can look away and say all day long that I wasn't abused.

I wasn't tyrannized.

I wasn't neglected.

I have no such recollection.

They did the bare minimum as parents—

No, you couldn't even argue that in bad faith.

They only ever did the minimum as parents.

They only ever did the worst they could do.

That's how I should have thought about it.

They'd abused me in the most heinous way, by not loving me—I'm sure they had their excuses.

But what did those kinds of excuses have to do with their child?

A parent's love for a child isn't a duty to be fulfilled, it's a feeling, and you shouldn't get married or have children if you aren't capable of feeling it.

If you never had to feel pain or know sadness, then you'd be free of stress and always perform well, whether in school or in athletics, whether it's ethics or morals.

If you never had to feel the pressure of failing or anxiety over meeting a terrible fate, if you could ignore all pain whether physical or mental, you could be perfect all-around.

That is the truth of Tsubasa Hanekawa, model student.

The boring answer to why I have been me.

I could ignore the taste of blandness.

How unfair could it get, right? I was tossing the darkness and suffering that every person is burdened with onto someone else's shoulders.

I bet Miss Senjogahara would be furious if she heard that.

When I think of her two years of suffering—when I think of her two-year fight to in fact acquire her pain, and then look at myself and the way I put it all on you, never having to know suffering, never having to feel pain, never having to fight.

"Frustrating" doesn't begin to cover it.

And while it's very interesting that the form known as Black Hanekawa would be created by a person like myself getting involved with an aberration called the Afflicting Cat, aberrations are nothing more than triggers as I said earlier.

You are you.

Of course, this third edition of you is more powerful than the last two, and you seem to be severed from me. As I said earlier, I'm getting "better" at this the more I do it.

When I asked Tsukihi what the trick was to making a house of cards, she told me, "This kind of thing is just about practice. It's not about technique, it's how many times you've tried. I'm sure you'd be good at it if you did it twenty times," and the same goes for everything. So I must have uncoupled you from my heart better than I did my first and second times.

I made you into your own personality.

Call it nonsense if you want, it's a terrible story.

No, it's more terrible than a terrible story.

After all, like I've been saying, you're not the only thing I cut loose from my heart as an independent aberration this time.

Should I call it another *one*?

Or should I call it another breed?

I unleashed the Tyrannical Tiger before I let you loose.

If you are an avatar of my stress—then the Tyrannical Tiger is an avatar of my envy.

Just as I wouldn't have come upon the idea of a new breed of aberration if I hadn't talked to that library employee, I never would have come upon that keyword had I not talked to Karen and Tsukihi. But now that I have, it seems so fitting it feels like the only possible word for it.

Envy.

To be honest, though, I really had no association with this word, envy, until just two days ago.

I didn't even need to cut it loose.

I'd never envied anyone.

Because I was a disgustingly good model student able to ambitiously tackle any problem without feeling any stress at all.

I never felt like I begrudged others.

If anything, what I did feel was something like dissatisfaction: "Why doesn't everyone try harder?" or "They should all just do more."

The feeling had been enough to make Araragi mad at me, and now I realize just how self-absorbed I was. Unlike me, everyone else had to battle their stress as they lived their lives. He didn't need that from a cheater like me.

"You can do anything if you try hard enough."

I'd been able to do anything without trying, precisely because I wasn't trying, and I must have been looking away from even Araragi's feelings as I uttered those words to him.

Which is why I never needed to have anything to do with envy.

No, I wouldn't say that envy and I were completely unacquainted, but the amount of envy I had felt, that had built up in me must have been far less than any regular person's.

The total envy I had cut loose from my heart was a minimal amount.

But it crossed a threshold all at once three days ago.

I remember now.

That day, the first day of the new term.

Just like any other day, I was awakened by an automatic vacuum cleaner, I washed my face, I made myself presentable, I headed to the dining room for breakfast, and what I saw there were the persons who should be called my father and my mother already having breakfast.

The sight struck me as a normal one, and I began to make my own meal. But that only means that I immediately severed it from my memory, that I rewrote my memory, because I saw it, clear as day.

He and she were having the same thing for breakfast.

The three of us lived in the same house, but separately—that's how it was supposed to be, but for whatever reason, one of the two had made breakfast for the both of them and they were eating together.

When I recall it now—yes.

I *selected* my own cookware to make breakfast that morning—which was a strange thing to be doing.

After all, there should have been no need for me to select any cookware because I was the last person to enter the kitchen—the other two would have used the other two sets.

In other words.

It meant that one of them had made food for two for the other's sake—it could only mean that they were having breakfast together.

And leaving me out.

That's what made me jealous.

I felt a clear sense of envy.

I realize this is a ridiculous thing to say… These were two parents who abused me, two persons who lived in the same house as me but could never be called my family, and you'd wonder why I should ever care what they did, whether that meant eating together or anything else.

But it's not about logic.

And this illogic also explains why I began to feel so averse to the idea of us staying the night at a hotel as an emergency measure after the Hanekawa residence burned down.

I didn't want to be isolated in a cramped room.

Maybe if we were one and one and one.

But I didn't want it to be two and one.

It's not that I wanted us to be three—I didn't want it to be two and one.

I didn't want to see that, even if it meant sleeping outdoors.

I wanted to look away.

My oh-so-kind hope that those two would use the fire as an opportunity to begin reconciling was basically nothing but the flip side of these emotions.

There was practically something wrong with me? No.

There was absolutely something wrong with me.

I was scary, creepy—and foolish.

I was unable to notice my own feelings, and when I did I let them loose, only wishing that the two would get even closer and reconcile, in fact—you couldn't call my heart a human's.

You'd have to call it an aberration's.

My true, honest feelings were the result of looking away toward the flip side.

I was the reason that their relationship had cooled off, of course, and since I would be leaving Japan in half a year, it wouldn't be odd if they began treating each other differently. This was a couple who had become husband and wife because of a connection they felt existed between them. Or maybe another non-aberrational trigger for the change was the time they had spent in the hospital together during Golden Week.

In that case, I was envious of their relationship despite all of this evidence pointing to me being the cause. It didn't stand to reason.

So like I said, it wasn't logical.

I was thinking about how much they should just separate.

Yet I was also hoping that the embers between them would reignite.

But I didn't want to see the two of them getting along.

Whatever the case, I was jealous of their reconciliation.

I was envious to the bottom of my heart that they were now

trying to become a family again after all this time.

I was burning with envy.

That was enough for my envy to cross a threshold and give birth to the Tyrannical Tiger.

I gave birth to a tiger at the beginning of the new term, just as I gave birth to you during Golden Week.

If I was able to create a completely original, new breed of aberration this time without relying on a base like an Afflicting Cat, this must be another talent I'll only hone with practice. You could say that I was attached to the saying "Tyranny is fiercer than any tiger," but I also feel that Miss Senjogahara was somewhat right, and I was led to the name by Miss Gaen.

And one more thing on that subject. My guess is that the Tyrannical Tiger never would have been born if I hadn't met Mayoi on the way to school that day.

The tiger was born because my conversation with Mayoi *let me know that Araragi's whereabouts were unknown*, which is to say that *she let me know that he wouldn't be able to exorcize the Tyrannical Tiger* the way he'd done to you during your last two appearances.

Araragi must have been acting as the brakes on my heart. I'd been more excited to meet him in class that first day than I knew.

It was a case of terrible timing.

But I know for a fact this is why that tiger appeared right after I met Mayoi.

The responsibility is all mine in the end.

The Tyrannical Tiger is a monstrous animal that took form because of how fragile my heart is.

The all-consuming flames of envy.

It was of course envy toward my parents that caused the Hanekawa residence to be engulfed in flames, and it was envy that caused the abandoned cram school to burn, too.

My feelings toward Miss Kanbaru, the only person Araragi had asked for help.

I was angry at Araragi then—at least, I thought I was, but in reality I think I was intensely envious of Miss Kanbaru, the way I was of Miss Senjogahara.

That's how it should be.

I had learned of the emotion that was envy—and it suited me very well.

But it must not have been long before I cut that envy loose from myself and transferred it to the Tyrannical Tiger. My envy already had a convenient escape route.

Earlier I described the Tyrannical Tiger as an aberration that is independent, just like you, but autonomy might be a better word. Because unlike you who are bound to my flesh, the Tyrannical Tiger is able to move and act freely.

And as a result.

The abandoned cram school, which had a place in all our hearts, burned down.

Miss Senjogahara's line of reasoning that said any building I slept in would immediately catch on fire was wrong in the end, but the Tyrannical Tiger has what you might call a unique trait that makes her theory look like an attractive alternative.

Because, you see, that tiger burns down everything I envy.

Both Miss Senjogahara's apartment and Araragi's home could easily go up in flames at any moment. Not because I stayed the night, but because I was envious of them. I saw the unshakable bond between father and daughter at the Senjogaharas' and got that rare inside view of the Araragi family, built on its solid foundation of trust. I've forgotten it by now, but how could I not feel envy as someone who's never known home or family?

I wish I could curse myself to death for the way I'd looked away from that envy and forced it onto the Tyrannical Tiger and so optimistically thought about how great it was to feel included in a family. But it seems my curses are only pointed outwards.

If I can say there's any saving grace here, I suppose it would be that the Tyrannical Tiger's fires are limited to buildings and that it isn't an aberration that burns humans, similar to the way you acted during Golden Week. It seems that one of my firm values is that you should not kill humans.

I say that because I think I know just how much Araragi suffered over spring break caught between human lives and saving lives.

No, that's not it.

I'm whitewashing it when I say that.

No part of me during Golden Week was bothering to look at others, at victims including my parents. I did nothing but look away and was desperately working to do nothing but dispel my stress. Life was secondary (in fact, I tried to kill Araragi at the end), I was self-centered and nothing more.

That goes for this time, too.

What I'm truly jealous of, truly envious of, must be places, not people.

Places to live.

Which is why you can say it's dwellings that I've been targeting and not just any building.

Places where people live with others.

I burned down the Hanekawa residence and the abandoned cram school because I was someone who didn't even have a room and slept in the hallway.

I created that tiger.

I want a place where I belong, and I'm jealous of people who act like it's natural for them to have those kinds of places.

That's why I burn homes over humans.

It took all of it on, my destructive impulses of wanting that house to just disappear, my envy that transcended jealousy—and set it all ablaze.

Feelings ablaze.

Yes, I offhandedly asserted that I have the same kind of destructive impulses as everyone else, that I wished for that house to just disappear.

But the same kind of feelings as everyone else?

I hadn't even known what it feels like—how painful it is to feel like everyone else.

I'd taken that insipid destructive impulse that had already been cut loose and detached from myself to be the way I felt—and convinced myself that I was normal.

It was like I was overprotective of myself.

It was like I was abusing myself.

Yes, that's right.

I was abused most of all by myself.

I've been killing my self all this time.

While I think this self-analysis is correct, that isn't to say there's no risk at all of anyone getting burned, like it went during Golden Week.

Both the Hanekawa residence and the abandoned cram school just so happened to be empty when they went up in flames. If anyone was inside, I'm sure they would have suffered the same fate.

If Araragi or Miss Kanbaru happened to be in the building when the Tyrannical Tiger was invoked…

The thought sends a chill down my spine.

And this thought could still become a reality with Miss Senjogahara's apartment or Araragi's home.

The relationship between Miss Senjogahara and her dad?

The relationship between the Araragi sisters and Araragi?

I can't say I'm not jealous.

I bet it's a lie that I've never known envy. I've begrudged every person I've ever been jealous of.

I wanted a dad like that.

I wanted little sisters like them to wake me up every morning.

Those feelings—turn into flames.

I think we can say it was a very good move on my part to have never slept over at friends' homes until now. Well, maybe we should call that another thing I was unconsciously avoiding.

No.

If the Tyrannical Tiger got "better" at what it did—if it set fire after fire and grew proficient, then forget sleeping over at one home after the next, every house in the world could very well burst into flames.

Schools.

Libraries.

Parks.

I could see them all burning too.

That's how it was for me.

That's how jealous I was of warm homes.

Jealous enough to want to take that warmth and burn it to a crisp.

To be honest with you, I don't know what kind of values you, which is to say the aberration known as Black Hanekawa, have. We may share memories and knowledge, you may be able to face even the things I once looked away from, but it seems like we have completely different personalities. (What would be the point in having a split personality otherwise?)

So I'm also unsure of how you feel about this Tyrannical Tiger's presence or about my line of reasoning. Maybe you think things are fine the way they are, and I think that would be correct from an aberration's point of view.

Maybe you would tell me that there's nothing to be worried about because while arson may be a grave crime, this isn't the kind of thing that can be judged by the law.

Yes, that's one opinion.

And I won't lie, part of me wants to be comforted by those words.

But I just want to put an end to this.

I'd be cutting loose a piece of my heart every time something happens, endlessly creating one aberration after another, offloading any responsibility to elsewhere, and forcing others to meet terrible fates while being completely unaware of any of it, living a happy and carefree life. Could there be any worse nightmare?

I've torn so many people to shreds since Golden Week, spread so much damage, and been ignorant of it all.

Like I was pinching my cheeks but they didn't hurt.

Can't you say that's the life I've been living?

It's not as if I want to be a good person or a virtuous person. Being moral or ethical doesn't mean anything if you have to use something else to get you there.

You.

Or the Tyrannical Tiger.

I don't want to live if it means stepping on others.

Even if we resolve this issue with the Tyrannical Tiger, I'm just going to give birth to a lion or something next time, and then maybe a leopard after that, over and over, right?

I can imagine all of you saying that you don't mind, it's what you were created for, and that's why I've made my decision.

I've made a decision in my heart, this thing so whittled down that nothing is left, even its core.

I'm putting an end to all of this.

No. I'm going to begin at last.

I'm going to stop looking away and point my eyes straight forward.

Not only at the Tyrannical Tiger, but at you too.

I'm opening the eyes I've kept closed.

Sleeping Beauty has slept for eighteen years now, and she needs to wake up.

So please, Miss Black Hanekawa.

I want you to return.

I want you to go back inside my heart.

I want you and the Tyrannical Tiger to come home.

Please, I'm begging you.

My heart is your home.

I won't leave you to be on your own, so please, don't leave me on my own.

If Mister Oshino is right, when I turn twenty—or maybe even before that—you, and the Tyrannical Tiger too, might disappear.

My girlish, adolescent fantasies might die off and disappear once I become an adult.

Even now, you must be something like an echo.

So eventually.

I'm sure you'll vanish and disappear.

I'm sure that's the way it's supposed to be.

But please. That's why I'm asking you.

Please don't vanish. Please don't disappear.

Please. Come home.

Let's stop living apart.

I know there's not much space in my heart, but let's live as a family, colliding and crashing into one another inside of it.

I won't ever tell you again to just go to sleep if you're feeling sleepy.

I swear to you now that I'll love it all, my stress and my envy, my anxiety and my suffering, the bad possibilities and the deep darkness.

I know it's a shameless request.

But I've decided to live shamelessly.

I'm sure Araragi is going to be disappointed.

What he values in me is what Miss Senjogahara would call my pure whiteness, my deficiencies as a creature.

To be honest, that's the one thing that I can't do.

I don't want to disappoint Araragi.

In the end, I never once told him that I love him.

I was the only party to our love, from beginning to end.

It was frankly strange to me that I was so attracted to him when we'd never even spoken until spring break, that I still pine for him like this and refuse to let him go. But now I finally understand.

No one that I know confronts his own weakness as much as he does, and I find him dazzling.

Almost blindingly dazzling.

I can think back with fondness to that night when Miss Senjogahara and I excitedly badmouthed Araragi—and while I think Miss Senjogahara feels the same way, every insult I uttered about Araragi somehow became praise.

Like calling him a chump.

Everything I said came out sounding like that.

All of my anger for him was nothing more than fondness, and at face value too.

My feelings for him were the one thing I couldn't cut loose.

I've always loved Araragi, always, even when I become you.

He says he saved the dying Shinobu even as he cried about not wanting to die.

I bet I would have been smiling as I saved her.

Yes, I think that if you were to pinpoint the moment when I fell in love with him, it would have to be when he was crying in that battle to the death with Shinobu.

After all, I've never cried before, not a single time.

I doubt I even cried when I was born.

That's why I fell in love with Araragi, the crybaby.

Episode said that I had become normal, but the bigger question is what if I stopped being me?

If I became me, would Araragi cry yet again?

I wouldn't be able to stand it.

But I'm not going to look away anymore from whatever it is that I can't stand.

I want to become one with the two of you, never looking away from the reality that doing so would disappoint Araragi.

So that I can keep loving Araragi, too.

That's what I want to do.

Miss Black Hanekawa.

No, that's such a formal thing to call you now that I think about it.

The me inside of me.

Or maybe I should call you another me?

No, that somehow seems wrong, too.

I have a feeling that you're something like a little sister to me. I started to feel that way when I saw Karen and Tsukihi.

I'm sorry for being such an awful big sister.

I'm sorry for making you worry all this time.

This really is my final request.

This is the last time I'll force you to play such a difficult role.

Please save our other sister.

I know she's a troublesome girl, a pyromaniacal runaway, but I'll wait for as long as it takes for her to come home.

I love you both, and myself.

Yours in haste.

—

…And then.

That was it for the letter my myaster wrote before going to sleep.

It was hard to nyoh what to say.

I'd always thought my myaster was a smart anyimal, nyot an idiot like me—but nyow it looked like she myight've been just as stupid, or maybe even stupider.

I'd nyeed to be stupid in order to make my myaster smart if you went by the logic in her letter, but even that seemed fishy to me.

Since the way I work as a character is that I only ever do as my myaster wants in order to protect my myaster's intentions, she didn't have to write such a letter—all she had to do was go to sleep like nyormal and I would've gone out there to beat that tiger down.

I share my myaster's memories, so if she realized what the tiger, the Tyrannical Tiger, really was, I would absolutely nyoh about it too.

Nyo, my myaster was fully aware of that—she said so in the letter.

So that meant she nyew but still nyeeded to ask me?

In the end, my myaster nyever realized that that's exactly what people call her fastidiousness and nyot being like everyone else.

Nyow that is the biggest tragedy of all.

"Meow."

I placed the nyotebook on top of the desk.

Really, I had her memories of writing the letter, too. That meant there was nyo real reason for me to read it, but I took the time to anyway. I guess I'm in nyo place to say anything about my myaster.

Whatever the case, I nyow had a general idea of what was happening.

The Tyrannical Tiger.

And the source of my myaster's illness.

I had all the details nyow.

But even my myaster seemed to be mistaken about a few things— nyot that she could have avoided those mistakes since she was building a case without having everything she needed to come to a conclusion.

Both the style and context of my myaster's letter were out of joint—there was nyo way she wrote it in a collected state of mind.

It'd be impawssible for her to get a purrfect score in this situation, but she still myanaged to get decent marks, an eighty out of a hundred. Nyot bad.

"How does she nyot see it? You'd think she would. You'd think she'd question why nyo jealousy ever sprouted about Hitagi Senjogahara and Koyomi Araragi going out even though she burned with envy about her home and family."

The strongest emotion in my myaster was romantic love.

I don't think I nyeed to explain. Just think back to the transformation before the culture festival.

Basically, that annyoying little human's little sister was right when the first thing she associated with fire was feelings of love.

So the very furst thing my myaster should have burned wasn't the Hanekawa residence or the abandoned cram school, it was Hitagi Senjogahara *the purrson*—

Did my myaster really nyot nyotice?

Nyo.

I guess that meant she was looking away from the fact.

Then I suppose my myaster would eventually run into that reason once she's able to stop looking away from the truth and look straight at it instead.

I wonder if she'll be able to take it, though.

It's a cruel truth—and my myaster wouldn't be able to cut her heart loose anymore.

"Loving me and the Tyrannical Tiger—loving herself. I doubt my myaster knows just how hard that is. She's an extreme case, but doesn't any human look away from their stress and envy to one degree or anyother?"

Nyot many people are able to look at the world head-on. Why did my myaster have to be the one to wear such heavy shackles?

Me and the Tyrannical Tiger nyeeded to carry that weight.

Just because she cut her pain loose.

That didn't mean her pain never hurt.

In fact, just imagine how painful it is to sever a piece of your heart.

"And her biggest mistake was calling someone like me her family—mya-haha. I'm nyothing more than her pet."

Nyo, I was a stray.

And it was weird to call me her sister to begin with, I was a male when I was run over on that street—but then again, I was made from a cut-off piece of my myaster's heart even if I'm based on an Afflicting

Cat, so I guess my gender is a little fuzzy. Little sister, little brother—being called either doesn't feel wrong.

Why ask what an aberration's gender is to begin with?

Actually, the most impurressive thing was that she could call that gigantic tiger her little sister. She nyew the females are fiercest when it comes to wild animals, right? Wanting me to attack it and exorcize it was one thing, but asking me to bring the tiger back to her heart as family was a ridiculous request.

Nyot dead or alive, but alive and well?

She was asking for too much.

I was planning on beating it down even if my myaster didn't ask me to. But then she went and asked for even myore.

But if that Hawaiian-shirted jerk expert heard me, I'm sure he'd say, "What violent thoughts. Aberrations and humans need to figure out how to coexist" or something. Isn't that the kind of thing that little human said?

Sure, we were both nyew breeds of aberrations, both aberrations born from my myaster, but unlike me, that thing wasn't based on any aberration—its spirit didn't possess anything. My nyon-aberrational myaster didn't seem to nyoh what exactly that meant.

She didn't nyoh how freeing it was to a nyaberration to nyot be written about, to have nyo records, to nyever have been spoken of.

Honestly, I didn't even want to imagine it.

One thing I could say—is that the tiger had nyo blind spots, nyo weaknesses.

Furget bringing it back, just opposing it was difficult.

I'd have to face it head-on.

And destroy its strengths.

"Ah…" I sighed.

Nyow what a heavy burden.

Right on my shoulders, too.

"It doesn't really myatter to me. I'm just a nyaberration that works for my myaster's sake. Whether my myaster's parents' home burns, or some myemyorable building burns, or her friend's home burns, or even this home burns, it doesn't myatter to me at all. If anything, those rising flames look refreshing to me."

Because there wasn't much of a fundamental difference between the Tyrannical Tiger, the avatar of her envy, and me, the avatar of her stress. It called us similar aberrations, too—so if anything, I understood the Tyrannical Tiger's feelings better.

The only real difference between the two of us is whether we were independent of our myaster or if we couldn't separate ourselves from her. It didn't seem to mean anything to me.

Just like my myaster understood, I was just a nyaberration who was going to disappear sooner or later—so maybe there was nyo nyeed for her to take me back inside and burden herself with me.

Myaybe it was also true for the Tyrannical Tiger.

If she did nyothing, the flames of emotion might all just get expelled and vanish—so there might be nyo need for my myaster to take it all into herself.

Nyot just nyo nyeed.

Doing so myight even backfire.

Me coming out had to be its own kind of burden for her—so instead of accepting me, she nyeeded to erase me.

She needed to extinguish me.

It wouldn't be hard to do. In fact, it'd be very easy to make me disappear, my myaster only had to wish for it to happen.

But that wasn't what my myaster chose to do.

She'd set us loose, but nyow she was trying to get us back.

What a funny thing.

Me. The Tyrannical Tiger.

We were just nyewsances to my myaster.

Instead of stubbornly trying to accept us—if she really was smart, my myaster should be able to—

"So—it's pointless."

Hitagi Senjoghara must have changed.

That annyoying little human must have changed, too.

And my myaster also changed.

But nyo matter how much you change, there's something that doesn't change. The world.

252

Hitagi Senjogahara changing doesn't mean her past nyever happened. That little human changing doesn't mean his past nyever happened.

It doesn't change. It's not replaced. It doesn't become something else.

Humans are themselves for as long as they live.

We, who were created by my myaster who wandered around town during spring break wanting to meet that vampire, didn't change anything. So—it really would be right and good for us to just disappear.

That annyoying little human and that Hawaiian-shirted jerk would agree.

I was just in the way.

And so was the Tyrannical Tiger.

"But, well. She asked."

I didn't nyoh what this feeling was.

I nyew I should be doing the same thing whether she asked me to or not—so why did I feel so inspired?

The burden on my shoulders should have only weighed me down.

So why did it feel so comforting?

All that happened was that for the first time, I had a place waiting for me—I had somewhere to go home to. That was it, but why did I nyow feel like I could accomplish anything? What had she done?

It made me happy.

It made me want to cry.

"Nyot that I'm gonna cry—I'm a cat. I don't cry, I meow."

Meow, I meowed—and unlocked the window.

My myaster figured out that I'd come out the night before because I'd forgotten to lock it (she probably would have figured it out anyway, there was a lot of other evidence), but I didn't think I nyeeded to be careful about that now. I wouldn't be coming back to this room as me.

It seemed like my myaster had chosen my current appearance because she thought these clothes would be easy to mewve around in, but really, I mewved around best wearing nyothing at all. I felt bad doing that to my myaster, though (I even felt sorry nyow for going around in just her underwear during Golden Week), so I'd accept her act of kindness.

She was gonna have to let me go barefoot, at least.

And just as the bottom of my paw hit the windowsill, I remembered something.

Just a cat's passing fancy, really.

Nyo matter what ended up happening, my myaster wasn't going to be my myaster anymore, and I wasn't going to be me either.

This wasn't about individual differences between Black Hanekawas—it really would be the last time I surfaced.

After being put off in May and June, the aberration nyown as me really was going to be resolved this time.

So I'd write something down for her, too.

Would these count as final words in my case?

Nyo, probably nyot.

I wasn't going to die or disappear, I was just going home.

But what a long way back it was.

"Nyalright, time for my final service to my myaster."

It's nyot like I can write long sentences.

I added one little line to the end of my myaster's letter before flying out of the wide-open window into the mewnlit nyight.

"I'll be off."

062

I am a tiger. I have a name: the Tyrannical Tiger.

I have an idea of where I was born, but all I remember is that I saw sobbing and weeping in a dark, damp place—I am made of not envy alone but of all dark emotions.

I am a product of darkness.

The kind of darkness that makes you want to avert your eyes.

But it does not matter to me what I am, what my name is, where I was born, what I am made of.

In fact, the name Tyrannical Tiger is almost a nuisance. They say that a dead tiger leaves its skin behind, while dead men leave their names behind, but I am made of nothing but darkness, I have been all but dead from the beginning, and I intend on leaving behind neither name nor skin.

I do not intend on leaving a single cinder behind.

Like a raging fire that leaves not a single pillar or post behind.

I will burn everything to nothing.

All that I hold important is this heated, burning obligation in my frame.

This tiger of tyranny cares not for the past.

I must burn it. I must burn it.

Burn what?

Everything.

The moment after I was born into this world, I saw my mother who had brought me into it.

No, perhaps I should say my twin sister.

It seems that the flames that burn in my chest come from this sister of mine—my strong, wise, frightening, fragile, pure-white sister.

Innocent and unblemished. White, transparently white.

My beautiful sister, who looks not a thing like me.

She truly was beautiful.

That beauty.

That whiteness. When I think of how it is I who protects it—I feel proud.

But that matters none.

The spark can be anything.

The fire can grow in any way.

The one and only thing I have is this obligation.

While I have no sense that I am doing something for her sake, I also do not intend to cause her any harm, just as the cat born in the same way from her said.

I have no background, no motivation.

One could say that I am nothing but a flame.

I am a white flame.

I have been given neither consciousness nor will. While I may appear to be speaking my thoughts, I am only feigning to, only pretending to.

I am a natural phenomenon.

I simply burn what needs to burn.

No.

There is nothing in this world that cannot burn.

I must burn everything.

Inside, I am jealous of everything.

I am jealous of fathers, mothers, friends, juniors.

They ought to disappear.

They ought to vanish.

They ought to suffer, they ought to lament, they ought to feel down.

They ought to mourn, they ought to languish, they ought to feel worthless.

They ought to cry.

They ought to cry like me.

Perhaps those tears will help abate the flames.

Now, what should I burn this evening.

Though all may go up in flames with time, there is still an order to be followed.

There is still a process.

So I suppose for now, this building will be next.

As I thought this, no, before I thought it, I was already there.

I have no will. I have no intentions.

This is I.

I am this.

There is no getting there ahead or behind.

I appear anywhere.

My fires spread anywhere.

I looked carefully at the target, inspecting it.

Hm.

I see.

It seemed easier to burn than a house or a building.

But whether it would be simple or difficult, it was all the same.

Hesitation was meaningless once I acquired a target.

Everything was the same.

I do not know everything.

But everything burns.

I opened my mouth wide, baring my fangs.

And then the flames.

The flames—

"Mrow!"

Then in that moment, standing between me and my target—was a cat.

A single silver kitten came flying from the sky as if it had grown wings, and seemed to stand in my way.

063

Just like I expected, the Tyrannical Tiger was nyow right in front of the Tamikura Apartments, where Hitagi Senjogahara and her dad lived. Even if I was wrong, I was planning on just climbing up to the roof and searching the town like I did last time—but it's nyot like I wasn't certain about it.

I nyew.

After all, the Tyrannical Tiger and I used to be one and the same. The same thing, born from the same place.

So.

"Hey there, tiger," I said. In greeting. "I'm here to get you. C'mon, let's head back together."

<......>

But, once again like I expected, the Tyrannical Tiger was nyot even going to answer me.

She was just silently glaring at me.

Ah.

Nyow that I was facing her, it made me realize all over again just how huge tigers are. Nyo, she was a monster—real tigers weren't ever supposed to be that big.

It almost felt like I couldn't tell how far away she was.

I nyew this wasn't a fairy tale like Pinyocchio or anything, but it made me feel like the best way to defeat her might be getting swallowed and then fighting my way out of her guts.

I could try that if I was going to defeat her.

But that's nyot what I was here for.

<Move,> the Tyrannical Tiger finally decided to say after a long pause. <You there. I will burn you. You are in the way.>

"…Hah."

I didn't nyoh exactly why—but I laughed.

Maybe it was a chuckle? Nyo, it was a snicker.

It was weird, this tiger looked so huge and was so intimidating, which made everything she said feel so solemn—and even last time we met, that was enyough to scare me on the inside as we talked.

But nyow I realized it was different.

She—wasn't solemn at all.

She just lacked any sentiment.

She didn't have the tools she needed to speak and communicate, like a nyewborn baby—that's why we couldn't have a discussion.

I guess it's obvious that she was a nyinfant since she was only born a few days earlier—but an originyal aberration, huh?

An originyal, one with no history.

That's what had been cut loose from my myaster's heart.

A new breed of aberration.

Actually, though, originyal aberrations, aberrations made by individuals, aren't that uncommon—an old painter named Sekien Toriyama who made his living by drawing yokai apparently snuck in some of his own among all the other "traditional" ones.

Nyo matter what age they live in, every creative person must dream of making something of their own that can rival tradition.

Of course, it must take an enyormous amount of talent, nyo, enyergy to create something that can rival a traditional yokai.

So what was it in my myaster's case?

Her stress and dark emotions, nyo doubt—though I guess it's a little ironic for the Tyrannical Tiger, nyewly born from that, to be lacking any sentiment.

Or maybe nyot?

Maybe it wasn't that she lacked sentiment because she was nyewly born. Maybe my myaster unconsciously but intentionyally created the Tyrannical Tiger to be that kind of aberration.

Purrcisely because it was born from emotions—

The tiger was shorn of emotion.

It was lacking as a creature.

<Burn. I will burn you. Move. It is all too late. I will burn all. And I will burn that house first.>

"You nyoh that's not what our myaster wants."

<Hah,> the Tyrannical Tiger dismissed my words with a single laugh.

Nyo.

It was hard for me to believe she even understood what my words meant.

I didn't think she was as stupid as me, but she was even less flexible than me.

<I care not whether that woman does or does not want this. You are free to call that woman your master, but that woman is *nothing to me.* She is merely—>

The spring from which my need to burn arises, the Tyrannical Tiger finished.

"The spring from which your need to burn arises... That's a mixed myetaphor," I quipped.

Nyot that it made any sense to.

Sure enough, it didn't seem to land at all.

So I was right, she wasn't trying to be funny.

But still.

"You nyoh she's nyot nyothing to you, tiger—she's our birthparent."

<Our birthparent? How truly tedious,> the tiger grumbled heartlessly.

You couldn't call this a conversation we were having.

<And is it not that woman who knows better than anyone just how tedious a birthparent is?>

"Oh, you might be right."

Nyow that one hurt to hear.

I guess it went to show just how monstrous our myaster was as a "spring" if a nyewborn aberration could be so sharp.

"Maybe that's why our myaster called us her little sisters and nyot her daughters."

<Little sisters—>

"I don't nyoh how it works, but apparently they're a real hot commodity these days. According to what that little human told me."

Nya-haha, I laughed.

"So it myight be a perfect tag for you, since you're a real hot oddity, sister."

<Hmph... I have no interest in tags or the like. I am a natural phenomenon that burns whatever I wish to burn. I am like an automaton,> the tiger said.

Hard-headed, through and through.

<I am not interested in hot commodities.>

"Oh."

Hmm.

This conversation was really going nyowhere.

And I felt like I was trying pretty hard—in fact, I'd say I tried pretty hard the time before the culture festival, too.

I nyoh you might nyot believe me, but I do feel like I went too far during Golden Week.

So if we could bring this to a peaceful end, that's what I wanted—but when I faced that annyoying little human before the culture festival, I was dealing with a human, while we were two aberrations this time. Nyot only that, we were created by the same myaster, and we still couldn't commyunicate. It was really getting me down.

It seemed like I couldn't blame it all on the Tyrannical Tiger, though.

Well, nyothing I could do about that.

Nyot that it seemed like my myaster would be able to convince her. So I guess I was the right cat for the job.

Someone had to bring this runaway girl back home.

And it seemed like that was my task.

Unlike me, the Tyrannical Tiger didn't share memories with my myaster—or emotions, either.

While I said we were similar aberrations, she was still a different breed.

And that's why.

I had to use words to commyunicate with her, but—

"Hey, tiger."

<What is it, cat?>

"I should go ahead and tell you that I personyally don't intend to say one thing or anyother about the stuff you've done until now. I'm nyot planning on criticizing you and saying it was a crime to burn down that home or that building. Arson being a crime is a human idea, after all."

If they went around cracking down on that kind of thing, they'd be purrsecuting most aberrations out there, and that included me during Golden Week.

And anyway, while there might be a decent nyumber of tiger aberrations, you can find even more fire aberrations out there. A countless nyumber, even. Seriously, there's so many you might start to think that you could just group them all together.

You can't possibly crack down on all of them.

Just like how you can't crack down on every parking violation in the world.

<I assumed as much. In that case—>

"But," I interrupted the Tyrannical Tiger mid-sentence.

I cut her off—and glared at her.

"I told you before, nyo? I'm nyot going to forgive you if you hurt my myaster."

<What a funny thing to say.>

The Tyrannical Tiger had a puzzled look on her face. Nyot as though my words weren't getting through, but as if she truly didn't understand them.

<I do not care about that woman—and so I have no intention of harming her in any way. But you realize the feeling of wanting to burn down this apartment came from none other than your master herself.>

"……"

Yeah, pawbably.

That was the truth to this tiger.

Nyo—it was the absolute truth.

My myaster envied the Senjogaharas' home.

To the point of wanting it to burn.

That was the truth.

And it was also the truth that she envied those two organyisms known as her "parents" that I'd sent to the hospital over Golden Week. And she was envious that the little human asked only the monkey girl for help.

But still, you nyoh.

"Her feelings of trying to hold back that envy were also true—tiger. And you're ignyoring that fact."

<Enough. That woman's self-denial was what gave birth to me, was it not? So she is only reaping what she has sown. My flames do not take into account such circumstances.>

They can only burn. They burn.

As if to wash it all away, as if to sweep it into the sea.

They can only reduce everything to nothingness—as if it never existed.

They can only make it so that it never happened.

Saying this, the Tyrannical Tiger took a step toward me.

Meow.

Surprisingly, she seemed to be the furst one to get all hot and bothered—then again, she was rooted in flames.

"Well, between us two aberrations, you're in the right here," I said.

There was nyo denying it.

I was the one who wasn't acting like a nyaberration—I mean, I used to be an Afflicting Cat, which is supposed to be more about getting payback than paying anyone back.

If you thought about it, at furst I was the one who'd been trying to harm our myaster.

I just happened to have a change of heart.

And nyow—I was risking life and limb for my myaster's sake. You nyever nyew.

It was almost like.

I—was a human or something.

"Our myaster's friend lives in the apartment you're about to burn down—and at this hour, I don't think it's going to happen to be empty like with your other two fires so far."

They were pawbably sleeping in there.

That woman might have talked about how she was concerned that her home or the Araragis' could catch on fire, but I nyew that wouldn't keep her from going to sleep.

I nyew that from going through my myaster's memories.

That's how much she trusted my myaster—

I nyew.

And that's why I nyeeded to fight.

As Black Hanekawa.

As Tsubasa Hanekawa.

"I nyoh our myaster will cry if that woman dies. And I nyeed to do anything I can to keep that from happening."

<Hah. That will not happen, I guarantee you,> the tiger said, paying no heed to my words. <That woman does not cry. When she feels like crying, she sets loose the part of her heart that wants to cry. When she is bothered, she sets loose the part of her heart that is bothered. That—is how she has lived for eighteen years, giving birth to me and you. No. She'll only continue to—>

She'll only continue to live that way.

Giving birth to countless monsters.

Keeping only herself pure and white—clean and pretty.

Never hating another, never resenting another.

Kind and loving to all.

She will live a beautiful life.

Ever the real deal.

Said the tiger.

"Nyo."

And then I—

Hold on.

This was nyot me speaking—that's not who it was at all.

It was me.

I—

Tsubasa Hanekawa—denied it.

"No. I decided to stop already. I want to become someone who hates others. I want to become someone who resents others. I want to be unable to be kind and loving to others the way I have been until now. I'm sure people will start to dislike me and detest me. I'll probably become short-tempered and unforgiving. I think I'll start getting frustrated and annoyed. I might become dumber. I might not be able to laugh anymore. I might start weeping and sobbing."

Yes.

Araragi would be really disappointed.

I'd no longer be able to overlook the way he messed around, I bet—oh, but maybe that would still make him happy.

Because that's the kind of person he is.

A kind person.

I really did feel—so jealous.

"But that's fine. I'm fine with that."

I'd looked away from reality.

I'd forced you two to do all of my dirty work. And I'm sick and tired of it.

What I was doing to you.

How was it any different from what had been done to me?

"I don't want to be the real deal, I want to be real," I said. "I don't need to be beautiful. I don't need to be white. I want to get dirty, just like the two of you."

I couldn't be a girl who never knew what it meant to be stained for my entire life—I wanted to know filth.

I wasn't saying I wanted to become black.

But I wanted to take the black and the white together.

I wanted to become an adult who was gray as ash.

I was tired of living this life—

Where I couldn't cry, even with a broken heart.

"Come back, won't you? It's—past your curfew."

Let's have dinner together, I offered.

Extending my hand to the Tyrannical Tiger.

Extending a hand to my past.

<......>

Enough, spat the tiger.
It bared its fangs and leapt toward me.

064

That same moment, I fell over and of course I was nyow back—but I was facing a bit of a problem.

In short, the aberration that I'm based on, the Afflicting Cat, is one of the weakest yokai out there, myore or less useless in a fight.

I'm nyot a fighter.

So it kind of begged the question: how was I supposed to face off against the Tyrannical Tiger, a nyaberration with a lot of freedom and nyo base at all? (Yes, I nyoh that's not how you're supposed to use the phrase "beg the question," but does it really matter? I nyoh I'm misusing it but you still nyoh what I mean! Why do I nyeed to go back and figure out anyother way to say it?! I'm in an eat-or-be-eaten situation here!!)

I might have been the earlier-born aberration, but I wasn't even sure if you could call the Tyrannical Tiger my little sister. Aberrations can be aberrant, okay?

My myaster had described that little human and his sisters as triplets born apart, and I felt the same way about me, my myaster, and the Tyrannical Tiger—but the Tyrannical Tiger definitely didn't feel like the youngest of us three.

After all, stress is born from emotional friction—so if the Tyrannical Tiger was right and my myaster was the spring she drew from, then the spring that I drew from might turn out to be the Tyrannical Tiger.

I might have been born first, but that didn't mean the Tyrannical Tiger couldn't be the furst one to exist.

So even a simple comparison could rank the Tyrannical Tiger as a better aberration than me, Black Hanekawa. To complicate things further, the Tyrannical Tiger was also my successor.

They say that the later myachines like computers are built, the better, right?

And if you follow that same logic, there was no way I could beat the Tyrannical Tiger using nyormal methods.

And nyaturally my myaster was more experienced in creating aberrations when she created the tiger—and that's why she was a tiger, just like the nyote said.

Anyone could see who'd win in a fight between a cat and a tiger.

Anyone could see.

It made you want to look away.

…But my myaster wasn't looking away—she was facing it head-on, so I couldn't turn tail and run nyow.

After all.

Afflicting Cats are cats with nyo tail—

"Phew…"

I dodged the Tyrannical Tiger's fangs by the skin of my own teeth—and snyuck under its gigantic body as if I was going straight into the beast's den.

My strategy was to use her size against her.

You nyoh there's a saying, the cornered rat can even bite a cat, so what's wrong with a cat biting a tiger? And—also!

"Mrr…OWWW!"

I had something.

My secret weapon as an Afflicting Cat—my enyergy drain!

It always worked nyo matter my opponent, even against aberrations—so I could achieve my goal if I sucked the enyergy from the Tyrannical Tiger and brought that back to my myaster.

My myaster's request.

I could grant it then.

Sure, it was a pretty rough way to bring a runaway girl back home, but we could talk it over once we were all there.

There's nyo miracle cure for family problems.

It's nyot like you can reconcile with your family at the drop of a hat like some kind of melodramatic garden-variety domestic drama—for eighteen years, our myaster had kept cutting loose and been cut loose.

We couldn't go straight back to the way things were.

Nyo, there nyever was a place for us to go back to.

We would have to build it from scratch.

Today was just the first step towards that—and so.

I was pawsitioned under the Tyrannical Tiger's belly—and I embraced it.

With my whole body.

With my whole strength.

I made sure to touch as much of my body as pawssible to the Tyrannical Tiger's to maximize my enyergy drain's purrformance.

<Mmf—>

"Mrr—ROWWWWWWWWWWWWWWWW!!"

Where the Tyrannical Tiger groaned—I screeched at the top of my lungs.

Nyot a scream to motivate myself, like I was saying I'd nyever let go.

Nyot that.

While my enyergy drain, my special ability as a nyaberration, was the one opening I had to defeat the Tyrannical Tiger, using it also meant you needed to think about what her special ability was as a nyaberration.

A fire aberration.

The Tyrannical Tiger.

There are three ways that might work.

The easiest pattern for modern-day people to understand is what you might call pyrokinesis, where all it nyeeded to think was <burn> for something to burn, making it closer to a psychic ability than a nyaberrational phenyomenyon. So it feels more like a human skill than a nyaberration's? (Putting aside the question of if you believe in psychic powers.) There really was nyothing that I'd be able to do if the Tyrannical Tiger was actually using pyrokinesis to cause fires—because nyo matter if it was me or anyone else, you'd be turned to ash as soon as you entered her sight.

For that reason, though, I nyever believed it to be that pattern, and in fact, even when we talked, nyo part of my body or even my clothes caught on fire, plus its first attack was an anyamalistic bite. I could count that one out by nyow.

So, pattern nyumber two.

Another one that's easy to understand, or maybe easy to imagine, where the Tyrannical Tiger breathes fire from its myouth—or shoots flames from its claws, that kind of pattern. And because this one works together with biting and scratching, it lined up with being a predator.

Fire-breathing monsters show up all the time in anyame and monster movies, right? So from that point of view, this was the most likely reason the Tyrannical Tiger could create fire.

Well, it was the pattern I was hoping for.

But I was wrong.

It wasn't the furst pattern, the worst one of all—

But it was the third pattern.

"Mrrow—hot, hot, hot!!"

I nyearly took both my arms off of the Tyrannical Tiger's torso but realized what I was doing and just barely held back on.

To something that was nyow ablaze.

To the Tyrannical Tiger's torso.

"So that's the pattern here. *Your whole body is flames*—I shoulda nyown it!"

While there are some fire-breathing aberrations out there, this was the more common way it worked!

My myaster is a stickler for the rules, so of course she was gonna stick to precedent when making a nyaberration!

She wasn't going to show off her originyality, she was going to be orthodox—

Her aberration was a strange and suspicious fire!

<It's useless, cat,> the Tyrannical Tiger said. <It is in a beast's nature to fear flames. To say nothing of grasping onto a flame—your actions deviate not only from those of an aberration but also from any creature's.>

She sounded—calm.

Of course she did.

For the same reason that vampire girl—Shinyobu Oshinyo—could sit in my arms and look lively even though my enyergy drain worked on anything I touched, whether I wanted it to or nyot.

In other words, while my enyergy drain may look invincible at first glance, it has a weakness.

Or maybe I should say a structural flaw.

A nyecessary structural flaw.

If my target had a nyear-endless supply of enyergy, absorbing all of it would be like trying to dry a dam—and while I didn't think the Tyrannical Tiger's enyergy as the avatar of our myaster's dark emotions could rival a vampire's, still.

Still, its enyergy was like thermal enyergy.

Literal flames.

It was clear as day that I'd be roasted alive before I could absorb it all up—

"Aww, shut it! Of course I nyoh that!!"

Which was exactly why.

It was exactly because it was clear as day—that I screamed.

I yowled—as a cat.

"It doesn't myatter how stupid I am! I at least nyoh that a cat can't beat a tiger!"

While a cornered rat might bite a cat—it was only a bite at the end of the day.

It's nyot like the rat could win or fight off the cat.

It would just make the cat myad and then get eaten, right?

And nyow it was the same for me.

To be honest, I didn't even half-believe that this enyergy drain was going to work, that it would be an opening—I nyew this wasn't even a gamble.

I was just acting like I didn't nyoh.

<In that case,> asked the tiger. She looked at me, pathetically hanging off of her stomach, and asked, <In that case, why—why do this? It's senseless. It's reckless. It's pointless.>

"Because," I said, "our myaster asked me to."

<......>

"Our myaster asked me to."

You probably wouldn't understand.

You were just born, you probably wouldn't understand.

You don't understand just how happy it makes me for our myaster, who always wants to do every little thing all by herself, to rely on me—how happy it makes me for our myaster, who always tries to do every little thing all by herself, to rely on me without any concern for embarrassment or honor, about how it looks or how it reflects on her—when I was just a plain cat who had been run over by a car.

And she shamelessly relied on me.

She called me her little sister.

She called me her family, you nyoh.

"She asked me to take care of this—to take care of you!"

And—I thought as I looked at the Tamikura Apartments.

Hitagi Senjogahara asked me the same thing, too.

She asked me to take care of my myaster—

"...MEOOOOOWWWW!"

I.

I held even tighter to the Tyrannical Tiger's torso, so hot that I had nyoh idea what tempurrture it could even be—and buried my head in it like I was rubbing my cheek against her.

My clothes had gone up in flames long ago.

Hot. Hot. Hot. Hot.

Hot. Hot. Hot. Hot.

It felt like I was embracing the sun.

And in fact, maybe that's what I was doing.

I could see the flames of my myaster's pooled and accumulated envy gathering into a mass of that scale—which was why.

I nyeeded to swallow it all.

The hotter it was, the bigger it was.
The more I couldn't let go of it—
The more I nyeeded to hold onto it.
That's how I felt.

"Mrr…OWWWWWWWWWWWWWWWWWWWW
WWWWWWWWWWWWWWWWWWWWWWW
WWWWWWWWWWWWWWWWWWWWWWWWW!"

<Shut up.>

Swoosh.

The Tyrannical Tiger shook its body like it was wet and trying to dry off—and that's all it took to send my flying.

My body smashed into a nyearby concrete wall.

"Meow!"

Hearing my own scream, I nyearly fell unconscious for a meowment from the sudden change in tempurrture.

Nyo. I couldn't pass out nyow.

I was practically covered in flames.

If I lost consciousness in this state and switched back to my myaster's, she would probably die on the spot from full-body burns—I could somehow withstand this tempurrture only because I was a nyaberration.

"Agh…"

Still…what amazing power.

I was nyothing in comparison.

You nyoh, there's a nyaberration that's good at sumo wrestling nyown as the *bake-no-hi*, the changed flame (sounds ridiculous, nyo?)—but she was just as monstrously powerful as one of those.

Doggone it—though I nyoh that's a weird thing for a cat to say.

While I barely managed to stay conscious, one attack was all it took to immeowbalize me.

I couldn't mewve a finger.

Really?

I prepared myself, came here ready to attack, and look what happened—talk about lame.

Myaahaha.

Then again, that annyoying little human was always risking his life like this—he must've done a lot of fighting by nyow.

With tears in his eyes.

Crying foul.

And crying.

You nyoh what.

I wish my myaster would've cried, too—

If she was sad.

If she was lonely.

If she was bitter.

Who nyohs, maybe she wouldn't have had to give birth to me or the Tyrannical Tiger—and things could have still gone well.

Nyo, maybe it was the other way around.

Could my myaster not cry because we existed?

Well, yeah. That made sense.

If you had little sisters like us.

You couldn't cry, nyot as their older sister—

<What a weak being. So it's over already?> the Tyrannical Tiger said.

Expressionlessly.

Emotionlessly.

As it sizzled—and sidled its way toward me.

<Your gratitude or whatever you call it—that is all it was worth?>

"……"

<Hmph. Very well. Then as an act of kindness from one born from within that woman to another, I will personally drag you down to hell.>

The mass of fire was calmly muttering some really scary stuff.

Hell?

I wondered how much better that would be than a nyightmare.

Still, how many times would it be—I didn't want to die again.

I'd been run over by a car and killed.

I'd been won over by my myaster and killed.

And nyow it was over, with this tiger, too?

How many times was I going to die?

They say that death is the only cure for stupidity, but that's a lie. I'll always stay stupid, I bet—

"Ahhh. It really did make me happy, though."

Maybe it was what you'd call my nyature as a creature, but looking toward the Tyrannical Tiger as it carefully approached me cautious of my enyergy drain—

I muttered.

Were they my dying words?

Nyo.

It was just me being a sore loser.

"A life-or-death fight with you and all I managed was to delay this arson by ten seconds—I can't stand how weak I am."

<I told you so,> the Tyrannical Tiger told me.

There really was no sentiment there at all.

Churning emotion—devoid of sentiment.

<It's senseless. It's reckless. It's pointless.>

"It was syenseless. It was murreckless. It was purrointless."

Ahhh.

I never got a chance to say it, in the end.

Even though I loved him so much.

Loved him so much I became a monster.

I was never able to tell Araragi that I loved him—

"It was senseless. It was reckless. It was pointless—"

"That's not true, Hanekawa."

And then.

That moment—a lengthy sword came swooping down from the night sky.

It pierced straight through the Tyrannical Tiger's neck to stitch it to the ground.

That great katana—I nyew it.

I knew what it was.

Its name—the enchanted blade Kokorowatari.

The aberration slayer, unparalleled in all history—

"……ck!"

"It might've been senseless. It might've been reckless. But—it wasn't pointless. If you hadn't risked your life and delayed this tiger from burning this place down by ten seconds, I wouldn't have made it in time."

His dark hair had grown so much longer since spring break.

His body was small and fit.

He was already in tatters, from his skin to his clothes, and he was missing a shoe.

How terrible the torment and trials he must have endured to be standing here now—his appearance was enough to tell the tale.

"And that would have made me cry."

Then, with the hilt still in his hands.

Araragi—smiled.

065

"...Ah, ahh—"

Araragi.

Araragi, Araragi.

Araragi, Araragi, Araragi—

I felt a burning pain all along my skin.

The burns covering my body hurt now that my consciousness had thrust its way back to the surface—but it didn't bother me one bit.

I burned far hotter in my chest.

Oh.

So Tsukihi was right after all.

Envy was nothing—compared to the flames of love.

Just look at how the mere sight of Araragi made this fire roar—and it had only been a few days.

It felt like we were meeting for the first time in a century.

"Araragi...why are you here?"

"Hey, what sort of stupid question is that, Hanekawa?"

That hurts, he added.

"You're in trouble. How could I not come running to your side?"

"Ahaha… Listen to you."

I couldn't help but laugh.

Seriously, listen to you.

You were off on some grand adventure with Mayoi and Miss Kanbaru until just now.

Look at how battered you've gotten yourself again.

Hurt all over, covered in wounds.

No doubt having done many senseless things.

No doubt having done many reckless things.

But...

You didn't do a thing that was pointless, did you.

"Well, actually," he said, "I tossed everything aside and came running when I saw you in casual clothes in the pic you sent me!"

"Hold on, hold on, hold on."

I really wanted that to be a joke.

And those clothes were his, too.

Plus, most of it had gone up in flames.

<G-Ghhh...>

And there, under Araragi—growled the tiger.

The Tyrannical Tiger growled.

<Aaaaagh... It hurts. It hurts. It hurts. It burns. It hurts. It burns. It burns. It burns. It burns—>

"Oops."

Araragi saw this and pulled the blade from its throat in a single motion.

He seemed used to it.

How much hell had he been through over these few short days? Was his warrior level higher, or was I just imagining it?

"Um, Black Hanekawa...I guess? At the moment. Wait, you'd be Hanekawa either way... But you still have those ears and stuff, and your hair is white—"

"It's all me."

"I see."

Nodding, he took the Tyrannical Tiger, on the verge of death—grabbed that mass of my emotions, still stubbornly smoldering, by the neck and dragged it in front of me.

He took that heavy, massive beast that seemed to weigh easily more than a thousand pounds.

And brought it to me.

"You're not exorcizing it, are you?"

Sorry, but I went and read that whole letter, he said.

So he'd gone back to his room before running over here—no, that's exactly why he knew where "here" was.

"I pierced its vitals with Kokorowatari, so it's not gonna last long. If you want to absorb it, you'd better do it fast."

"……"

If he read that…then he understood everything.

Including the fact that I would be gone.

Or at least—that I would no longer be the same me.

He knew that as he was saying this.

"Are you okay with that, Araragi?"

Even so.

Even though I knew he did, I asked him in words if he knew.

I clung on to his kindness.

Save me—

I, who refused to speak those words until the very end.

"Are you okay with me not being me anymore?"

"Like I said—what kind of a stupid question is that, Hanekawa?"

Yet he replied immediately.

"You just said it yourself. No matter what happens, it's all you. You might change, but you're still you. Don't worry. I'm not going to make any special exception for you. If you become a bad person, I'll hate you. If you do bad things, I'll get angry at you. If people resent you, I'll stick up for you. If you get stupid—well, I'll even help you study."

If you cry, I'll comfort you.

Saying so, he—

Patted my head.

"………nkk!"

This one act.

Caused my heart—to be engulfed in flames.

I couldn't even describe it as hot anymore.

Right.

I always—wanted someone to do that to me.

I wanted someone to stroke me gently like that.

I wanted someone to touch me, gently.

"Hey, Araragi?"

"Hm?"

"I love you, Araragi," I said.

"Can we date with the intent to get married?"

I was finally able to say it.

Just that much—and it took me nearly half a year.

Araragi looked the tiniest bit startled by my sudden confession before his expression turned into a troubled smile.

"I see," he said. "I'm super glad to hear it. But I'm sorry. I happen to have a girlfriend."

"Yeah. I know."

I raised my head and looked straight ahead of me.

Room 201, Tamikura Apartments.

She would be in there—sleeping, alongside her dad.

"Do you love her more than you love me?"

"Yeah."

It was a mean question, but he gave an honest answer.

I was so happy that he did.

But of course, more than that, it hurt.

"Ahhh... I've been rejected."

Right.

This was it.

Correct.

Confess, then get rejected.

I felt so sad.

I'd been talking about traveling the world and discovering myself—when I'd never experienced this sorrow?

What self-discovery, what self-creation?

Without heartbreak—how could I go on a trip to mend my broken heart?

I was never able to say, "Save me."

But I did say, "I love you."

I was able to say it.

Araragi noticed my feelings a long time ago, of course. He found out before the culture festival.

Actually, he found out all over again if he read the note in his room.

But it wasn't enough that he knew it.

I needed to let him know.

I needed a reply from him.

He needed to let me know.

How he felt about me.

I finally got my reply—and.

I was rejected, and was able to feel hurt.

I reached out my hand and touched the Tyrannical Tiger's forehead—

I patted the head of this third me.

I was doing to the still-burning flames of my emotions what I was so happy to have done to me.

I stroked my smoldering feelings.

An energy drain.

For the last time.

The burns across my body began to heal—and as they did, waves of feeling began to surge into me.

Dark emotions that had pooled and accumulated for eighteen years.

And stress.

Everything I had forced onto Black Hanekawa, onto the Tyrannical Tiger, was now, with interest—coming back into me.

"Unh... Uh-unnnh..."

Why was it?

By the time I realized.

"Unh... Wuuuh... W-Waaahh."

By the time I realized, I was crying.

Maybe I couldn't bear the overflowing emotions, maybe it was the pain of the stress they brought with them, or maybe, after all, it was my sadly broken heart—but right in front of Araragi.

Without a care if anyone saw me.

Like a child.

Like a newborn child, I wailed.

"Waaaaah, ah, ah, unh, uwaaaaahhh, hic, hic... Waaaaaaaaaaahhhhh!"

Which is why I feel this was the day—

I could be born at last.

Just as he'd promised, Araragi comforted me until the tears stopped.

Not saying a word.

He spent the night gently stroking my head.

066

The epilogue.

Or maybe, let's consider everything until now the prologue.

My tale begins today.

First is the question of what Araragi was up to these few days, skipping school, but he stubbornly kept his mouth shut and refused to tell me a thing. Well, Miss Kanbaru was present the next day like normal (and aside from the bandage on her left arm, she didn't seem to be covered with injuries like Araragi); he also said I didn't need to worry about Mayoi and that the temporarily severed pairing between him and Shinobu was now back, so it all worked out well in the end—or at least that's the way it seemed.

I still had no idea how Miss Gaen and li'l Episode were involved, or how they had interacted, but this is Araragi we're talking about.

I'm sure something incredibly painful happened.

And that he overcame it.

I want to be that way too.

I also had a chance to speak to Shinobu, her pairing with Araragi now restored. Hearing of my experiences during his absence, she said:

"What ye've there is a *kasha*. While it may have no base, it was surely modeled on it or something of its ilk. I'd say 'twas an aberration created with something of that nature in mind rather than a *bake-*

no-hi."

"A kasha?" I asked, while also thinking about how this was the first time I was ever talking to Shinobu this way despite exchanging words with her multiple times as Black Hanekawa. "What might you mean?"

"Really, class president? Thou art ignorant of the kasha?"

"Oh, no, I'm certainly aware of what it is, but…" I was trying to be polite speaking to this aberration who had been alive for five hundred years, but it felt odd because she looked like an eight-or-so-year-old little girl. "…As I'm sure you're aware, it was a tiger."

"And I'd heard as much from the Afflicting Cat, which is why I had trouble coming up with this then—yet if this aberration was one of fire, then it surely must have been a kasha."

"Oh…"

The kasha, or the Burning Chariot, is an aberration said to drag dead bodies into hell—which, now that I thought about it, was something the Tyrannical Tiger had said, too—and it was described in many cases as a *cat aberration*.

A cat.

—That woman has seen me.

—That alone is essential.

More things she had said.

In other words, seeing the Tyrannical Tiger was directly linked to a trip to hell, no ifs, ands, or buts—

"It wasn't a cat, though, it was a tiger."

"Similar enough, are they not?"

"And it wasn't a chariot, but a tiger."

"Then what about a jaguar? Is that not a type of chariot nowadays?"

"……"

A Jaguar?

So she was trying to say—that a flaming chariot was just as likely to be a flaming tiger?

That seemed like a coincidence…but then the name came from Miss Gaen.

No, it came from me, after all.

In that case.

"After thy Afflicting Cat, that aberration drawn across the street by a vehicle, we have a flaming chariot that draws the dead to hell—what an elegant connection, eh? Haha, and 'tis just as that Hawaiian-shirted boy says, meet an aberration and you'll be drawn by aberrations."

"This feels like it's just turning into a word association game... Hmm—so if I understand you correctly, you're saying that while there may not have been a base aberration like with the Afflicting Cat, the Tyrannical Tiger still wasn't entirely original?"

"Not a thing exists that could be called entirely original—'tis the wall that any creator throughout history has inevitably encountered. Even Sekizen, in fact. The flaming tiger ye conjured is undoubtedly the product of all thy gathered knowledge and relationships, not some changed flame or flaming chariot alone. One may have a great deal of freedom, but one is never truly free."

"So it's like the saying, all art begins with imitation."

"Oh, but what a terribly timid and masochistic way of thinking." Shinobu shrugged and laughed. It was a gruesome laugh. "We ought to think of ourselves as continuing on in the tradition of our great forebears, should we not? Every one of us continues in the footsteps of another, and every one of us will have others continuing on from the paths we've tread. We take the ball we've received from our predecessors and pass it on to the next generation. Someday, someone may shoot that ball and score, but the match will only go on. 'Tis what we mean by lineage, and what we mean by tradition, and perhaps someone may follow after the Black Hanekawa or Tyrannical Tiger ye thought of."

"Hmm."

I wouldn't want that happening.

But maybe there was still meaning in my folly if it could go on to become a lesson for later generations.

Even this worthless tale of mine.

Maybe it could be of use, I thought.

Well, now that Araragi had returned, I of course needed to leave the Araragi residence, like dough being pushed through a pasta maker—but he said, "No, don't worry about it. I'll sleep on the floor, so you can keep using my bed. In fact, I'll sleep under the bed. I'll even be your bed. I promise to close my eyes when you change and stuff, of course."

His kind objection, though, only served to make me feel like my chastity was in danger, so I respectfully declined.

I was happy that he still treated me the same as always, but it also seemed to be his way of showing how unshaken his feelings were, and I couldn't help but feel pained, too.

If I let Araragi keep me there any longer, maybe it was his chastity that was going to be endangered.

Karen did say that "He should just leave so you can become one of the kids in our family, Tsubasa" (how mean!), but of course that wasn't happening.

Their family.

Consisted of them and them alone.

I couldn't thrust myself into it.

While it may have only been two days in retrospect, before leaving their home I politely thanked everyone in the Araragi family who had taken care of me.

From there, I ended up going back to Miss Senjogahara's place—the nearly incinerated Room 201, Tamikura Apartments.

Apparently Mister Senjogahara was going on a two-week-long overseas business trip—and he in fact requested me to stay with his daughter.

I knew it had to be an excuse.

There wasn't any way that he could so suddenly be assigned such a trip—not unless he asked for it.

She must have explained the situation to him, and this was his way of handling the situation. She must have known that I couldn't stay at Araragi's for long, regardless of when he would return.

In other words, that too—was part of her scheme.

"Hitagi, I've always told you that you should become the kind of person who helps her friends when they're in trouble," Mister Senjogahara said just before he left, his largish travel bag in hand. "And that's exactly who you've become. I've never been happier."

He patted his daughter on the head.

And I'll never forget Miss Senjogahara's expression as he did so.

Or his own.

While I cohabited with Miss Senjogahara for a while after that, it's not as if everything went perfectly.

Having taken the Afflicting Cat and Tyrannical Tiger in, I was, to be blunt, an emotional wreck. To say the least, I don't think I was pleasant to live with.

Miss Senjogahara, though, still did what she could to support me.

"I know how it is," she told me.

She let me know in detail how she'd overcome her churning emotions.

We clashed, and we even fought.

But we made up afterwards.

And as the days went on, I began to understand why, despite all the jealousy I should have felt for Araragi's girlfriend, she was the one person I never envied.

Right.

I think I understood from the beginning.

Araragi.

Miss Senjogahara.

They were going to end up going out.

They were going to end up going out.

I understood—and knew that.

I might not know everything, actually.

But I did know that.

So the supportive feelings I had for their relationship ever since Mother's Day—those, at least, weren't a lie.

"You know, Miss Hanekawa," Miss Senjogahara said, "I was thinking the complete opposite. Ever since seeing you and Araragi in April, I thought you two had to be going out. Or that you were at least in love with each other. That's why I was shocked when I asked Araragi if you were and he said no."

And now.

And now that I feel like I can be honest with you, she said before continuing.

"I thought Araragi was going to reject me when I confessed how I felt. At the time, I was of course prepared to do anything to get him to say yes, but I can't deny that somewhere in my heart, some part of me felt resigned. I mean, Araragi was so clearly in love with you—and that's when I felt like I'd fallen in love with the guy who'd fallen in love with you."

"Oh. That really is the opposite of me, then," I remarked. With a smile, I think. "I doubt I'd have fallen for him so hard if it wasn't for the fact that he was going out with you."

Yes—I know it's the most cliché thing to say.

But we fell in love with his kindness.

He never cuts anything loose, he never throws anything away.

We fell in love with how many-loved he is.

Good—so my sense that I had never begrudged Miss Senjogahara over Araragi was the one thing that I hadn't cut off, it was my one true feeling.

I still couldn't deny thinking about how great it must have been, though, so I did tease her at night, and her reactions were so wonderful.

Oh.

So I did love Araragi.

But I loved Miss Senjogahara too.

And only when I was able to admit that to myself did I feel like my heart was well and truly broken.

Pain and heartbreak—I'd managed to experience them.

Having lived thus for about ten days.

The moment arrived at last.

The news reached me that a rental had been found to replace the burned-down Hanekawa residence—which meant I needed to go. Miss Senjogahara seemed worried and said, "You don't need to leave so suddenly. Why don't you take your time until you feel like you're ready?" but I was fine now.

She didn't need to worry at all.

"Thank you," I told Miss Senjogahara, "I'll come over to play again soon," as I made my dashing exit from the Tamikura Apartments—

no, that's a lie.

What really happened is that I broke down crying.

It hurt to have to leave Miss Senjogahara, and I felt helpless when I thought of my life to come.

So the Tyrannical Tiger was right.

I really was fragile.

Quick to break down and cry.

But Miss Senjogahara cried too, so maybe we were even.

And you know, I ran into Sengoku on my way from the apartment to the rental house.

Nadeko Sengoku—a middle-school student with ties to Araragi.

We had never interacted much with each other, though, and she was with her parents, so I didn't call out to her. She probably didn't notice me.

They seemed to be such a close family.

The thought passed through my mind—and I felt jealous.

No, no, I thought as I suppressed the feeling.

Nope, I shouldn't be suppressing it.

I'm the kind of person who sees that kind of thing and feels jealous.

My first step was going to be accepting that.

As I went on living, I'd check to make sure that a fire still burned in my heart—after all, flames are a part of civilization, no matter what the flames may be.

I knew I could evolve.

I wasn't Miss Kanbaru, but my view had widened to the point where I could at least walk by a happy family like that and see them—so it felt like I was beginning, indeed.

If you were wondering, the cases of the Hanekawa residence and the abandoned cram school burning down were chalked up to spontaneous combustion, as close to an accident as you could get—window glass acting as a lens or something, unusually dry air for summer or something.

Huh.

So the world did work itself out.

Contradictions did get resolved.

Even so, I don't think I can allow myself to forget what I did.

While no one ever tried to find me guilty, I was not innocent.

That was something that needed to be fresh in the mind of every living thing—

Pure, white innocence was impossible.

The rental house I arrived at wasn't too big. They must have seen it as a temporary abode for the duration of the new home's construction. In fact, it seemed like it was on the smaller side for the neighborhood.

It didn't have many rooms, either.

But I had already faced the persons who should be called my father and my mother and told them in no uncertain terms.

I told them when I heard that they decided on a rental—

"Dad. Mom. Please give me a room."

And so.

And so, for the first time in my life, I had my own room.

I didn't want the sisters in my heart to feel cramped.

Yes.

It's not as if she disappeared.

It wasn't as if the Tyrannical Tiger disappeared, either—

They were in my heart.

And I hadn't disappeared either.

The old me was in me, too.

A thought crossed my mind.

A model student, a class president among class presidents, kind to all, fair, smart, like some kind of saint—maybe the old me whom Araragi described in such terms was the first aberration I ever created.

The girl that Araragi called the real deal.

And the girl that Miss Senjogahara called a monster.

That was the very first time I created myself.

The ideal me—for whom I had killed my self in so many ways.

It was probably something that I shouldn't have done.

The very first thing that I had cut loose from my heart was my self—it was never about real or main, about dominant or controlling.

It was all me.

And so—both the current me and the past me.

The future me, too. Maybe there was no essential difference among us.

Just as Araragi would always continue to be Araragi, no matter how much he changed—I would never change, no matter what me I became.

That's how it was.

Nothing changed.

That was—not the epilogue, but the punch line of this story.

I am me.

Tsubasa Hanekawa.

My cat ears were gone now and I wasn't seeing Tyrannical Tigers, but about half of my hair was still white, almost like a tiger's stripes. That seemed like proof.

I dye it black every morning now, since going to school looking that way would be a little too avant-garde, but it never feels like a bother or a waste of time.

It's my way of communicating. With them.

With my own heart and mind.

It's the honest truth that I find it fun.

Yes.

I have a feeling—this is how my life is going to be.

Changing, even when nothing changes.

I used the key I had been given to open the front door—it looked like those two hadn't come back from work yet, and no one was home. It was a completely unknown house to me, but for some reason, it didn't feel like I was sneaking into a stranger's residence. If anything, it felt familiar. Was unlocking a front door enough to make you feel that way?

Wondering, I began by climbing the stairs.

One step at a time.

Like I was chewing over the act.

When I climbed up the last stair and reached the second floor, for some reason I suddenly thought of Mayoi.

The girl who'd been lost for a long time when I first met her.

The Lost Cow—right.

So just maybe the very first source I had cited in creating the Tyrannical Tiger hadn't been any flaming chariot or changing flame, but the Lost Cow.

Mayoi had of course been parted from the Lost Cow by now, but I could see it as being something of an echo. Perhaps learning of Araragi's absence wasn't the only reason I had met the Tyrannical Tiger just after coming across Mayoi.

There was apparently a time when cows and tigers were confused for one another—so it didn't seem impossible.

I had lost sight of family and home—so it seemed like an appropriate aberration to meet.

Ever since that day.

No, ever since I met Mayoi in the park that day in May—I had been lost.

Wandering back and forth, here and there, around and around.

I must have been roaming.

I thought to myself.

I'd talk to Mayoi about it the next time I see her.

I really had gotten myself lost, hadn't I?

As lost as one could be.

But thanks to that, I got to meet a lot of people.

So, so many people.

I witnessed various families.

I witnessed various me's.

Which is why I could become me.

If the past me is me, then the future me is me, too.

There's no moment when I'm not me.

Then, what me will I be tomorrow?

Looking forward to things, I place my hand on the doorknob.

It's my room, given to me.

Western-style, hundred-or-so square feet.

Though only for the six short months until graduation—this place is, without a doubt, for me.

A place for us.

Out of nowhere, I remember the passage added to the letter that I left in my notebook that day.

No, it isn't long enough to be called a passage—a line, or just words.

Just a brief little greeting from a white cat that always stayed with me, that protected me at all times.

A common expression.

One that passes through everyone's lips as a normal part of the day.

But it's the first time in my life that I ever mouth them.

"I'm home."

I enter my room.

Finally I've made it back.

Afterword

There are a lot of cases in manga where the protagonist gets so over-whelmed by, say, summer homework and pleads for something ridiculous, like "If only I had two bodies," or "I want there to be another me." Most such stories, however, seem to settle on the punch line that both of you slack off when you have two bodies or another self and don't get any more work done. That sounds plausible, but when I really think about it, I don't know. The issue there is that both bodies have free will, and if a single will could control plural bodies instead, wouldn't there be a dramatic improvement in efficiency? In other words, a single chain of command operating both body A and body B, like a left hand and a right. You might think I'm being ridiculous here, but in fact I'm not; given the incredible advancements in wireless communication in our world, I guess I just can't deny the feeling that some extremely mechanical solution might serve. A *manipulator*, to put it simply. But then, if we expand ourselves limitlessly like that, we might no longer be able to tell where we end. Should we consider the shoes we wear when we go outside a part of ourselves? Are nails part of us before we clip them, but not after we do? Couldn't we just say the books lining our shelves are us? Is what we know part of us, or is it mere knowledge? The question of what the self is and how far it extends has been exercising many humans for ages, and when you think about it, maybe no times can do so like present-day society.

Despite the title, *NEKOMONOGATARI (WHITE)* isn't meant to form a pair with *NEKOMONOGATARI (BLACK)*, not in particular. Whether it's *(BLACK)* or *(WHITE)*, each tale can stand on its own, and they have different narrators in the first place, don't they? Say, I guess if *BAKEMONOGATARI, KIZUMONOGATARI, NISEMO-NOGATARI,* and *NEKOMONOGATARI (BLACK)* were the first season, then this *NEKOMONOGATARI (WHITE)* would be beginning a second season. I'm exaggerating on purpose, but I feel like up to the previous volume, the narrative already "existed" when I began the series (whether or not I actually wrote it all out), while the tale from this book on was a future unknown even to the author. I wonder if this is what they call characters acting on their own, but in any case, the plan is to release another five books or so. What will their story be? Okay, this has been a novel I wrote cat-percent to entertain myself, *NEKOMONOGATARI (BLACK)*. Pardon me, *NEKOMONO-GATARI (WHITE)*.

We've requested VOFAN to keep drawing the front covers and insert images for the second season. Miss Hanekawa is getting too many covers, though. Three in the series? What if she's on the next one, too? I can see it happening. Well, please look forward to the coming installment, including who's going to be on its cover. Actually, I'd be surprised if it was anybody other than Hachikuji.

I hope you'll continue to join me, everyone.

NISIOISIN

NOW!

AUTHOR NISIOISIN

BAKEMONOGATARI
MONSTER TALE

01 | 240 PAGES | $13.95 | 9781942993889
02 | 328 PAGES | $14.95 | 9781942993896
03 | 224 PAGES | $13.95 | 9781942993902

BEHIND THE HIT ANIME!

DECAPITATION
KUBIKIRI CYCLE
The Blue Savant and the Nonsense User

A dropout from an elite Houston-based program for teens is on a visit to a private island. Its mistress, virtually marooned there, surrounds herself with geniuses, especially of the young and female kind—one of whom ends up headless one fine morning.

The top-selling novelist year by year in his native Japan, NISIOISIN made his debut when he was only twenty with this Mephisto Award winner, a whodunit and locked-room mystery at once old-school and eye-opening.

$14.95 US / $17.95 CAN

Story by **NISIOISIN**
Retold by **Mitsuru Hattori**

Imperfect Girl

Legendary novelist NISIOISIN partners up
with Mitsuru Hattori (*SANKAREA*) in this graphic
novel adaptation of one of NISIOISIN's mystery
novels.

An aspiring novelist witnesses a tragic death, but
that is only the beginning of what will become a
string of traumatic events involving a lonely
elementary school girl.

Volumes 1 & 2 Available Now!

"With a huge collection of light novels to keep up with, I currently don't read many full-length novels, but *Anime Supremacy!* has proven itself a must-read for an anime fan like myself. Well written, informative and charming... 9/10"
-Anime UK News

As three women, a producer, a director, and an animator, survive in a business infamous for its murderous schedules, demoralizing compromises, and incorrigible men, moments of uplift emerge against all odds. More than just a window into an entertainment niche, here's a kickass ode to work.

ANIME SUPREMACY!

MIZUKI TSUJIMURA

Paperback • 416 Pages • $16.95 US/$18.95 CAN
ON SALE NOW!